ALSO AVAILABLE FROM JAMES WADE

All Things Left Wild

RIVER, SING OUT

A NOVEL

JAMES WADE

BLACKSTONE
PUBLISHING

Copyright © 2021 by James Wade
Published in 2021 by Blackstone Publishing
Cover and book design by Kathryn Galloway English

The characters and events in this book are fictitious.
Any similarity to real persons, living or dead, is coincidental
and not intended by the author.

Printed in the United States of America

First edition: 2021
ISBN 978-1-9826-0108-9
Fiction / Literary

1 3 5 7 9 10 8 6 4 2

CIP data for this book is available
from the Library of Congress

Blackstone Publishing
31 Mistletoe Rd.
Ashland, OR 97520

www.BlackstonePublishing.com

For Coy and Dorinda
In memory of Peggy Hageman

PROLOGUE

In an age far removed from the age of men, the world was yet unsettled, and the land drifted overtop the sea, and beneath the soil ancient lithospheric complexes of rock collided and pulled apart and collided again. Mountains did emerge, oceans rising and falling away, and steam erupted from the bowels of the earth where great fires burned in that inner furnace. And always they had burned, since the first whit of calcium came spilling forth from the cosmos, fleeing the last gasps of dying stars, abandoning its elemental hosts so that a new form might come barreling into existence—an astronomical explosion passing through the vestiges of forgotten galaxies, gathering to it allochthonous minerals and energies ripe for creation.

And in that great long ago we were all of us water creatures, and such truth held within us for millennia as we did gather and pool along the sea. And as the rivers reached out across the dry world, we followed—never straying too far from the flowing life what created us.

For the world we know now is a world receded. The very ground upon which we stand is a borrowed commodity, loaned to us by the ocean and its tides. The ebb and flow of earth and all its creatures brought about by the shadows of moons and the dust of stars, the consequence of elemental warfare on celestial plains.

Thick deposits of marine salt were drowned by the growing coastal waters and their waves of green. Silt to sand to swamp. Marshlands and hardwood forests spread north from the widening gulf, nine hundred miles from the great ocean to the east. And there the yellow pines made their last stand against the desert valleys and jagged uplifts, and there in such climate all their own, the forests grew and thrived and covered the country in deep, impassioned glories of green—eclipsing the horizon, veiling away all markers of the world without.

One such nativity leading to another, until at long last the river did manifest. In what would become Eastern Texas, the Neches was born dripping and gathering, collecting and pooling and drawn by gravity into the dirt, and there carving out its own bearing—a great pathway to the sea. From the hills of Van Zandt County, then some four hundred miles to the Gulf of Mexico, and along the way joined by creeks and rivulets with pathways of their own, and all connected in this selfsame destiny, wherein all stories share an ending, all lives a like fate.

And through these ages untold, the river did act as the lifeblood of those alongside it, those sons of Adam who pulled from its basin rice and timber and great tracts of each. Then came the oil and refineries and the promise of fortune, and the river was dug deep and unnatural along the estuary where it spilled into the ocean, and the water turned at once brown and polluted.

Soon the dams and spillways were built for the creation of lakes and reservoirs and the populations to come. And come they did, and forests felled and banks muddied; and the people abandoned the river, lost in some modern notion of promise and progression. So the river drew to it a sinister force, and along its banks grew deep roots of poverty and perturbation. And there the story begins and ends and begins again, as each rhythm of the earth's turning draws the water darker still.

1

The bank man lived in the sort of house befitting his position. A man handling money must be trusted to make smart decisions. His decisions had resulted in this house, that was the thinking. It was built on a hill above the rest of the neighborhood. Elevated. Imposing. Proper. The lawn was kept green and mowed, and the brick siding and stone columns were pressure washed each season.

Appearances were important.

He'd brought in a woman from Houston to decorate. She told him about layered design, feng shui, and statement pieces. She showed him the difference between granite and quartz countertops, between aspirational and reimagined layouts. In the end, the bank man told her to do whatever looked best.

It was a Tuesday. The soft light of the morning leaked through the bedroom windows, and the bank man studied himself in the mirror.

"What's my first appointment?" he asked without looking away from his reflection.

"Nine a.m.," his phone answered. "Janice Howe."

The bank man furrowed his brow. The widow Howe was long overdue on her mortgage. He wasn't sure she understood what that meant, or that she understood anything at all. He'd tried to explain the way of things to her. She would smile a faraway smile and nod.

"Edward's the one handles these things," she'd say. "He and Jack Copeland grew up together."

She'd say these things to the bank man, and he'd tell her Edward was dead these last ten years and Jack Copeland of Copeland Bank and Trust had passed some five years before that.

The bank man did not look forward to such conversations. No, to speak to the elderly was something altogether unsettling, under any circumstance. To converse with someone so near to death's door felt unnatural, as if by his very presence he may be revealing himself to death so that death might know him and return for him in some dark hour before his peace could be made.

And what a struggle such peace had come to be. As a child there was no worry of death, of nonexistence. Then slowly the fear manifested and evolved, and the bank man's brain propped up the tried-and-true defense mechanisms of man. He would put off the thought, plan to confront it later in life, once he had accomplished those many things that would make him happy, bring him peace. Perhaps he would even believe in the things he sang and the things he heard on Sunday mornings. What greater peace could there be than knowing death was only the beginning?

But as the years passed, such comfort had not been found, and so many suppressed fears would come flooding back as the man stood in front of these once-young lives, so near to their end, so sad in their being.

He breathed in then out, nodding, and leaned closer to the glass to inspect a stray hair. He took it between two fingers and plucked it from his head. He studied it.

"Kicking that old woman out of her house got you going gray?"

The bank man wheeled toward his bedroom door and saw the two men watching him. One shorter, one impossibly large.

"Christ Jesus," the bank man said. "You scared the hell out of me, Mr. Curtis."

"Morning, Mr. Klein," the shorter man said, stepping into the room.

"Well, good morning. You mind me asking what it is you're doing here?"

"I need to make a withdrawal."

"That's fine, but—"

"I know it's fine," the man said, cutting him off.

"—but you got to come down to the bank, Mr. Curtis. That's how it works."

John Curtis smiled. His teeth were a gnash of thin yellow bone.

"I know how it works," he said.

"Alright," the bank man said. He looked at his phone, measuring the distance between where he stood and where it rested on the dresser. "So, I'll meet you down there."

"Down where?"

"At the bank."

"For what?" the man asked. He slid his hand down the length of the dresser top, stopping it on top of the phone.

"For you to make a withdrawal."

"I can make it right here."

The bank man swallowed hard. Swallowed the truth of the situation, and it sunk into his stomach and landed so hard he thought he might shit himself.

"Well, Mr. Curtis, I don't—I don't have much cash in the house."

He tried to swallow again but couldn't.

"That's a lie." John Curtis shrugged. "Don't matter though. I ain't here for cash."

"What, uh, what is it that you're here for?"

"Done told you."

"I don't understand," the bank man said. He spoke softly. He closed his eyes.

"No, you don't. Most don't. Most don't understand because they can't understand. They've spent their whole lives living in a world full of choices. Just like you."

John Curtis looked up.

"What shoes are you going to wear today, Mr. Klein?" he asked.

"What?"

"You're shoeless, Mr. Klein. You've got no shoes upon your feet. But I'm guessing when you walk into that bank this morning, you'll have some fancy shoes on. So which pair is it gonna be?"

"Uh." The bank man looked around. "The brown pair, those there."

"The brown pair. Good choice. Sharp. So how come?"

"What?" the bank man asked again.

"Follow along, haas. This ain't accounting or whatever the hell it is you do down there in your little glass office. How come you to choose them shoes?"

"They, uh, they go with my suit."

"Really? Brown shoes with a gray suit? That goes together does it?"

"Yes. No. I don't—"

"Easy, Mr. Klein. Take you a breath. Folks is having heart attacks at awful early ages now'days. And you got yourself a stressful bank job and all. Just breathe, and tell me if them brown shoes match up with your gray suit."

"Yes, they do."

"Well, alright then. Go ahead and slip into 'em then. Put 'em on."

The bank man steadied himself on the dresser and slid his feet one after the other into the brown dress shoes.

"Fine job, Mr. Klein. Fine job. Myself, I'm partial to the tradition of black with gray, but I must say, the brown shoes do look handsome."

John Curtis turned to the large man still standing silent in the doorway.

"They do look handsome, don't they, Cade?" he asked.

Cade crossed his muscle-bound arms. "Look like fancy shoes."

John Curtis frowned and looked back at the bank man.

"I can't tell if he means that as a compliment or not," he said. "Now tell me, did you make that choice or did the suit?"

The bank man was in a full sweat. He felt his breath coming faster.

"I—I made the choice."

"But you needed to match the suit, ain't that right?"

"Yes, but I picked the suit."

"Ahh, you're sure right, Mr. Klein," John Curtis clapped his hands on his knees. "You're sure right. But how come you to choose the suit? Is it because you like the color? Did your father wear a suit like that? His father before him? Did the girl at the shop tell you it looked good? Did she smile at you? Did you think to yourself, if only I had this suit, this gray suit, I bet this little ole gal would spread right open for me?"

The bank man shook his head. He fought the tears.

"Mr. Curtis, do you believe I wronged you in some way? Is that why you're here in my home, trying to intimidate me?"

"Intimidate? Whoa, Mr. Klein, we're just talking. Talking about choices. If you don't want to tell me about the suit, that's okay. Nobody's getting ugly here. But think, Mr. Klein, about why you wear that or any other suit. Think about why you do anything a'tall. How much of this life is truly your choice?"

"I am here by the grace of god, if that's what you mean."

"It's not." John Curtis laughed and shook his head. "It is decidedly not. Another choice you never made, your god. You think you chose between Heaven and Hell, you think you chose forgiveness and salvation over sin. But if you were born amongst the sand niggers in the Iraqi desert, grew up over there with the goats and jihadis and the like, you'd be praising Allah and fucking camels at this very moment. Now tell me I'm wrong."

"I don't know, sir. I can't speak to that."

"Can't speak to it."

"No, sir."

"Well."

"Mr. Curtis, can I please, with all respect, ask you to leave my home. If you have business, I'd be happy to conduct it at the bank, which I am running late to as we speak."

"Alright, alright, I know I'm keeping you. But I'll make you a deal. Let me tell you a story, and at the end of the story, I'll say goodbye, and you won't have to worry about me dropping in on you anymore."

"I assume I don't have a choice."

"Hot damn, he's starting to get it now, Cade. Starting to get what all this is about. Choices, Mr. Klein, true choices, are a rare breed. You wear brown shoes, black shoes, no shoes, who gives a rat's ass? That's not a choice. That's just culture and trends and narcissism and egos and all the bullshit you were born into. But I wasn't born into it, nossir. And that's where the story starts."

John Curtis motioned to the edge of the bed. The bank man sat, his knees near to collapsing in on themselves.

"Along the banks of the Neches, high up on a hill, there used to set a pine-planked shack. It was my first home. I guess you'd call it that, even though it was a terribly short period of time that I was there.

"My momma was twelve years old, which didn't much matter to me at the time. Certainly her age made no difference to my daddy. He was some old boy she'd seen over in Groveton. She'd been roller skating with her friends, how girls do. Or at least how they did. I'm not so up on the times. Anyway. By the time he got her back to the river shack she was in bad shape. He'd hit her too hard, you see. Misjudged his own strength. Her own frailty. Either way, he wanted her present and in the moment for what was to come. So he forced her to snort up a line or two of cocaine, and then he went to work on her. He kept her there for however many days and kept on with the powder and the rape and everything else. Then, after however long, he started to notice something. You know what he noticed?"

The bank man shook his head. He was shivering.

"He noticed she was liking it. At least she was liking the coke. She may not have liked the sex, but she wasn't fighting him. She was addicted, and he was the one with the supply. And one day she told my daddy— the same man who'd stole her away like she didn't no more belong to this world than a piss pot—that she didn't never want to go home, wanted to stay with him in that shack for however long he'd let her.

"Turned out, that was about three months.

"Then she started to show, and he put her out. Well, okay. She went home, but her folks wouldn't take her back. They'd been worried about her, had the police looking for her and all, but she wasn't the same girl they'd lost. No, sir, that little girl had died. They didn't want nothing to do with some drug-addict slut got herself knocked up. Can't blame 'em. Times were different. What would folks think? Hell, what would they say?

"She hitched down to Houston. Big city, big parties. She feeds the habit. Finds a couch here or there to crash. But then she gets so big she's about to pop, and nobody has the room. Not for her. Not for some baby bound to come out deaf, dumb, and blind.

"She could've gone to a hospital, or a women's shelter, or anything else. But she knew the deal at places like that. No drugs. And that just couldn't be.

"Anyway, poor Momma, she showed up back at that little river shack.

Daddy wasn't home. So she went on inside, pushed out a screaming baby boy, then proceeded to die right there on the dirt floor. Who knows how she died. Maybe she bled out. Maybe I was scratching and clawing at her, caught something important. I've heard that's been known to happen. Maybe she overdosed, some last, little bastion of freedom. Maybe my daddy found her there and killed her, rather than explain anything to anybody. As I was fresh into the wide world at the time, I honestly can't say. I don't know how long I was there, but it couldn't have been long. They guessed as I'd only been alive a day or two when I was dropped at the hospital. Hospital to the state, state to the foster system, foster system until there was nothing left.

"And that, Mr. Klein, is what I was born into. I had no choices, no decisions to make, save whether to die or survive. I chose the latter. Been choosing it ever since. That one choice, that first choice, is the only one I've ever made. Every single action I've ever taken has been in service of that first choice. Do you understand now?"

"I'm sorry," the bank man cried. "I'm sorry that happened to you."

"You don't need to be sorry about all that. You just need to tell me where my money is."

"What?"

"My money, Mr. Klein, where is it?"

"I don't—it's in the bank."

"Not that money. I gave you ten thousand dollars to buy me a stake in that timber plot before it caught fire and the whole thing went belly up. Now I want my investment back."

"But, Mr. Curtis, you just said yourself, that project is bankrupt. That money is gone."

"That may be true for everybody else you're in business with, but that ain't how it works with my money."

The big man in the doorway pulled from his waistband an eight-inch blade with a deer antler handle.

"Mr. Curtis, I don't—I can talk to the insurance, see what can be done. I can maybe get you back five thousand dollars."

Cade advanced.

The bank man trembled. His suit pant darkened the length of his thigh.

"You'd kill a man over ten thousand dollars?"

"Twenty thousand," John Curtis told him.

"But . . . you only put in ten."

"I want a return on my investment."

"Mr. Curtis, please, I can't—I don't know what you want me to do. Please. Whatever it is, just tell me and I'll do it."

The bank man's knees hit the floor and he pulled at John Curtis's hands and arms, and the room filled up with the smell of urine.

John Curtis knelt and touched the man's cheek.

"You still think you can talk me out of what has to happen," he said. "Even after everything I've said, you still think there's a choice to be made."

John Curtis twisted away from the bank man's grasping. He nodded at Cade.

"It's a lovely home you have here, Mr. Klein," he called over his shoulder. "Very well appointed."

2

The sun set and the world died another small death, and those upon it the same, and all growing closer to what ends may be met. The boy watched the darkness spread as the hills before him turned from shadow to black and the red-hued colors of the horizoned sky took a last smoldering gasp and disappeared into the stale gray of dusk. The crickets and cicadas started up almost in unison, as if being urged on by the invisible hand of some almighty conductor. The boy sat cross-legged atop the trailer's roof and closed his eyes and listened to the insects and the night and the humming of the window unit in his father's bedroom.

The big doe came again. The day had fallen into the west, and he could scarcely make her shape but he knew it was her. She'd come each night in the spring, and the boy had studied her and her swelling belly and he had taken to putting out corn against his father's wishes. He would watch her eat and each night he'd creep closer, and always she was wary of him. He could never get more than a few yards from the trailer before she would perk her ears and stare at him for a time, undecided, then bound back into the tract of loblolly and sweetgum, turning again from the safety of such cover to look at the boy as he looked at her.

She had not returned in several days, or maybe weeks, and the corn was eaten by squirrels, and the boy thought about shooting one of them to cook with dumplings to surprise his father. But he had no gun of his own and would have to ask his father's permission to borrow one, and then the surprise would be expected and really no surprise at all. Still, the boy scattered the corn each afternoon after his father left, then drug the old picnic table with its rotted wood and rusted frame up against the trailer and stood on it and reached up and, careful not to grab the gutter, pulled himself onto the roof and sat.

Now she appeared once more, and he saw her step out from the darkened tree line and move slowly toward the corn. She smelled it, put her head down to eat then raised it up again and glanced over her shoulder. A fawn emerged from the woods and took awkward, spilling steps toward its mother. The big doe looked past the young deer and back to the food and began to eat, and the fawn waited and hoped for milk, and the boy watched them both with great interest.

The back of the trailer pushed up against a grove of cypress and oak which guarded the Neches river. It sat clumsy and diagonal, and faced the small clearing, looking out at the world as if someone had left it there and never returned, and whether the abandonment was accident or circumstance made no matter to the rust and the rot. The corrugated siding had been overwhelmed by watermarks and a copper color still spreading with each rain, and the door hovered three feet from the ground where years ago there had been steps and maybe a porch. There was mold and flood damage and a waterline from when the river spilled its banks and flooded the bottomlands. Markings of things past and things that perhaps would be again.

The road in was grass and soft dirt and often mud, and for days at a time it would be impassable. The boy would look toward it and fix his eyes between the sentry pines on either side and study the space therein until the path bent up out of the bottoms, bending and disappearing toward where the path turned to gravel then blacktop—which was as far as the school bus would come. Then, further on, the highway, where mothers and fathers drove to pick up their children from school and baseball practice. Where they wrapped them in their arms and told them things. *Nice things*, the boy would imagine, as he stared at the road.

The fireflies parried about in the gloam of the coming night. The deer flicked their tails. The boy sat with his chin in his hands and watched the evening unfold.

Beyond the trees, somewhere in the darkness, the river outstretched in winding sequence. The boy wished he could feed it. Wished he could empty bags of corn and oats into its swarthy gullet and watch it grow and rise, and the world in full descending beneath this new ocean of retribution. He imagined it spilling out across the bottoms, each tributary and shallow waterway flooding until all were linked and one and uninterrupted. And he imagined himself swimming atop the sunken soul of all that was, peering down through the brown water and watching everything fall away.

Below him the window unit shuddered and let loose a mechanical cry then sputtered to a stop. The deer looked up, frozen, eyeing the dim lights of the trailer, then turned and retreated into the forest and left the boy to tend to human matters and broken things.

The boy stood in front of the air conditioner and frowned. He turned the knob from On to Off then back On again. It sputtered and choked and died out. He walked into the kitchen and opened the cabinet under the sink and pulled out a toolbox and a wire brush and took them both back to his father's bedroom. He got down to his knees then set the box on the floor and opened it carefully and looked at the screws on the air conditioner brackets and picked out the screwdriver he thought was the best match.

He loosened the screws with a flathead screwdriver and took them out and sat each one on the carpet next to the brush. He pulled the brackets off and laid them alongside the screws, then he grabbed hold of the coil panel and swung it outward from the rest of the unit, making sure not to damage the rusted freon lines. He looked at the inside of the panel and ran a finger along the buildup of dirt and grime. He wiped his finger on his shorts and rose to his feet and went back to the kitchen. He found an old dish rag and brought it into the room and spread it out underneath the window unit.

He picked up the wire brush and went to work, scrubbing the panels as best he could. When he finished, he sneezed, then looked at the panel and frowned again. It had been improved, but there was still all manner of dirt lodged around the coils. He closed the panel and replaced the brackets and screws, then tried the knob again. The unit kicked on, and the boy felt cool air on his face but he could hear the congestion from within. He turned it off and went into the kitchen and found a flashlight. He climbed down from the trailer and turned on the light and used it to spot the westward trail. He followed it for near a mile before the old man's porch light came into view.

The cabin roof was visible through the trees, two levels of rusted tin, the first sloping in sheets across the main structure, then another, less angled, coming down over the porch. The wood was primarily pine, but there was some oak and hickory too. Some of it going back seventy years. Some of it going back much further.

The porch might have been three feet off the ground, and there were rotted steps on the end closest to the road. A more suitable set was placed in the middle of the porch, lining up with the door to the cabin. In the back was a row of small sheds, some more used than others. Weeds grew up through bent chicken wire wrapped around an old coop. The grass was overgrown, and the shrubbery had taken over most of the yard, save for a half-trimmed path to the outhouse. Smoke rose from the piped chimney, even in June.

A half-dozen cats lounged in various positions between the porch and the dock. None of them paid the boy any mind as he approached.

"Who's out there shining a light?" the old man called as the boy came closer.

"Jonah Hargrove, Mr. Carson."

"What's that?"

"It's me, Mr. Carson, Jonah Hargrove," the boy said, louder.

"Jonah Hargrove," the old man repeated. "What are you doing coming into camp in the middle of the damn night?"

"Was wondering if you had a can of coil cleaner."

"A can of what?"

"Coil cleaner."

"Coil cleaner?"

"Yessir."

The boy was in plain view of the porch now, the old man sitting bare-foot in a wooden rocking chair, a pair of denim overalls with nothing underneath, and a black and gold ballcap telling of his service in Korea.

"Well, I'd asked you what you want with coil cleaner, but I reckon that'd be an ignorant inquiry."

"I guess."

"Come on up, come on up and set for a minute."

The boy looked back the way he'd come.

"Your coils can wait," the old man said. "Come set."

The boy clicked off the flashlight and put it in his pocket and walked up the steps to the porch and sat down in the rocker next to Mr. Carson.

"Ought not be out in the woods after dark," the old man said.

"How come?"

"Well, lots of reasons."

"Alright."

"When I was growing up, our parents would tell us a lion was gonna drag us off and eat us. If we was running around after dark, that is."

"There aren't any lions left though."

"No, not in a good many years."

"I dreamed there was a panther in the bottoms. A black one."

"Well. A good place to keep things alive, I suppose. In dreams."

"You ever see one?"

"Several. Used to be they was all over."

"What happened to them?"

"Same thing happens to all of us, I imagine."

"You think there's one might have come back?"

The old man shook his head slow, as if in some great sorrow. As if the fate of the animal's existence was in some way tethered to his own.

"No," he said. "Once something's gone, it don't ever come back."

An ash-colored cat with a crooked head rose up from the corner of the porch and stretched its front legs out and raised its hindquarters and came trotting toward the chairs. The old man shooed it away, and the cat yowled and slunk over to the boy and arched its back and pressed up against his leg and purred. The boy reached his hand down and the cat clawed and bit at it as he jerked it back up.

"Don't give her no attention," the old man said. "She's liable to jump in your lap and curl up just so she can get close enough to tear your eyes out."

"Where'd these cats come from?"

"Hell if I know. Where does anything come from?"

"Do you feed them?"

"Sure. When they're hungry."

The boy stared at his feet.

"How's life treating you, son? You doing good in school?"

"School's out. Summer break."

"Ah. Best time to be a youngster."

"I guess."

"What's your daddy up to?"

"Work. He gets back tomorrow."

"Hard living. Good money, I hear. But a hard living, no doubt."

"Yessir."

"I got some coffee in yonder, if you want."

"No thank you."

"A can whoop us up a biscuit or two."

"That's alright, I was just hoping to borrow that coil cleaner off of you."

"One track mind, huh?"

"I guess."

"Man on a mission. Well, alright then. I'll get up and fetch it for you here in just a minute."

The old man showed no sign of his intention to rise, but eventually he did just that, groaning at the process. He stood and looked down at the boy and paused, smiled, then went inside. He came out with an old spray can with rust around the rim.

"About half gone," he said, and tossed it to the boy.

"I won't use it all."

"Use it all if you want. My air blower ain't likely to give out before I do."

"I'll bring it back tomorrow."

"You can keep it. Come on back in the morning if you want though.

I'll cook us some breakfast. Got some deer meat I'll get out of the deep freeze."

The boy nodded. He switched the can for the flashlight in his pocket and started toward the trees.

"Hey, son," the old man called after him. "That ain't one of them cans where you can go sniffing at it in a paper sack. Just so you know."

"Okay."

The boy sat in front of the air conditioner and repeated the process. This time, with the panel swung open, he shook the can and sprayed the coils. He let the cleaner sit while he took the dish rag and shook it out over the trash bin. Then he wet the rag and went back into the bedroom. He scrubbed off the cleaner and the dirt with it. It still wasn't as clean as the boy would have liked, but he was satisfied enough to close it up again and put away the tools. The unit sounded better in its running. He sat in front of it and listened to it hum. He closed his eyes against the cool air.

That night he dreamt the earth was water alone and he floated atop it and from the center of the endless sea rose enormous a single oak and upon its bark and branches clung thousands of gray and green tree frogs and none moving or trilling yet all somehow calling to him and the boy spoke in a voice they understood.

"Where am I?" he asked and the frogs did not answer and they stared at him in legion from above.

"What is this place?"

On a low limb, inches from where the tree disappeared below the surface sat a three-toed box turtle. Its head speckled with orange and yellow spots. Its high, dome-like shell adorned in faded designs of brown and red and rust.

"This is the last," the turtle said and his words were an echo across a wall-less world.

"The last what?"

"Place," the turtle answered.

"Where is she?" the boy asked and the frogs began to sing and croak and trill and the noise grew so loud the boy covered his ears until the turtle bid them back into silence.

"Gone," the turtle said.

"Where?"

"Where we all go," the turtle answered and again the chorus of frogs began a rousing clatter and one by one they leapt from the tree and into the water and the boy watched them splash about him until the oak was barren and the turtle slipped slowly from his branch and into the sea.

"Wait," the boy called but he felt himself being pulled under the dark surface and he could not swim or fight his way to the top and the pressure in his head grew and his breath gave way and as the water filled his nose and eyes and lungs, a hand reached down and grabbed his arm, pulling him up above the surface and the water and the world. Pulling him past the lone oak and into the clouds and the stars and the great energies of all that is guessed at. There was at once life and death and awareness and the boy felt his life slip and float and there in the ethereal darkness a warmth of light and color attached to his mind like leeches and bled dry the knowledge therein, and he watched his soul fall away to some realm unknown and what was left was empty and weightless and as he tried to take a breath the black water poured from his mouth and into his bed and he opened his eyes and coughed away all that had been seen.

3

The boy used to come around when his daddy was gone, which was a lot. I liked him coming around. We took to one another in some sort of way. Not like a father and son, I don't believe. But like a pair of souls, adrift, nodding one at the other as if to verify the experience of our own existence. As if to make sure the world was still the world, and we were still of it.

That last summer the boy was here, we got as much rain as I could remember. There was some folks believed it was the end times, and I guess I can make some sense of that. In the classics, they say water represents salvation. Into the water we carry our sins so that they might be washed away, so that we might be cleansed. And in the Bible the Lord God did submerge the Earth so that it might be remade, and the Caddo People were saved from a four-headed monster when a great flood came. And in our myths and stories the rain comes always to purify, and in such manner we seek out the water as our redemption. We look upon it and see ourselves reflected and the things around us and in such images there is prophecy of a time when all must return to the sea.

Still. I don't care much for lore and religion. Some might say I got a grudge against god. Maybe I do. Maybe that would be better than not believing at all. In the end, I guess it doesn't really matter. When the black water rises, and the last breath of the world is drawn, what difference does it make who sent the flood.

But sometimes I'd sit a johnboat in the middle of the river and watch the fog come off the still water and the morning sun drying away the night. Near *the shore, a reflection of every plant and tree and piece of sky spooled out across the surface, as if ahead of me were two mirrored worlds and either one I chose would allow me my shortcomings, would keep me as its own.*

Then the birdsongs would start up, and it's hard not to think there's something greater. Something we likely wouldn't understand even if it was laid out piece by piece right in front of us—which, I believe, it probably is.

4

Splithorn Hill was the second highest peak in Neches County. It rose up from the western banks of the river, out of place and in great contrast to the lowlands that surrounded it. Pines grew from the slopes of the hill, and some grew up straight and others grew out sideways as if they belonged to some counterworld with different rules than our own. Deer shaped intersecting game trails along those same slopes, but rarely did they venture up toward the ridgeline as it was there that lions had once roamed. And though the great cats were long since faded from the bottomlands and the country entirely, their prey were still weary, as if the deer were governed by the ghosts of their ancestors who dictated to each of them the protocol of survival. As if the spirits of the lions themselves might lay in wait, stalking the ridgeline in some eternal quest for death.

The Caddo people called it *Hahtinu*, Red Hill, because of its clay loams, and they believed the hill to be the burial mound of a long-forgotten god, driven to ground by the great sky father *Kadhi hayuh*. Like the animals, they too dared not disturb the sanctity of such a place, lest the discarded deity arise from its slumber and lay waste to the earth and all upon it. Only the *xinesi*, or high priest, was permissioned to approach the hill where he would perform rituals to keep locked whatever evil existed within.

But these fears appealed not to the settlers, who worshipped their own god and wrote a history different from the Caddo and from the animals and different even from nature itself. And their god of blood and greed drove away the Indians and the lions, and they conquered the hill and named it as their own.

Parts of the cabin had stood for near one hundred years. Some of the same boards John Curtis was thought to have been born on still remained, stained with his supposed mother's blood. But John Curtis had brought the cabin into the new times. He'd made sure the county ran electric lines up the more gentle western slope of the hill, and he'd built a road, put in a septic tank, and upgraded the old, handmade water catchments. He also added on new rooms and a porch, essentially building an entirely new structure around the old one. Splithorn Hill, once known by locals as the seedy congregating point for druggies, burnouts, and low-level criminals, had become something far more sinister.

They stood in the darkness on the slope of the hill, smoking, the two of them looking down into the hole where the light from a headlamp played off the dirt. Frank tapped on the butt of his cigarette.

"You keep on with the digging, you ain't gonna be able to climb outta that hole."

"Don't be jealous," Lonnie said. "Just 'cause I'm gonna climb outta here a rich man."

"It starts raining here after a while, that sucker's gonna fill up and you'll be a drowned man."

A shadow moved across the light from the porch. The girl stood and looked out.

"Hey, girl. You come to watch Lonnie dig his way to China?" Scooter called to her.

She stood for a moment more, then turned and went back inside without speaking.

"Well, fuck you, too," Scooter muttered. He licked his lips over and again.

"Don't let the big man hear you say that," Frank warned.

"Shit, I'm not as stupid as you look," Scooter said. "I will say though, I think it's a mistake having her around."

"I always knew you put peckers over pussy."

"You go ahead and laugh, but that girl ain't as harmless as she puts on. I seen how she makes eyes at John Curtis every time Cade ain't around. Now tell me that wouldn't be a clusterfuck of epic proportions."

"Like I said, you just keep your mouth shut and don't worry about anybody's business but your own."

"I'm just saying. Besides, you can't trust nobody from Louisiana. Bunch of backwoods coonasses."

"Aren't you from DeQuincy?" Frank asked, raising an eyebrow.

"That's how come me to know."

Lonnie stopped digging and leaned his shovel in the dirt and picked up the detector and swung it in either direction in front of him and it chirped and calculated and made all manner of mechanical suggestion.

"You boys hear that? That's the sound of my fortune calling to me."

Scooter shook his head.

"Ain't no fortune buried that far under the damn ground."

"O, ye of little faith. That's why I won't be sharing. A pious man, no matter the obstacle, continues about his labors. Leave the doubters to their . . . doubting."

"I've always said it, Scooter, some folks just can't handle drugs. Got them two sketchers in yonder, can't make sense of a word they're saying, and here's ole Lonnie ready to live with the mole people."

"Hey, don't you lump me in with them crazy sumbucks inside."

"I'm not sure you get to make that sort of demand, bud. What with you looking like a reverse Andy Dufresne."

"If I wasn't in this hole, I'd whip your ass."

"I can wait 'til you're done digging, if that helps. But I imagine you'll be double disappointed when you wake up with a busted jaw and still as broke as a politician's promise."

"Y'all knock that shit off. John Curtis wants us ready when he gets back. Says there might be trouble with the Mexicans."

"Well, there's something should come as no surprise," Lonnie said. "We should've never been running their dope to begin with."

"That's your measure of it, huh?"

"It is, indeed."

"Alright, go on and tell John Curtis to his face, then. Mind you, you might as well stay down there in that hole, since he'll be putting you right back in it."

"Maybe I will. Maybe I'll unearth this here buried treasure, then tell John Curtis he should have never went into business with them bean-eating bastards."

"You eat beans too, you dumb shit," Scooter said.

Frank scowled.

"I can't set here and listen to y'all no more. I'm gonna try to catch some rest. I'd advise you to do the same."

"Rest is for the weak," Lonnie hollered up at him. "Fortune comes not to those who dally."

Frank drew in the last of his cigarette and shook his head.

"Out of pure curiosity, have you tried that detector without having them steel-toed boots on?"

He flicked the butt into the hole, and it spirited through the black air with a flaming tail and landed among the curses of Lonnie's revelation.

He and Scooter turned toward the cabin and there they caught a glimpse of a figure moving through the darkness beyond the flood light.

"Hey," Frank called. "Where you headed with that satchel?"

5

The boy moved beneath the canopy of trees, a visitant of men long past. He thought of such men. Men with black hair, long and braided, their ears and necks adorned with feathers, beads, and shells from an ancient sea where people once lived with gills and fins and gray, foggy eyes.

The thick trellis of branches parried with the sun and cast upon the earth a quiltwork of shadow and light. The boy looked at the pattern on the ground before him and each section aglow as if all the fallen stars had returned from their banishment and sought new residence on the forest floor, shimmering in the dirt with each gust of wind, waiting on nightfall so they might look to the sky and see some long ago reflection of themselves.

He looked to the river and could feel there all the souls who'd passed by and passed on, each blending into the other and existing vague and veiled, as if the spirit of this place was a forgotten dream come calling. And the boy was awash with such emotion, yet none of it named or reasoned, and when he looked down at the brown water he saw only a quivering mirror of himself, leaking into the surface as if he too were destined to join the parade of phantoms trapped beneath the wickerwork canopy what hung above the river.

His toes dug into the muddy bottom. He felt something hard and smooth touch his foot, and he bent to pick it up. The ghosts of the Caddo nation slipped through the thin membrane of time, taking to the woods of their once-home, and the boy could see them in his mind. The boy ran his finger along the edge of the arrowhead and wondered if it had been used, if it held within it the murdered soul of some man or woman or wild animal. Or had it simply been created to wait, fashioned and forgotten, burying itself in the ground until the complexities of this strange new world collapsed violently inward and the ancient ways were restored. The boy closed his fist around the crude blade and squeezed until he felt the warmth of his own blood.

The river road twisted and squirmed up from the lowlands, a nondeliberate mix of gravel and sand and spots of always mud. The kids would come in their trucks after a good rain and tear it to shit. Jonah would hear the custom mufflers, the country music, the hoots and hollers from the older boys and the delighted squeals from the girls.

Others, closer to the boy's age, came with their dogs and their fishing poles, and two boys carried a cooler and a girl smoked cigarettes and left lipstick stains on the filters. Jonah watched them from his tract of sand. They were at ease with one another. Laughing and teasing and existing as a collective. An old cur dog with his tongue lolling came trotting through the underbrush and stood panting in front of the boy. The dog was a mutt if ever there was one, with wire scrub hair and a bobbed tail. The boy leaned forward to touch the dog's head, and it darted to the side and barked and sunk its front shoulders in a play bow, then leapt back in front of the boy and barked again.

"She botherin' you?" a girl asked, appearing in front of him.

"No."

"Good."

"She's nice," the boy said.

"She's a bitch."

"Oh."

"What are you doing out here?"

"Nothing, I guess," the boy replied, looking around as if there may be an answer he'd not yet seen.

"Well, I mean, you gotta be doing something."

The boy shrugged.

"You're bleeding," she said.

He looked down at his right hand, then switched the arrowhead to his left and wiped the blood on his shorts.

"Cool arrowhead. Is that what you're doing?"

"What?"

"Looking for arrowheads."

"Sure."

"Well. Do you want to come hang out? We have beer."

"Um."

"Do you live on the river?"

"Yea. Just through there."

"Most of us do too. Over in Timms County, though. I'm Katie."

"I know."

"You know?"

"I seen you around, some. At the Pick-It-Up, different places."

"You stalking me?"

"No."

"Good. So you want to come over or not?"

"Katie! Get your ass back over here. Don't leave me with these boys!" the cigarette-smoking girl called.

"I'm coming. I'm talking to . . ."

"Jonah," the boy said, wiping the blood from his hand and reaching it out toward the girl.

She took it, then hollered back over her shoulder, "I'm talking to my friend Jonah. He lives on this side of the river." To him, she said, "C'mon. It'll be fun."

The girl led him by the hand and they emerged from the thicket and onto the bank, and the other boys sized him up and dismissed him.

"I know you," one boy said. "You're Hargrove."

Jonah nodded.

"Oh my god, Katie, you found a pussy. That's great, now there's three guys and three girls."

"Shut up, Patrick," the girl scolded. "Don't mind him, Jonah. He's just an asshole."

"It's okay."

"Katie, come pee with me," the other girl said, and the two of them disappeared giggling into the woods.

"Hey, man, I'm Trevor."

"Hey."

"Patrick really is an asshole, but he's our asshole, you know?"

"Okay."

"Yeah. Anyway, you having a fun summer?"

"I guess."

"Anything beats school, right?"

"I don't know. I kind of like school."

"Jesus fuck, man. Are you like a smart kid?"

"No. I mean, I don't think so."

"My old man says if I don't go to school, he'll beat the shit out of me. That's the only reason I show up. 'Cause I know he means it. But as soon as I turn seventeen, I'm headed to the oilfields. Make some real money. You know?"

"That's what my dad does."

"No shit? That's badass. I can't wait, man. My cousin said he'd get me on, making like sixty grand right off the bat. I'm gonna buy the meanest fucking truck in the world."

The boy called Patrick had dropped a line near a bed of tall grass, he flicked the rod a couple of times and laughed.

"If you want to drive the baddest truck in the world, you'll have to ask me nicely," he called.

"Maybe I'll ask your mom after we're finished," Trevor replied, then turned back to Jonah. "Patrick's just being a bitch because he's home-schooled, so he can't quit. His parents are some sort of weird Jesus people. Not like normal people who go to church, but like, the crazy kind."

"Oh."

"Yeah. Micah over there—he don't talk much—he says he ain't going back to school at the end of the summer. I think he's full of it."

"What about Katie?"

"Oh, Katie's cool as shit. She'll be in high school next year, over at Timms. I'll be in eighth grade, me and Katy with a Y."

"They're both named Katie?"

"Yeah. They're like best friends."

Jonah nodded and watched the other boys. They were his age, but they all looked much older. They wore jeans and boots, even in the summer. They carried Skoal cans, drank beer, and called each other terrible things and then laughed.

The girls returned, stepping delicately around the thorn bushes and vines. They climbed atop a red moss boulder and unfurled towels.

"Hell yeah, let's see some titties," Patrick hooted as the girls began to undress.

"You're so gross," Katy said.

Jonah watched Katie shimmy out of her shorts and reveal green bathing suit bottoms with ruching in the back. She left her tank top on, while the other girl took off her shirt but left on her shorts, as if the two had picked their best assets to show off, or perhaps chosen to cover their biggest insecurities.

Jonah had never seen a girl in a bathing suit. He'd seen a few of his father's girlfriends, and once he'd seen his aunt Tracy, but none of that counted. Or if it did, it certainly didn't compare to this. He found himself in no way prepared for what was before him.

Katie caught him staring. She smiled. He turned away.

"Can I have a beer?" he asked Trevor.

"Yeah, man, of course. Katie's brother can get booze anytime, so we always have some."

Micah reached into a red cooler with a white lid and tossed the boy a beer and nodded at him. The boy nodded back.

"Whoa, whoa, wait a minute, dude," Patrick said, leaning his fishing pole against a tree. "You can't just open it. You gotta shake it up first."

"Shake it?"

"Yeah, dude. If you don't shake it then it doesn't taste good. It's like Gatorade or a Yoo-hoo or something."

"My dad doesn't shake his beer."

"What kind does he drink?"

"Pabst."

"Well, see, there you go. These are Coors Light. They're different. Look on the side where the mountains are."

"Okay."

"Are they blue?"

"Yeah."

"Okay, then, that means you gotta shake it up."

The boy began to shake the can.

"Yea, really shake it. That's it."

The boy opened the can and the beer sprayed onto his face and his shirt and he dropped the can and it sprayed onto his legs. The other boys laughed and clapped their hands.

"You fucking retard," Patrick said.

The boy bent down and picked up the can and it was full of foam and the rim was covered in dirt. He held it from the top between his thumb and forefinger and watched the beer drip down the side.

"Even holds it like a pussy," Micah said.

Jonah looked up at the girls, and they whispered and giggled and shook their heads.

The boy turned and began to walk away as Patrick and Micah continued to howl with laughter.

"Hey, man." Trevor ran to catch up with him. "They were just joking with you. It's okay."

Jonah spun and faced the other boy.

"Did you know what would happen?" he asked.

"What? Like did I know the beer was about to fucking explode? Yeah, man, of course. I can't believe you didn't."

Jonah's face was red and flushed and his fists were balled.

Fuck you. Fuck you. Fuck you. Fuck you. He screamed inside his head.

He turned without saying anything and Trevor shrugged and rejoined the group and the boy imagined them all laughing at him and talking about the weird kid from the river and how he'd never had a beer or a girlfriend or a mother. He hated them. He hated them all, and he hated his father, and he hated himself, most of all.

Dwayne Hargrove sat in the well-worn recliner, sculpted into the growing indentation of his own making, and watched the light from the evening sun as it sieved through the broken blinds and fell across his lap, painting the leg of his jeans in disjointed stripe and shadow.

He drank Pabst Blue Ribbon beer because that's what his father drank, and he thought about his life and his father's life and how the old man had died young, never having to deal with the changing times.

He thought about his ex-wife, who was still legally his wife, and he wondered whether there was such a thing as common-law divorce. He thought of her often, and rarely were his thoughts pleasant. She was weak, and he saw her weakness in everyone, in all the world except himself. He saw it most in their son, standing in front of him as if he expected something. Everyone always expected something. It was, in Dwayne's estimation, the downfall of society.

"It was a shit two weeks, so I need some time to myself. I don't want you bothering me with questions. You understand?"

"Yes, sir."

"Goddamn foreman thinks the sun shines out his ass. I been working this job since that little prick was your age. Thinks he can tell me how to go about it."

Dwayne took a pull from his beer and sat it empty on the ground next to him.

"Another fallen soldier," he mumbled to himself, then looked up at his son. "Go get me another can out of the ice box, boy."

Jonah nodded.

"Better make it two," his father called after him.

The boy opened the refrigerator and saw milk, a case each of PBR and RC Cola, a jar of pickles, a carton of eggs, and a block of cheese.

"You didn't bring any more groceries?" the boy asked.

"You know what the problem is? Nobody's got any common sense anymore," the man said, ignoring him. "They read all these books about this and that, but that don't prepare you for what it's really like. Your momma was like that. She was book smart. But what does that get you? Not a goddamn thing. And now half the hands out there are Mexicans who don't speak a word of English. Gonna get somebody killed is what they're gonna do."

The man's eyes were glossed and narrow. He pulled a small Bic lighter and a soft pack of Marlboros from his shirt pocket and flicked his wrist so that one cigarette rose halfway from the pack. He leaned forward and clasped the filter between his lips and lit the end opposite. He rocked back in the recliner and inhaled.

"How was school?" he asked, as if the thought had just come to him. He kept the cigarette in his mouth and it bobbed up and down with each word.

"It's summer break."

"Oh. Well. Good."

The man looked on either side of the chair for an ashtray. Seeing none, he leaned over and tried to ash his cigarette into one of the empty beer cans, but most of it missed and disappeared into the carpet.

"Anybody come to the trailer a'huntin' me?" the man asked.

The boy shook his head.

"Good." The man nodded. "That's real good."

"You expecting somebody?"

"There was just some ole boy I'm partnered up with, and I thought he might've come by to see if I was here."

"Partnered up?"

"Yea, an investment thing down in Livingston. He loaned me—" The man stopped himself. "You know what? Mind your business."

The boy looked around, hesitant.

"Your air conditioner broke, but I think I fixed it," he said.

His father stared at him and smoked and said nothing.

The boy's heart raced.

"You went in my bedroom?" the man asked, finally.

"Yessir, but just to look and see if I could fix it. It's working again, now."

"Goddamnit, boy. You know the rule."

"Yes, sir."

"Hell, it ain't like I ask hardly anything of you. Most kids would love to be in your position."

"Yes, sir."

"Why can't you do what you're told?"

"I just wanted to make sure it worked when you got home."

"Are you talking back?"

"No, sir."

"Did I ask you why you broke the rule?"

"No, sir."

"Go to your room. And don't come out until I say so."

The boy went to his room and shut the door and listened to the droning of the television and counted the times his father got up to go to the refrigerator and the times he got up to piss. The boy worked it out in his head and figured his father pissed once every three beers. The man had gone into the bathroom five times before he passed it and opened the door to Jonah's room.

He stood in the frame. The boy sat on the edge of the bare mattress.

The man nodded.

"Alright, then, let's get on with it."

"Please," the boy said, moving toward his father. "I just wanted to fix it for you."

The man slapped him and the boy staggered backward and steadied himself on the bed.

"Don't talk back," the man said, as he slid his belt out from the loops of his jeans.

The boy shut his eyes and gripped the mattress with both hands.

Don't cry. Don't let him see you cry.

6

The room was bright white, then fading. Pulsating. Two of them, Dustin and Ryan, sat with crossed legs and rocked back and forth in front of an unplugged stereo.

"No, you can't, you can't just do that," Dustin said, his skin tingled, his breath cold. "You know? You can't just do it like that. They get angry. They get so angry. And Cade. Man, you just, you just can't."

"Yeah, alright. But. 'Cause this has gotta be fixed, though. This is . . . I mean. It's gotta be fixed. Okay?"

"No, listen, you're not listening, and you have to listen, they'll get angry. Fucking pissed."

"Let's fix this shit, man. Let's just fix it."

"Where's Lonnie? Wasn't Lonnie here?" Dustin asked. He started grinning, then laughing. "I'm sorry, man, I'm pretty out there, right now."

Ryan joined in the laughing.

"Those cartel boys sure know how to cook up some roosk."

They laughed harder.

"Powerthirst," Dustin said, his voice full of faux intensity.

"Geeter."

"Gak."

"Cracker crack."

They fell backward onto the floor and held their stomachs as they laughed.

"We need music," Dustin said.

"That's what I'm trying to say," Ryan insisted. "This stereo is broke as shit, man. Let's fix it. We can fix it right now. I want to hear some music."

"I don't think we should. I don't know. Where's Lonnie?"

"He's digging, man. He's digging in the earth."

"What? He's digging in the—hey, hey, we should ask the girl. Where's the girl?"

"She's, I don't know. I think . . . I think she's in the bathroom. Hey, are you in the bathroom? Fuck it, man, let's just take it apart man. We'll fix it, we'll put it back together. She don't care."

"It's not her, dude, it's Cade. Cade will kill your ass. He's crazy. He's crazy, but you gotta ask the girl. She's his girl. If she says yeah, then it's on, okay? It's on."

The girl heard them beating on the bathroom door. She couldn't think. Everything was different now, and they wanted something from her and she couldn't think. *Yes*, she thought, *give them whatever they want. Make them go away. I just need to think.*

"Yeah," she called. "Do it. Fix it."

"Yeah?"

"Fucking yes. I don't care."

She didn't care. She couldn't care. Everything was different, now. She hadn't thought it would be. She told herself it wouldn't matter, but it did. She hadn't believed it before, but she believed it now, and now it mattered.

I'm so high. I can't do this.

The bathroom had red bulbs over the sink and the wood panels glowing like they were on fire, and the girl wondered if this was Hell, if this is where she would go.

I can't breathe.

She tugged at the slipknot of the black cord she wore around her neck.

The faucet knobs were marked hot and cold, but it was summer and the water ran hot no matter which one was turned. The girl turned them both. She cupped her hands and let the water fill and watched as it ran over and into the sink. The drain was filled with beard trimmings, black mold, and all manner of waste. She bent over the basin as it began to fill, and she splashed water onto her face and let it run down her neck.

She stared through the caked grime at the face in the mirror above the sink. Her cheeks were sunken, her eyes hollow. Her bleached, matted hair fell past her shoulders, uneven streaks of purple dye reflecting near black in the dark red light. She could see the bones in her shoulders, the veins in her neck. She could feel each droplet of water as it slid along her body.

She shivered.

She pulled her phone from the pocket of her jean shorts. The battery was at 2 percent and there was no service, and even if there had been, she didn't know who she'd call. She stared at the cracked screen and the background of a white sand beach with impossibly blue water. She cried.

She slunk down along the wall and cried for a good while, and when she was finished she stood and wiped away the tears and wiped away a swath of dirt from the mirror and looked again at herself.

She thought of her mother and her mother's frailty. Of the victimhood in which she weltered.

No.

Not me.

She gripped the edge of the sink with both hands, her jaw clenched. She nodded at her reflection. Tense and flexed and nodding, she was a long time in deciding her next move.

She walked barefoot, her feet shuffling over the short, loop-pile carpet like voltaic emery boards. The stereo was in pieces as she passed by. The two boys didn't look up.

"Y'all know when Cade gets back?" she asked.

"No."

"Nope."

"You gotta phone charger?" she asked them.

"Uh-uh."

"I don't got a phone. That's how they track you."

"Did Cade ride with John Curtis?"

"Naw, big man took his truck."

"Shit," she said. "Y'all know where John Curtis keep his keys?"

At last they both looked up from the floor.

"Why?"

"Nothing. Forget it."

She walked barefoot out onto the porch and squinted at the figures in the darkness.

"Hey, girl. You come to watch Lonnie dig his way to China?" Scooter called.

She crossed her arms over her chest and shook her head. She stumbled back inside. *I should drink water or eat something. I should take vitamins. I'm so fucking high.*

She went into the kitchen and opened the fridge and stood staring for a while and there was nothing she wanted. She closed it, then forgot what she was doing and opened it again. Still nothing. She felt the panic creeping. There was a backpack on the counter. She unzipped it.

It was more crystal than she'd ever seen in one place. Maybe more than all the crystal she'd ever seen in her life added up. She zipped the backpack up and stood there at length. Again she was a long time deciding. She picked up the bag and put the straps backward over her shoulders, holding the bag in front of her as if it were a small child, and walked out of the cabin without putting on her shoes.

She moved slowly along the side of the structure, trying to avoid the reach of the flood lights. She started across the yard and toward the treeline. She could hear Lonnie cussing from down in his hole.

"Where you headed with that satchel?" Frank called to her.

She froze. The men were just silhouettes. Shadows. She was crying, again. She'd been crying, but she didn't know how long.

"Hey, come here," Frank said and started toward her.

She was twenty yards away from him, another twenty to the trees.

Lord protect me.

She ran.

Dustin wasn't much count at fixing stereos. But running? That he could do. He'd been all-district in centerfield, and only a sophomore. Before meth, running had been as close to free as he'd ever felt. He'd stolen twenty-six bases that year, and tracked down dozens of fly balls that should have been hits. His coach thought he could play college ball at Neches Community, maybe even somewhere bigger. That was another life though, and he worked hard not to think about it. As if the memories didn't belong to him.

He was the youngest in John Curtis's crew, and he relished the chance to prove himself to the older, harder men around him. He pulled ahead of the others. He could hear them shouting, see their lights dancing off trees, but they weren't fast enough to keep up with him. He was so spun he'd half-forgotten what it was he was chasing. Then he saw her, clawing at the underbrush, panting and crying.

"Hey! Stop," he called.

She turned in a crouch and looked at him with animal eyes. A creature swallowed up by terror and confusion.

"Get away from me!" she screamed.

"Whoa, it's me. It's Dustin. It's okay."

He'd always liked the girl. Felt sorry for her. She was the closest to his own age, and she'd already been through more than any one person should.

He shined his flashlight on his own face.

"See? Just me."

"Let me go," she said, a begging whisper.

He frowned.

"What's going on?"

"Please. Just let me go."

"I can't help you if you don't talk me. And I can't let you go. Not with that backpack."

She clutched it tighter to her chest.

"You have to. Please."

"Why? What's wrong?"

She told him.

A few minutes later the others caught up to him near a clearing. He was waving his light back and forth across the topgrass.

"Where is she?" Frank asked.

"Couldn't catch her," Dustin said.

"Goddamnit."

He put his hands on his hips. The others followed suit.

Dustin avoided their eyes.

Frank continued to stare at him.

The night was filled with insect songs and the heavy breathing of men.

7

Cade stood alongside one of the marble pillars meant to separate the dining area from the grand living room. He'd never been in a house, or any other building, with such refinements. The grandeur was unsettling; the space too open, too vulnerable.

The men at the table played their game of postures. Cade ignored them. He wasn't there to negotiate. John Curtis brought him in case things went wrong. In case the masks of civilization were pulled back and the true nature of men unveiled. Fancy talk, he called it. When in the end it was still the soldiers who won the war. It always comes to blood, sooner or later.

He was growing impatient. They still had a long drive back from the city, and Cade hated driving in the dark to begin with. Too many things hidden in the shadows.

On the far wall, framed in gold styling and hanging above a stone fireplace, was an enormous canvas whereon some great battle played out in oil paints and varnish. Cade stared at the scene.

"You know this painting?" a man whispered.

Cade glanced at the man and then back to the far wall. He shook his head.

"The Battle of Ciudad Juarez," the man said.

"Juarez," Cade repeated.

"The great Mexican Revolution," the man said. He scoffed. "And yet, what did it bring us? Death and division, and what else? Brothers killing brothers."

"We had one like that," Cade said.

"Yes. The war of the slaves."

"Wasn't about slaves."

The man looked confused.

"The Civil War, no?" he asked.

"It was about the rights of the states, the rights of the people."

"The rights to own slaves?"

"What was you all fighting over?" Cade asked, ignoring his question.

"The soul of our country."

"Who won?"

"Death."

"Well."

The two men stood one next to the other and looked at the painting. From the table came an exaggerated fit of laughter from John Curtis.

"Your boss is a funny man," the Mexican said.

"Well, he don't particularly see himself that way. I wouldn't let him hear you say that. Hell, you ought not be letting me hear you say it."

The man laughed.

"My friend, I do not mean to insult. You are the muscle, as am I. Can we not speak freely of our employers to one another?"

"I'm not one for speaking. Freely or otherwise." Cade looked the man up and down. "But you don't much seem like the muscling type."

The man smiled.

"Americans. Always they are thinking the biggest must be the best."

"Worked out for us so far."

The man smiled again.

"Perhaps one day it will not."

"We can find out right now, if you want, haas."

"No, my friend, I am not wanting to fight you, here. If it is meant to be so, we should let it happen naturally. After all, anticipation is the sweetest fruit."

"I'd rather just get to the point."

"Yes, I see this. This is a shame for your women. Or your men."

The big man turned and stared down at his grinning counterpart.

"Cade," John Curtis said, "time to go."

"I'll be seeing you again," Cade said to the man.

"No, I think we have seen the last of one another. But if not, I look forward to our meeting again."

"Cade," John Curtis repeated.

8

She ran blindly through the bramble and burs and stinging nettle, the thorns tearing at her clothes and her skin. She stepped on the stunted side of a fallen branch and went tumbling down the slope toward the river. She crashed into a tree with her hip and covered her mouth to keep from screaming. She pulled herself to her feet and followed the river southeast, limping and crying silent tears.

By dawn she was lost and exhausted and she needed a hit. She sat back against a thick cypress trunk and opened the backpack. The crystals looked as if they belonged in some gift shop where kids can fill their bags with different colored rocks and gems. She dug through the bag and there was no spoon or syringe or anything else to mix a hit. She unzipped the front pocket of the pack and found a small steel pipe and a miniature Bic.

Her heart was pounding as if it was something she'd locked away, something that did not belong to her, now demanding to be set free. She rolled the pipe across her palm, then back the opposite way.

She watched the red sky through the trees on the far side of the river. The outline of a dozen limbs lay across the rising sun like fault lines, as if the sun itself were fracturing from within. She imagined her own body fracturing, her beating heart exploding from her chest, scattering pieces of her along the bank.

The birdsong closely followed the light, and the girl watched the world awaken and the clouds moving in with their purple underbellies against the pink hues of the morning. A doe emerged on the east bank, silhouette against the sunrise, and drank from the river and raised her head and looked across the water. A fawn came in behind her, looking both ways as if making ready to cross a busy street. The doe urged her forward and the young deer stood above the water and lowered her head and began to drink.

The girl was a long time watching the pair, and finally, once the sun had unfastened itself from the horizon, the deer moved back into the woods. The girl stood and watched after them. She threw the pipe into the river and the lighter as well for good measure. She zipped the backpack and began to walk on raw and bloodied feet as the first drops of rain fell from the swollen clouds above her.

9

"Well, let's get right to it. You all come up here for a reason. What is it?" John Curtis asked.

The two older men looked at one another, then at their younger companion. One of the men leaned over and whispered into his ear.

The young man nodded and brought his hands together atop the table.

"We believe there is a problem," he said.

"Not on my end."

"We believe it is on your end. You are taking certain, uh, liberties, that are not good for business."

"Not good for business? Hell, son, I've expanded my territory to cover the whole damn river basin. From the Gulf all the way to Van Zandt County, the tweakers in East Texas are buying pure Mexican ice. No shake and bake, no Nazi labs, just me. Which means just you. How in the hell is that bad for business?"

"It is true, you have grown the clientele, expanded the market. We appreciate your sacrifices in the territory wars. But—"

"A war which we won. Me and that big sumbitch in yonder. We were the last men standing. We were the ones putting our lives on the line. Y'all Mexican motherfuckers didn't send one goddamn gun up here, let alone a soldier or two."

"Yes. And again, we appreciate this."

"Well, what's the problem then?"

"There is the matter of the murdered banker."

"What matter?" John Curtis asked.

"You killed this man, yes?"

"I don't know what you're talking about."

"You don't know of the dead banker?"

"I heard about it. Don't got nothing to do with me."

"It has caused several issues with our business."

"Sorry to hear that, but like I said—"

"Yes, I heard you, you did not kill the banker. Still, it has caused several issues. The first is the authorities who will investigate this death. They will link you and the banker together. Whether they can prove you killed him is not relevant. If they link you, they might link us. You can see how we do not want to be associated with the murder of an American bank man."

"Well, I can tell you right now—"

"Second," the man continued, cutting off John Curtis, "this banker did more than your modest timber dealings. He was used by several friends of the business for certain . . . purposes. These friends are now asking for answers, you understand."

"Yeah, I hear you, it's just that I don't give a shit. You understand?"

The young man looked to his elders who did not speak, then he turned back to John Curtis.

"Mr. Curtis, I am sorry this is not going well. I am sorry you are upset."

"Like hell you are. You're just sorry I'm not gonna be your little monkey on a string. Y'all may be hot shit in Mexico, but this is Texas, amigos. It's not Mexico, and it's not the United States for that matter. This is something different. Purgatorio, if you will. Our people have always done things our own way. Independent like. And on my river, I'm the judge, jury, and executioner. You want to stop that flow of cash coming back to you, by all means let's replay the Battle of the Alamo; but I'd warn you, gentlemen, the sequel ain't likely to go your way."

The young man pressed his hands together.

"Mr. Curtis, we too are judge and jury, but we are not executioners."

"Tell that to the headless bodies piling up on your side of the river."

"Unfortunate outcomes. But, as I said, we do not advocate for violence. However, we are businessmen. And we take very seriously every aspect of our operations. If there is something not working properly, something, say, out of order, then we make the adjustments necessary to fix it."

"Adjustments? That's what you call it?"

"It does not matter what I call it. The only thing that matters is that you understand what will happen to you, and your men, if you are not agreeable to our terms."

John Curtis sighed.

"And what are these terms, that you would offer me here under threat of adjustment."

"You will increase your payments by five percent, on top."

John Curtis laughed and pounded the table. The glasses rattled.

"Hot damn, boys, if you'd told me we were going to a comedy show, I wouldn't have ate so many beans at dinner. Cade likes them chain Mexican joints, but they make me gassy as all get out. Especially when I laugh at something as funny as paying five percent off the damn top."

No one spoke.

"Oh, I'm sorry, please, continue with the sketch."

"You will increase your payments by five percent, as a means of placating our partners whose business interests were buried with the banker. Also, you will pay one hundred thousand dollars to us upon our next meeting. This is a one-time restitution. A penance for your recklessness, as well, if I may say, for your attitude here tonight."

John Curtis leaned back in his chair. The young man leaned forward across from him.

"I have watched you closely, Mr. Curtis, for many years. I know you are not a stupid man. I know this shit-kicking cowboy act is simply a ruse. You are too smart to mistake our civility for weakness, so I warn you, do not also mistake it for apathy.

"You see, it's true you mean very little to us. Our operation is run on a scale you could not imagine. You might, in your limited view of things, believe us to hold some position amongst our people. In other words, you might believe us to be in leadership. I assure you, we are not. But we do answer to leadership, and they in turn answer higher, and so on until we reach the top."

"And who's at the top?"

The young man rose from his seat. The two elders as well. John Curtis drummed the table with his fingertips.

"Not who, Mr. Curtis, but what. And the answer to that is the same in every gated neighborhood and crumbling ghetto in the world."

"Cade," John Curtis called. "It's time to go."

"You have one week, Mr. Curtis. We eagerly await your payment as a sign of our continued business together."

"Cade."

John Curtis mixed the hit while the big man drove. He waited for it to dissolve. No chunks, no cut.

"A little something to center ourselves after that clusterfuck," he said.

"Think they'll be trouble?"

"No. There's too much money to be lost by trouble. Told the boys to be ready though, just in case."

He filtered the hit through a cotton ball and drew it into the syringe. The liquid swirled then settled. He took an alcohol wipe from the console and passed it across his neck, flexing his throat like a war-ready reptile. He brought the needle point to a forty-five-degree angle and pressed it into his neck and brought down the plunger.

His eyes were open and opened more and opened to a world only he could see, as if every atom belonged to him and him alone. He clutched at the leather pouch. He let his thoughts go, let them run and saw them running each one before him and with the care of a surgeon he extracted the one he knew was right. He reached into the pouch and ran his fingers through the thin tuft of hair.

"You can get word to that cousin of yours in Ojinaga?" John Curtis asked.

"Yessir."

"Good."

"What do you want me to tell him?"

John Curtis breathed out, long and heavy. He cracked his neck.

"Go on and get your hit. Business can wait."

The big man pulled the truck over at a rest area called Lovers Lookout. One of hundreds, perhaps thousands of rest areas with the same name existed across the country. This one was on a ridge overlooking cattle land, pine trees, and the river valley below.

Cade was an oilman and he conducted each excursion accordingly. He studied his own body like a map of a shale, envisioning where he could pump and where he couldn't. He imagined small red and blue dots popping up along his forearm, between his toes, even on his neck. His very own Well Legend. He surveyed it. It was ripe for drilling.

His whole life there'd been injections. Liquid shot down at high pressure into subterranean rock. He'd break the earth and take its resources until there was nothing left to take, then the trucks would crank up and he'd move on until he was overtop of a new valve. Drill down, inject, turn on the spigot and watch money rise to the surface.

He squeezed his fist a few times and watched the veins rise up under his skin. They approached the surface like eager fish at feeding time. He thought of them as willing participants, friends on this journey. His network of tributaries. A sea of oil and gas under his feet and a river of blood inside his body. It would all be utilized—helping with production, satisfying demand, and keeping him moving toward whatever's coming next.

He leaned against the window as the dome light went from bright to Holy. His eyes avoided the glow and focused instead on the rain drops as they fell on the windshield like a growing pox. The drug was already crawling through his body like an insect, spilling from his ears and eyes and fingertips. He felt the familiar cold glide into his chest and throat as he worked to loosen the belt around his arm. He needed to cough, but his lungs felt like they were constricting. The drug weaved in and out of his ribs with every breath he took. The dopamine slithering around his brain made his scalp tingle like a menthol shampoo. The chills traded off with waves of heat, rippling through him, making him sweat. He was shaking too much to put the cap back on the needle.

He couldn't remember if he'd ever coughed, but it was too late. He was scared the drug would fall out of his mouth, so he breathed through his nose as the euphoria settled in. The drug slid its hand up his back and grabbed him behind the neck, pulling him close. He leaned in and smiled. The rush was subsiding, but the high had made a comfortable home for itself, and he could tell it would be staying for a while.

He held his arm up and inspected the fresh drilling site. There was a trickle of red smearing his map.

"How come you never get tweaked out like the rest of us?" Cade asked.

"What?"

"When you use, how come you don't get high?"

John Curtis grinned, slow, measured.

"I get high. I just do it on my own terms."

"What are those?"

"For most folks, the drug's in charge. It's doing the driving. See, they've got nothing inside of them strong enough to control something that powerful."

"But you do?"

"Yessir."

"Don't suppose you wanna tell me what it is?"

"It's hate, Cade. It's my hate for everything that keeps me strong. Keeps me from getting lost in all this shit. If it weren't for the rage inside of me, I don't believe I'd be able to take another breath. Wasn't always like that, of course. I used to think there was something wrong with me. Something missing, maybe. But the older I got, the more I understood what I had was a gift. There wasn't a damn thing missing. In fact, I had something extra. Something other folks didn't. And I used that to get through those years in the system. Used it to take over this operation and make it into something nobody figured it could be. It was hate, got me through the wars."

"Which ones?"

"All of them. The wars in the desert. The wars in Redtown. The wars still going on."

"I remember all of 'em."

"Yeah, I suspect you do. If it weren't for you, we wouldn't have all this. You know that, don't you?"

The big man didn't answer for a while.

"I didn't know if I'd ever see you again," Cade said at last. "You saved my life. I remembered it. But they put me on a flight, sent me to Germany, then back home, and I didn't know if you'd lived or died. Then you—you just came walking into that camp, and everything you said I knew was gonna come true. I knew it. I could feel it, that wasn't nothing gonna be able to stop us."

Cade looked out the window and there was only darkness.

"I don't feel that way no more," he said.

"How do you feel?"

"You ever think about getting out?" Cade asked without answering the question.

"There's nothing to get out of. Nothing to go into. This is my world. I built it. I control it. It revolves around me. That's how it feels, anyway. You wanna know if I get high? Sometimes. Sometimes I look down that hill and see the river, and I know, I truly believe, I could stop it from flowing if I wanted.

"Like the world is made of a fabric so thin it can be changed with a slow wave of my hand. Like reaching out and touching god. Having him touch me back. I don't know how else to describe it. I see the river and the trees and sky. I see the moon and the stars and the pictures taken from space. I know about matter and time and existence, and yet, if I close my eyes, it all goes away. Like the universe itself is mine to stop or start or erase altogether."

John Curtis took a deep breath.

"So, go on and call your cousin," he said. "Tell him East Texas is open for business, and we're looking for a new dancing partner."

"I ask you something else?" the big man said.

"This is a curious side of you, Cade," John Curtis told him.

"That story you told the banker, about your momma and Mac and everything. How do you know all that? I mean, if you was a baby."

John Curtis nodded.

"I was left at Pineland Heights ten months after Cindy Curtis was abducted. Her folks tried to keep it a secret, but word had got around that she tried to come home with a swollen belly and they turned her away. Game warden found her body on the Hill. I read about it, once I was older. I spent a lot of time in the library to avoid going back to whatever foster home they'd stuck me in that month. When I was old enough—man enough, you might say—I went up there and found Mac Stafford. Had some words with him. Filled in some gaps."

"Did he say he was your daddy?" Cade asked.

"No."

"Did you believe him?"

"It was too late for all that. I had a story—a narrative—that had kept me going all that time, all those years. And Mac Stafford was the man at the end of that story, whether he wanted to be or not. Actions breed reactions, and it ain't always clean."

Cade nodded.

"And what if word gets back to the Alanzo family? What do you think their reaction will be if they find out we're talking to another cartel?"

"You heard 'em. We're small fish. Made their point loud and clear. They want to disrespect me, fine. Mexico's full of Mexicans. It's time they learned they ain't the only swinging dicks can move any weight. Besides, if they want a war, they'd better send the devil himself up here to do the job."

10

The thin man rose before the first light of day and set about the composition of the morning: Café. Baño. Huevos rancheros. Mas café.

It was in these early mornings that the thin man was himself, for in the coming hours the children would wake, as would his spouse, and despite the often enjoyable nature of his interactions as a father and husband, only the darkness allowed him the freedom of the man he had always been. Would always be.

The mountains were more brown and jagged than their majestic blue counterparts to the north. The thin man liked it this way. It was, he believed, somehow more honest.

The first band of orange light traced the horizon. The cold wind came in off the desert and moved west, as if it were running from the sun; and with it was brought the smell of creosote and sage, and soon the night lizards would see their shadows cast long in the calm awakening of the world.

The thin man stood in the dirt and drank his coffee. The early light fell across his face and he turned away from it, toward the western ranges, and in a moment within this moment he was for a short time half light and half darkness. Then he walked up the steps of the porch and let the light pass him by.

He watched the dawn, and he was of the belief that no single sunrise was less than a miracle. Not because of a deeply held appreciation for life, nor due to any religious suggestion. But rather, the thin man had seen the whole of the world's offerings, and had long measured every outcome of his own species and found none to his liking; and so through such a prism he viewed his own existence and the existence of those around him—with no exemptions for even his own family—as a great plague upon the earth. And with each passing morning he gave his apology, in hopes that some future dawn would fall away in silence, leaving the world in the very darkness it deserved.

11

The boy woke before the sun but stayed in his room and listened to his father making coffee and watching television. When he finally came out, his father was smoking a cigarette and wouldn't look him in the eyes.

The boy went to the pantry and took an open sleeve of crackers and stood in the kitchen eating. His father came and stood, unsteady, next to him.

"I'm sorry, Jonah. Alright? I'm so sorry, buddy."

The boy was silent save his chewing.

"I love you so much. You know that, right? What I said last night, what I did, that's not me. It's not. And it'll never happen again. I promise you. I can promise you that, son. That was the last time. Okay?"

His father looked around.

"I asked for god's forgiveness, son, and guess what? He forgave me. But that's not enough. I don't care if it's blasphemous, I'm saying it. I need more than god's forgiveness. I need yours, too. C'mon, buddy. Give me another shot. Alright?"

The boy nodded.

"Alright," the man said. "That's my boy."

The man ruffled the boy's hair and opened the fridge and drank milk from the plastic carton and the milk ran down into his goatee and dripped onto the linoleum. He wiped at it with the sleeve of his shirt and set the milk back and grabbed a beer.

An hour later the boy's father had a productive buzz and the words of the early morning had spirited away with the dawn.

"I'll be at Shawna's for a while," the man said.

They sat, the two of them, on the worn sofa, dark green with torn fabric and stains new and old and mysteries. The boy stared at the rabbit ears atop the television and wondered how far away they went to retrieve the blurred images on the screen. His father watched the man on television, and the man told his father the country was collapsing and the only thing to be was angry. Maybe it was the man, or maybe it was everything else, but the boy's father *was* angry.

"You hear me?" he asked the boy. "I'm talking to you."

"How long?" the boy asked.

His father threw his hands into the air.

"I don't know," he said. "A while."

"Can I come?" the boy asked, still fixated on the antenna.

"No, you can't come. I gotta talk to Shawna about grown-up things. I can't have some little kid running around making it weird."

"I'll be thirteen on Tuesday."

The man paused.

"Tuesday, like tomorrow?"

The boy nodded.

"No shit? Well, I'll tell you what, I'll see about bringing you back a present. How's that?"

The boy nodded.

His father touched the boy's knee and rose from the couch and groaned and flipped up a cigarette from his pack. The boy looked down at his knee where his father had touched him.

"Well, alright then," his father said and put on his pinched-crease cowboy hat and nodded and opened the door and hopped down and cussed when he landed. The boy turned toward him and saw only his torso and head and his face buried under the hat, and the man closed the door without looking back.

The boy stood and gathered what few dishes there were and picked up his father's ashtray and took everything to the sink. The water dripped and sputtered and banged through the pipes. When it came out it was brown and roily. He used just enough to rinse a bowl and a spoon and he set them both out to dry on the counter. He emptied the ashtray and rinsed it as well and took the old broom and opened the door and swept the dirt and dead bugs into the yard and looked toward the road and tried to hear the last of his father's truck as it rumbled away, but he could not.

Another rainstorm, and the boy soaking wet and mud on his shoes.

The old man sat rocking and watching the rain and watching the water come off the roof. He looked up at the boy and felt at once a great sadness, such a pitiful sight as he was.

"Missed you yesterday."

"Yessir."

"Had to eat all that deer sausage on my own."

"Sorry. My dad came home."

Carson stared at him.

"He the one split that lip?"

The boy shrugged.

"Well. He ought not do that."

"I don't think he likes me," the boy said.

"He's your father. He loves you."

"What does that mean?"

"What does what mean?"

"Do fathers have to love their sons?"

The old man took pause.

"No," he said. "No, I suppose they don't. But fathers make mistakes. We build them up, you know, to be something they ain't. They're just men. And men are flawed."

They sat for a while on the porch, but when the rain ended, the day grew hot and humid and the old man motioned for the boy to follow him inside. There they sat again, on wooden bench seats on either side of an old red-and-white table from a bygone decade. Along the wall were rusted nails from which a half-dozen medals hung. The old man turned the knob on a window unit at the end of the table where it met the wall. The air conditioner sputtered to life and the boy and the old man each put their faces in front of it and let the cool air blow against the sweat on their foreheads. The medals swung slightly, bumping into each other with a series of soft "tinks."

The old man pulled strips of bacon come from a feral hog he'd trapped and laid them to cook in a cast-iron skillet set over a single burner propane cooktop. The boy ground roasted beans in a tin grinder and soon the small cabin was cooled down and smelling of bacon grease and fresh coffee.

They ate the bacon and drank the coffee and played two games of chess on an old pine board with the pieces carved from basswood. The boy lost both games, but the old man said he was getting better.

"You aren't taking it easy on me, are you?" the boy asked.

"Wouldn't even know how to go about it," the old man replied.

He rose and walked outside and flung the dregs from his cup into the grass. The boy did the same.

"I baited my trotline this morning," the old man told him. "What do you say we go check and see if there's a cat or two waiting to come up?"

"Is it far?" the boy asked.

"Just down about half a mile from my dock."

"That's okay, Mr. Carson. I should be getting back."

"You just got here," the old man protested, though the boy knew it was not true.

The boy frowned.

"You been here your whole life, Mr. Carson?"

"Oh yeah, yeah, most of it. Left a time or two, always came back. My home."

"You like living here?"

"Well, I got everything I need. Not as much as some. More than some others. Yeah, I guess I like it. I can't see myself living any place away from the river. Last place left where a man can find any sort of peace. Maybe on some mountain somewhere, but even then. Gets cold. No, I imagine I'll die right here. Right here on the river."

"Did it used to be different?"

"Different?"

"When you were growing up, I mean. Were things different than they are now?"

"Yeah, son, I suppose they were."

"How?"

"I can't say exactly. Lots of ways. The people, for one. It was just a different breed of folk. It's like, things were more savage and more civilized at the same time. For all the damn sense that makes. I guess, maybe, it was just less. Less people, less money, less choices. Things get all twisted up when there's choices. Too many of us making the wrong ones."

The old man watched a memory as it bobbed atop the surface of the river then disappeared.

"It's all backward now, from how it used to be," he said, turning back to the boy. "Soon as they found that first drop of oil, everything changed. The people changed, the river changed. Even the deer ain't the same. Smaller, if you ask me. These boys go off to the pipelines and come back addicted to meth or money, and most times both. Spending it as fast as they make it, and on what? Nobody cares about the old ways. The river ways."

"What were the old ways?"

"Well, to hear the old timers tell it, the river was all there was."

"What do you mean?"

"Everything revolved around it, everything depended on it. Up near the headwaters, the river was too shallow for the steamboats, so the farmers would have to load up their wares and take them by cart and mule all the way to Bunn's Bluff."

"Where's that?"

"Down south of Evadale."

"That's a long way."

"Oh, my, yes. They'd be gone weeks at a time. Much to the chagrin of them left behind. It was said a man could have himself quite a time at them old trading posts."

"You ever go?"

"How old do you think I am, son? No, I never went. Them days were long gone 'fore I was ever thought about. The railroads came in, became the preferred method of transporting goods. If folks couldn't trade along the river, they'd have to find some other way to live. So they turned to timber.

"They started sawing logs all up and down the basin, mills sprung up along the banks, a dozen of them overnight is what my daddy used to say. Down in the flood plains they started working the wetlands for rice. Food and timber, that's what the river gave us. Then it all went to shit, if the old waddies is to be believed."

"Are they?"

"What?"

"To be believed."

The old man considered the question.

"I'd imagine they are. At least on the more severe matters. My daddy used to say that first drop of oil was the end of everything. Looking back on it, I don't know if he could've pieced together how it would all turn out. But he was right anyway. They choked the life out of this place. Zinc, lead, phenol, just about every chemical you could think up coming from the plants and refineries. They dug out the bottom of the river where it meets the sea, salt water started flowing into its mouth. And all of it on top of the goddamned lakes and neighborhoods and everything else.

"One day, all this is gonna be gone. You watch. They'll flood these bottoms and start building gated subdivisions all along the edge of the water. They act like this land ain't worth nothing to nobody, but they get 'em another lake and you watch the money come in. They'll push us out. You just watch."

The old man spit off the porch and shook his head.

"I don't know," he said. "Maybe we ought to be pushed out. Maybe a great purge is the only solution. Either way, I hope to hell I ain't here to see it."

"How come you to stay this long?"

"Like I said, for better or worse, this is my home. Besides, where else is there to go?"

The boy looked out at the river and nodded his head in agreement.

"I don't know. Nowhere, I guess."

12

It's something folks nowadays don't understand. Can't understand. Some things just are how they are. They can't be held accountable for nothing, 'cause weren't no decision ever made.

They say it's a privilege, getting old. Maybe it is for some. But I feel only the continued burden of existence. Some cursed watchmen at his post, set about to oversee the desolation of a world I thought I understood. I never did, of course, never could—and it's in these twilight years that I come to know such a truth.

This world is not what we make it, as told to the children, some unmolested canvas upon which to create a future worth living. No. The portrait of our lives was begun in years too long ago to be numbered. It was etched and painted and painted over to some millionth degree, with colors overlapping or mixing or fading altogether into some forgotten story left forever untold.

And these images created over time did evolve, and in their evolution we looked upon them and to each new discovery we gave praise, and so on, and growing old until the picture of the world was no longer one I recognized, as it no longer looked like me. And only then did I discern my own life never belonged to me, my own world never a creation meant to last. Yet here I am, bitter and full up with regret, an old man privileged to die alone on an ever-changing canvas to which he no longer holds a brush.

In those olden times, as you lay dying beneath the roof of the selfsame shanty *wherein your entire life had been rendered, you could hear there, outside your very window, the composition of your own passing, the spadework upon the earth and the saw blade passing along the boards.*

Some poor boy, maybe your grandson, maybe just a boy, working a crosscut back and forth on a piece of wood. Bent over and covered with sweat, bracing himself on the table horse, pulling the teeth of the tool across the pine, and you hearing every bit of the mechanism gone into your own coffin.

It'll always be like that for old men. There may not be some poor soul digging a plot in the yard, but I can still hear such fateful approaches. Oh, yes. I can hear the saw.

And to awaken each day is to be reborn as an old man and to have a life lived over in the split second it takes to wipe away at half-hung eyes, and such eyes offering a bleak recanting of the world—a reminder of what waits outside of dreams. As if in some immeasurable flash, the brain must give an accounting of every breath ever taken, so as to bring to consciousness those memories lost each night.

The sum of such recanting is less and less these days. Certain emotions come up against, but no particular memories to pair them with. Some overwhelming chaplet of grief pulled down upon my head, and here I'm sent to bawling. Neurons firing, I'd guess. Wires being crossed as the system starts to shut down. We spend half our lives accumulating experiences, the other half forgetting them.

I don't know what else to say. Not because I forgot. That's the other part of old age: All the things you thought you'd learn, you don't. You don't find out who you are. You don't make some peace with the world or with god or even with yourself. You don't end up wise and content and ready to die. No. The truth is, in these final hours, the world makes less sense than it ever did before. And death is still something to be feared.

One of the few things I've learned is that believing in god is not something you try at. As soon as you start to feel unsure about things, that means you don't believe, even if you're too afraid to say it.

13

On Tuesday, the boy woke. He'd slept on the couch and his back hurt from where the cushions sagged in the middle. He'd left the television on and the picture cut in and out almost rhythmically and through the cascading lines of static he could see there were two women sitting in chairs on a stage and a man in between them. The volume was down but the boy watched as the women yelled at the man and at one another and then one of the women picked up her chair and threw it and other men rushed onto the stage to grab her. He stood and stretched and walked to the television and turned the knob to Off and opened the door and climbed carefully to the ground and stood there in his boxers and looked toward the tree line.

There was no movement, so the boy walked barefoot across the clearing and searched the ground for uneaten corn, but there was none. He nodded and walked back through the clearing and behind the trailer and to the shaded tin shed which sat at a tilt beneath two large cypress trees. There was a lock on the door. The boy yanked at it until he was convinced it would not open. He moved to the backside of the shed and felt the dirt at the base of the tin with his toes. He dropped to his knees and dug and it did not take long to dig past the bottom of the tin and further still until he could lay on his stomach and fit his arm into the shed. He felt blindly with his hand until his fingers touched a corn sack and he pressed his shoulder further into the tin siding and stretched his arm far enough to grab the sack and pull it into the hole. The sack filled the hole and would not fit under the shed, so the boy pushed himself up from the dirt and brushed himself off and went back to the trailer.

When he returned he held a pocket knife and his cereal bowl. He wedged the bowl into his side of the hole, letting it rest against the bag on the shed-side. He opened the knife and cut a gash into bottom of the sack and the corn began to pour out and into the bowl. When it was full he took the bowl and walked back to the tree line and scattered the corn and stood with his hands on his hips. He filled the bowl twice more and when things were completed to his satisfaction he shoved the dirt back into the hole at the back of the shed and hoisted himself into the trailer.

The discolored wallpaper above the bathroom sink took the shape of an almost perfect rectangle, holding dear the memory of the mirror that had once hung. There was no shower curtain and pushed against the outside of the cracked tub were several old and molding towels. The boy took off his boxers and stepped over the towels and into the tub. He turned the hot water knob and the clanking of pipes ensued, and when the water came spilling out it was brown and oily. He turned the cold water on as well but nothing changed.

He stepped out of the tub and over the towels and walked naked into the kitchen and turned the faucet on and watched it drip and saw the same grimy water emerge. He walked through the kitchen and living room and down the short, carpeted hallway and went into his own bedroom and stood above a small pile of clothes. He reached into the pile and sifted until he found the swim trunks he'd been given the summer before. They belonged to the son of a woman his father had been seeing. She was a nice woman, with red hair that curled and a face full of freckles. The boy liked her. He'd told the woman she looked like a spotted fawn. His father had slapped him.

He smelled the trunks and put them on and left the trailer and went into the woods past the shed and down the bank and into the river.

He walked until the brackish waters were at his waist. He reached out with both hands and touched the surface and watched it move and felt it as it tugged at him, counseling him with its current, some long-known warning of stagnation and survival and the rivalry between the two.

He let the river and the world flow around him.

The boy didn't know where the river started, only that it was somewhere north and whether it was Dallas or Denver he couldn't say. He knew at the mouth the estuary spilled into the gulf and the gulf into the ocean and all things connected in the end, but still the beginning remained a mystery. He knew the river's course held tributaries and watersheds and he imagined many creeks and coves, and in his mind he saw the river laid upon the land as a vein which carried the earth's blood, and such blood was muddy and brown and from it sprang a song of nature, persistent and tholing.

The river flowed and the world turned, cutting paths both new and old, overwhelming those things which came before but could not adapt to the constant movement, the everlasting change. The river and the world together, and both giving life and both swallowing it whole, and neither caring which, and neither having a say in the matter. The boy watched both passing by, his choice and his path each belonging to some current long set in motion.

He scrubbed the dirt from his hands and knees and stomach and the water was not too cold and there was no one and nothing around. The current was nonthreatening, and the boy walked further into the Neches and felt along the bottom with his toes. As the water passed his chest he tilted backward and spread wide his arms and there floated with his eyes closed and his ears half submerged as if he was listening to the world both above and below the surface.

A male wood duck passed overhead and the boy opened his eyes as it landed in the shallow water on the far side of the river. He watched the bird, its green crested head and intricate plumage, its chestnut breast rising and falling as it glided along against the water's easy flow. It was more stunted than a mallard, with a thin neck, boxed face, and short wings. His father liked to shoot mallards.

The boy floated and splashed and made sure not to veer too far up or down the river and then there was at once a rumble both in the sky and in his stomach. He swam to shore and walked from the river and stood in the clearing in front of the trailer and let himself drip dry as the dark clouds crept in and the coming storm gathered around him.

The drawer was overflowing with used envelopes, paper clips, and all manner of trinkets and forgotten possessions, and the boy pulled from it one of several lighters and lit the grease mantled stovetop and set about scrambling himself an egg. He could have eaten three or even four, but there were only half a dozen left and he did not know when his father might return or what he might bring when he did. The boy stirred the egg meticulously, first in a clockwise motion to the count of fifty, then counterclockwise for the same period, as if an imbalance in the procedure might render the product inedible. He slid the spatula along the sides of the pan and shook loose the edges of his creation then dumped the contents onto a paper plate.

The wind raced into the bottomlands and met there the ancient trees which bent and swayed but held their ground until the gusts broke through into the clearing and shook the trailer and the boy inside. Whatever magic the antenna drew upon had been blocked and the television darkened as did the world around him. The boy ate his food slowly, in small bites and chewing until there was nothing left and finally swallowing, and after, taking a long pull from his soda can. When he was finished he licked the plate and took the half-empty can with him to the bedroom and crawled atop his creaking mattress and lay on it perpendicular and on his stomach with his chin in his hands and the soda resting on the ledge where the bed met the window. He watched the road and the rain and the dancing trees and soon he was asleep and dreaming of a river full of mallards and wood ducks and he floated among them and called each one by name.

When the boy's eyes opened the rain had passed. An afternoon storm blown in from the west in a fit of fury and gone just as quickly toward the swamps of Louisiana. It was the nineteenth day of rain in a row.

He looked out the window to the road and then left his bedroom and called for his father. There was no one else in the trailer and when he hopped down from the door there was no truck parked in the yard. He felt the wet earth on his feet. The spores of sweet-smelling bacteria growing in the ground had been kicked up and into the air and the world was left humid and green and perfumed. The boy walked to the tree line and looked to see that the corn had not been washed away but if some of it had he did not notice or thought it not enough to bother with. He went back inside the trailer and looked at the clock and added the hour that had not been changed when the rest of the country sprang forward. He dressed in blue jean shorts, hole-riddled socks, and off-brand tennis shoes. He pulled on an oversized T-shirt of a band he had never seen and went outside and drug to its right spot the picnic table and climbed atop the roof.

For a time he lay on his back and closed his eyes and listened for the sound of the truck. When that time passed he sat up and looked to the road and the tree line and both were quiet and still. He watched the sky change above him, growing cold and blue gray in the east while the sinking sun layered the western heavens in an ombre of red and orange.

His father did not return, but the big doe did. The last of the day was slipping from the horizon when she stepped out into the clearing. The fawn followed. The boy perked up and sat still as the animals walked gingerly amongst the corn. Fireflies in quick glowing bursts of light appeared as though they were the last of a shower of falling stars, burning out just as they reached the earth's surface.

He thought about his father and about god and forgiveness and all of it. If god could talk to his father, maybe he could talk to the boy as well.

Give me a sign, he thought. If you're real. If you can control everything. Let me touch that deer.

The boy moved slowly, sliding from the rooftop onto the table and then freezing. The doe's head was up. He didn't move until it went down again. He eased his way off the table and took small, measured steps into the clearing. Both heads came up and the boy stopped, motionless, but the deer were not looking at him. Their heads looked past him, past the end of the trailer and toward the river and the big doe flicked her tail. Then, like the afternoon rain they were gone, vanished back into the wooded ether from which they seemed to materialize. The boy looked after them, though in the settling darkness there was little and less to see.

When at last he turned back to the trailer she was standing there in the flickering of the porch light and her silhouette came and went with each spasm of the bulb and he thought her some specter, a ghost or haint from times forgotten come to take his soul or perhaps just haunt him to madness and he thought it more certain as she reached out her hand toward him. He readied a scream but it stuck in his throat and he took a step back and she forward, still reaching, and then she collapsed onto the wet ground before him and her hair strewn about her in streaks of blond and purple and the boy stood, watching, as her back rose and fell with heavy breathing.

He walked slowly to her and bent down and studied her. She was barefoot and wore blue jeans and a camo tank top, and the boy could see her red bra straps. He reached out and touched the bare skin on her shoulder, and she jerked and cried and tried to get up but couldn't.

"Are you hurt, Miss?" the boy asked.

The girl looked up at him wild-eyed. She opened her mouth but didn't speak. She stared past him, like the deer, looking at something he couldn't see.

"Are you friends with my daddy? Do you know Shawna?"

The boy straightened up and looked around as if the answer might lay in wait.

"Water," the girl said at last.

"We don't got no water."

"Water."

"We don't—alright, you just stay here."

The boy left and returned with a cola, and the girl drank and coughed and spit and drank some more. She made it up to her hands and knees and then vomited. She began to shiver.

"Are you cold? You can come inside."

She looked at the trailer and then at the boy. Her eyes were full up with fear.

"It ain't nobody here but me," the boy said.

She nodded.

The boy squatted down and wedged himself under her arm and the two of them stood together and moved slowly toward the door. She crawled into the entryway and the boy pushed her legs and got her inside the door, then climbed up after her. The girl was writhing in pain on the den carpet.

"Do you have a cell phone?" the boy asked. "I can call an ambulance for you. There's a spot about a mile up the road that gets service. I can run up there."

"No," the girl shook her head weakly. "No ambulance. Bed."

The boy looked toward his father's door.

"You can sleep in my bed," he said, and again positioned himself as a crutch as they trudged down the hall.

"Um, my room is messy, so, I'm sorry," the boy said. "But there's nothing on the bed, and you can sleep there."

The girl collapsed onto the bare mattress and the boy lifted her head and slid a pillow under it and covered her with his one sheet and then brought a blanket from the couch and covered her with that as well.

"I have CDs," the boy said. "I like to listen to music sometimes when I'm in bed. I don't know what kind of music you like, though."

He wanted to say the right thing. His heart was pounding.

The girl didn't answer, and the boy watched her breathing, and her tank top bunched above the small of her back and there was a half-finished tattoo of a butterfly. On her left shoulder blade flew three blackbirds, and the name "Cade" was spelled out in script across her left wrist.

She was skinny, like the boy. He looked at the veins straining against her skin. He thought she was very likely the most beautiful person he'd ever seen.

"Are you gonna be okay, Miss?" he asked, but the girl was fast asleep and the boy reasoned that if she was breathing she wasn't dying, and so he sat up the rest of the night and watched her breathe.

14

John Curtis stood in the doorway and the sunlight behind him, a shadow framed with white. He stood in silence, the others looking to him as if he were some muted messenger of the last morning, a harbinger of the evil yet to come. He stood, unmoved and unspeaking, and drew from each of them the guilt of what had transpired. He stood until they could no longer take his standing and began to all of them beg for his forgiveness, his mercy, his understanding. They confessed their sins at his feet and he listened to all they had to say.

"So, then. You all let a little girl steal from me. Is that about right?"

They hung their heads like dogs.

"Any swinging dick here believe their life is more valuable than that satchel?"

Silence.

"Well, I guess that means killing you is out of the question. So, what now?"

The men looked up. They looked at one another.

"We find her," Frank said.

John Curtis turned and walked onto the porch and looked out.

The hardwoods grew tall and spaced along the steep incline of Splithorn Hill's eastern ridge. In the cold season when the branches were brought bare, a vantage of the river's bend could be had from most all of the eastern ground leading up the stunted shelf-land. John Curtis stuck his hand in his pocket and mumbled and nodded and looked out with wild eyes at something only he could see.

"Alright then," he said, turning back to the cabin door. "We find her."

He moved from the doorway and made a sweeping gesture with his arms.

"Everybody out. Go on. Get."

The men again mumbled their apologies as they passed by, eyes down.

"Not you, Cade."

The big man nodded.

"Hold up a second, fellas," John Curtis called.

He stood at the front of the porch and Cade beside him on the first step and the rest of the men below in the yard like some tattered army of miscreants, staggering and swaying with wide eyes and gray veins run along bone-tight skin.

John Curtis looked out at them.

"Now, for whichever of you fine men brings me the girl, I'll have a special commission waiting."

The men giggled and grinned through thin and rotting teeth. They looked to one another and nodded and rubbed their hands together. They bounced on the balls of their feet and clapped and cackled.

John Curtis waved his hand again and the men disbanded and their trucks cranked and rumbled one after the other down the hill toward the muddy river road and the highway beyond.

He turned back to the big man.

"I'm being tested," he said. "By what, I don't know."

Cade spit off the porch, then nodded.

"By god, I imagine," he said.

"God," John Curtis scoffed. "I don't get it. Call me an infidel, but I really just do not understand it."

"Which part?"

"We don't have that kind of time. The Trinity, the virgin birth, the words of god that were written by men. But I'd say my biggest issue is with myself."

"How's that?"

"If there's a god up there, supposed to be looking out for everybody, then why am I still alive?"

Cade laughed. "Dumb luck, I reckon."

"And I gotta say, if god exists, he sure ain't much of a businessman. It's a little insulting, really. I mean, ought not my everlasting soul be held in higher regard? A lifetime of misdeeds mitigated in mere moments. Speak the prayer. Ask forgiveness. Accept the Lord into your heart—and then, enter unto the kingdom of heaven forever and ever amen. I don't know. Sounds like a raw deal for god. Either that or he don't value my soul the way he should."

"Thought you said we ain't got time," Cade replied, shifting his considerable weight from one foot to the other.

"You know," John Curtis continued, "I asked one of my foster mothers—once, on such occasion that I was feeling abnormally curious, or perhaps even mischievous—what Jesus might have done with Adolf Hitler, had he prayed in those final hours for absolution."

"And?" Cade went along.

"If he was sincere, she told me, if his heart was open, then the Lord would forgive him. And he would go to Heaven. My mother told me it was not fairness or worth that determined one's place in the afterlife. Mercy, she said, and grace, are the pillars of god's love." John Curtis slipped his fingers into the pouch around his waist and stroked the brittle hair within. "All who believe in him, shall have everlasting life."

The big man leaned and spit, again.

"You ever think maybe we aren't meant to understand the ways of god?" Cade asked. "Like maybe we just aren't capable?"

"If gods are real, and we lack the agency of understanding them, then it's because they made us as such, to toil away in the ignorance of our own existence," John Curtis answered. "What are you, a preacher now?"

"I got as much chance at preaching as them peckerwoods do of finding your backpack."

"About that. We'll get the satchel back, and the girl carrying it."

"Alright," Cade said.

"And then what?" John Curtis asked him.

Cade shrugged.

"What do you mean, then what?"

"I mean what are we going to do about the girl?" John Curtis said. "Do you love her?"

Cade walked to the front of the porch and leaned against a cedar post, his back to John Curtis.

"I guess it don't matter now," he said.

John Curtis nodded.

"You want I should take care of it myself?"

Cade turned and looked at him. He sighed. "Yeah, you'd better."

"Alright then. It's done."

"Gotta find the little bitch first," Cade reminded him.

"Don't worry about all that. I'm about to head into town and take care of it."

15

The day passed unnoticed, the girl in the fetal position, sleeping or crying, the boy moving about the trailer like some nervous handmaiden, and all the while the afternoon rain grew harsher and stayed longer. The river began to rise.

The boy chased a snake from the weeds beneath the trailer and picked through the items collected there. A push mower he'd never seen in operation, old tin pans with rust and rot, ropes and chew toys belonging to a dog he remembered as a toddler, tarps with much of the lining eaten away, and several broken plastic planting pots made to look as if they were clay.

The boy drug from the pile an old folding chair and set it in the yard. He took the least damaged plastic pot and filled it with water from the river then added soap. He wet a wash rag in the pot and wiped down the chair, scrubbing the grime from the joints, then dried it with a towel and took it inside.

He set the chair near his mattress and took the box fan from the bathroom and propped it up in the chair and turned it on. The blades groaned but complied and the boy watched as the girl turned toward the breeze with wet matted hair and beads of sweat across her forehead.

"That's better, huh?" the boy asked, and the girl moaned quietly, and he took that as a yes.

"I'll make you an egg if you get hungry," he told her.

The girl did get hungry. She would wake, wild-eyed, and ask for food, and he'd scramble an egg and put pepper on top and bring it to her on a paper plate. Then he'd count the eggs and the plates and try to determine how long either would last. His father had taken the pickles and cheese, and the boy was worried they would soon run out of food.

"These eggs taste like shit," the girl would say, or, "Who's so poor they don't have ramen?"

Once she apologized and thanked the boy. He asked her name and she said not to worry about it, but he worried anyway.

The girl cried often. She would scream and the boy would come in the room and find her on the floor next to the mattress, sobbing.

"Go away," she'd sometimes tell him, then she would add a hesitant "please," as if remembering some lone manner she'd once been taught. Other times she wouldn't say anything, but would motion for him to join her on the floor and there they would sit together, and she would lay her head on his shoulder until she stopped crying and fell asleep.

The only thing she did more than cry was sleep. Sometimes she would wake and profess her starvation as if she were moments away from perish, but when the boy would bring her a scrambled egg she would have already fallen back asleep.

"No more eggs," the girl said, but she ate them anyway and then fell back onto the bed and slept again. The boy watched her and when she began to shiver he added blankets and when she began to sweat he took them away. He kept the plastic cup full of Coke.

He studied her as she lay there, as if she were some unknown specimen—which in many ways she was. He looked at the sharp bones near her collar and shoulders. He stared at the outline of her hips and at her bare legs, and he felt guilty but he didn't look away.

He poured milk onto a rag and washed the girl's feet while she shivered and moaned. Her feet were raw and cut up, as bad as the boy had ever seen. He dug through the old seasonings in the cupboard until he found a tin shaker of turmeric with a best by date from the first Bush presidency. The powder was clumped together and hard, so the boy shook it and separated what he could and took a handful back to the bedroom. He pressed the turmeric into the girl's wounds. She winced but said nothing.

The next day he chopped a quarter of an old onion and mixed it with a jar of honey and used his finger to apply the paste to each cut and blister on the girl's feet.

"What the hell are you doing?" the girl protested.

"Fixing you up."

"Why's it all sticky?"

"It's honey."

"You ain't gonna lick it off my toes or something, are you?"

"What?"

"Nothing. Ugh. It smells weird."

"It's the onions. Or it may be your feet, from the turmeric."

The girl snatched her feet away and tucked them under the blankets.

"It ain't my feet."

"Okay," the boy said.

The girl started to cry.

"It's not your feet," the boy said.

"I don't care what it is. I don't care about anything. I just want some water. I need water, okay? Please."

The boy's face twisted up with concern.

"Okay," he said after some time. "I'll go fetch water. I know a man who might have some to spare."

It was in the waking from those fevered dreams where the girl first found things familiar within herself. A simple feeling, like the comfort of closing her eyes for just a while longer, knowing she was taken care of, knowing she was doing something right and good and worthwhile. Guilt had kept her awake for what seemed months at a time. Guilt and drugs, and now she would work to rid herself of both.

But such solace in those first days was rarely more than a whisper, fading so quickly and completely, the girl was left to question whether it had been there at all.

The withdrawals seemed the one constant. And the boy. He was there when she opened her eyes, and there when she closed them again. He pulled her away from the dreams with Coke and over-peppered eggs. He covered her when she was cold, without her ever speaking, as if she'd somehow thought him into existence. Maybe she had. Maybe he was only an apparition, a cool spring in a desert of meth-fueled psychosis.

Now the boy was gone. He said he was fetching water. Or maybe that had been a dream. Was it all a dream, and she was back in the cabin on Splithorn Hill? Had she never left Louisiana? She couldn't remember, she couldn't breathe. She couldn't remember how to breathe.

She'd seen this before, with Sadie. Sweet Sadie. She'd had panic attacks almost daily. Panic disorder. She screamed and cried and thought she was dying. Maybe she was. The girl would hold her and they'd rock back and forth on the couch, sharing a quilt, staring mindlessly at the blue light from whatever weightless sitcom was on the television. The girl would rub her back and sing to her.

You can be a sweetie pie,
You can be a sweetie guy,
You can be a candy cane la-dy,
You can be a frosted flake,
And still not have the sweet it takes,
To ever be as sweet as Sa-die

The girl repeated the song to herself, just as she'd done so many times with her sister. She cried and sang and cried again, and soon she was asleep.

In her dream she walked along the riverside and there was no rain and the sun was bright but it wasn't hot and everything was green and splendor. Sadie ran ahead and looked back and laughed and ran faster still.

"Be careful," the girl told her. "Stay where I can see you."

But soon she'd disappeared from the trail and the girl called for her, but no one answered. The sky darkened and the rain and lightning spilled from the clouds. The girl yelled louder, but each time she opened her mouth the thunder came to steal her voice. She thought she heard a noise in the woods and she ran toward it, waving her hands in front of her face to ward off spiderwebs and thorn vines and low-hanging branches. At last she came to a clearing and her sister stood facing away and she spoke in a soothing whisper to the infant cradled in her arms.

"Sadie," the girl called, "what's going on?"

"He's beautiful," her sister said, turning. "He's so beautiful."

The girl took a step back and covered her mouth.

The child was covered in scales, and the scales were bursting with blood and maggots, and the child's head was two sizes too large and from each side grew black, spiraled horns.

"Put it down," the girl cried.

Sadie stepped toward her.

"Hold him," she said, smiling, as if she were fallen under the spell of some woods witch or hex.

The girl shook her head and took another step back.

"Sadie, please," she said.

"Aw, hold him," Sadie begged. "Hold him."

Her sister froze and looked at the girl with black eyes.

"Hold him," she said and her voice was a low growl. "Hold him. Hold him. Hold him."

She began to sprint toward the girl, holding the crying creature out to her. The girl turned to run and Sadie was already there, her mouth opening beyond her face, beyond the realm of any reality save that of some demon world.

"No!" the girl screamed and threw the blankets off of her and onto the floor.

"Sorry to bother you," the boy said, out of breath. He'd run the whole way.

"Ain't no bother, son," the old man told him. "C'mon up."

"You think I could get some water off of you?"

"Water?"

"Yessir, if that's alright."

"Got some rain water, all them storms we been having. You're welcome to it."

"I'd be much obliged. I think there's mud in the pipe water."

"Pipe water," the old man repeated softly, as if weighing the worth of the words.

"Yessir."

"Well. I got plenty of water, all this rain," the man said again. "C'mon in and get you a jug or two, and we'll go fill up yonder at the barrel."

"Thank you, sir. Like I said, I'm sorry to bother."

The old man waved his hand at the boy's apology, as if doing so might chase away the words. Inside, he bent over a sliver of space between the side of his refrigerator and the wall. He pulled out a plastic jug and popped the top and smelled the inside. He scrunched his face and turned away, then replaced the top and put the jug back where he'd found it. He emerged with two more jugs, each one passing the smell test, and they were on their way.

The barrel held fifty-five gallons and the old man judged it to be at capacity. It was mounted under the gutter and affixed to a flexible downspout diverter to capture the runoff.

"Ain't nothing we haven't seen," the old man said as he held the jug up to the brass hose bib near the bottom of the barrel. "Claudette hit in '78, or maybe '79. You would've thought it was the second coming, the way folks acted. Set the world record, from what I understand, down in Alvin. Rained forty-three inches in a day. That's something I doubt I'd even believe if I hadn't seen it."

The old man replaced the cap on the jug and handed it to the boy and took the empty one and began to fill it.

"Daddy used to talk about twenty-two inches that come down in two hours time. Of course, that was out west somewheres, near Uvalde. Still, floods come, droughts too. People always want to get stirred up about it, but I tend to go along as best I can."

He turned the spigot off and capped the second jug and wiped his hands on his overalls. He held the jug up and eyeballed it and pursed his lips.

"You'll wanna boil this 'fore you drink it. I got a screen in the barrel, but I think it might be about give out on me. Let's get us a biscuit and a cup."

"I ought to be getting back."

"Aw, c'mon now. You done pillaged my water supply and you ain't even gonna set with me for a bit?"

The boy bit his lip.

"Alright," the boy said.

"That's alright?"

"Yessir."

"Go on and set. I'll be right out."

The boy sat on the edge of the porch and his feet dangled above the ground. The old man made the stairs, slow and groaning, and drug the inside of his right foot across the floor boards with each hobbled step. The boy could hear him mumbling inside the cabin. When he emerged he handed the boy a blue tin cup with white speckles three-quarters full with lukewarm coffee and a cold biscuit wrapped in a paper towel.

"Got some mayhaw jelly in there."

"That's alright. Thank you."

Mr. Carson sat back in his rocker and put both hands on his knees.

"Well. You been doing any fishing?"

"Little bit. I'm not allowed to use Daddy's rod, but I got pretty good at grabbing with my hands and tossing them on the bank."

"Noodling."

"Huh?"

"Called noodling. Any river man worth his salt can catch a fish with his bare hands. Good for you, boy. Real good."

The boy nodded and bit into the biscuit.

"Mr. Carson?" he asked, his mouth half full. "You ever been in love?"

The old man laughed.

"You're too young for all that. Hold off on it. Hold off as long as you can."

"But have you?"

"Yes, I suppose I have. I loved my wife very much. Delores. She was a beauty."

"She died?"

"She did, but not here. She left me. They all leave. Nothing lasts," the old man shook away the feeling and smiled at the boy. "Like I say, hold off. Save yourself that pain until you're older, more able to deal with it. It's one thing to be in love. Quite another to think you deserve it back."

"Yessir."

"You understand what I'm saying?"

"Yessir. I think so."

"We go through life, every one us, measuring our experience. For better or worse, we hold our own world up to the one next to us, or to the one somebody wrote about, or to the idea of some world that's been stuck in our head for however long. Then, sometimes, somebody comes and helps us with bringing each of those worlds to account—puts the measuring into a different perspective. When that happens, it's up to us to buy in and be a part of a new determination. Cause if we don't, well, that's how come some folks to stay together and others to not.

"Love—a lasting love, that is—is the reconciliation of two separate accountings of the world, and a promise to use like measurements going forward. That, and dancing."

"I don't know how to dance."

The old man gave him a look of faux concern.

"You'd best learn."

The boy tossed the dregs of his coffee into the yard and looked up at the gray sky. "I'd better get on, before it starts raining again."

He put the paper towel inside the cup and handed it to Mr. Carson and thanked him again.

"I would've give you the water even if you hadn't stayed," the old man said.

"I know it."

16

Dustin didn't fit the narrative. John Curtis had told him that once.

"You don't fit the narrative," he'd said.

Dustin was born middle class and could've stayed that way. But he was a sweet kid, and sweet kids aren't long without being broken. His parents fought and his old man scared him and he grew up skinny and shy and awkward around girls. A few were nice to him, but he took it wrong and things always ended badly. When he finally found one to run with, she was part of a more sinister world. But he thought he was in love, and such thoughts come pre-equipped with bad decisions. He tried methamphetamine on a cold day in early November. By Christmas he was a full-on addict. To make matters worse, his girl found Jesus. Got clean. Said he wasn't good enough for her.

Something like that ought to harden a man. Maybe it did. He dropped out of high school and started dealing. Small stuff at first, but John Curtis took a liking to him and it was a quick ascent from there.

"Half these boys are dragging chains of mental deficiency behind their every step," he'd told Dustin. "You may be a pussy, but at least that means you're scared. Takes a brain to be scared."

It wasn't unusual for John Curtis to call him out to the cabin just to shoot up and have him listen to wild philosophical theories about Native Americans, or how men might soon evolve into the superhuman.

Dustin didn't understand much of what was said during those times, but John Curtis seemed to think he did. Or maybe he just appreciated the company.

This day was different though. He felt it on the drive up. The truck sliding in the mud, the wet branches reaching out over the road like the arms of a thousand errant souls. He'd had panic attacks when he was younger. Now he couldn't tell the difference between a panic attack and a withdrawal. When he could, he stayed high enough to keep both at bay.

"Dustin."

John Curtis sat on the porch.

"Boss."

"How you been, brother?"

"Okay. You?"

"Oh, I'm always alright. Here, come sit down and let's watch the rain."

"Okay."

They sat on the porch in wooden chairs opposite one another and looked out, both of them, at the parcel of world in their frame. The storm clattering on the tinned porch roof sounded as though each raindrop were made of steel, such was the enormity of the noise. The rain fell in great droves and fell straight down until a gust of wind would pitch it sideways, and then it would work to right itself. The wall of falling water made saturated the green trees near the cabin, but muted the colors of those further off, the rows of pines going from blue green to gray to nothing at all.

Dustin shifted his eyes to look at the other man. John Curtis sat staring straight ahead with a blank expression that made Dustin more nervous than he'd started out. He turned away. Before him, the storm had created a gray curtain upon the land, as if this were some sacred convergence, a hallowed meeting place where one reality was veiled off from another.

Soon the rain lightened and the veil dissipated and Dustin saw the world behind the curtain was the same as his own, and when he turned back, John Curtis was staring at him and had been for some time.

"Did I ever tell you about an old boy named Harlen I used to run with?" John Curtis asked.

"No, sir."

"I never did?"

Dustin shook his head.

"Well. Harlen was a wild man. A good man, according to most, but he had a temper on him that would get hotter than two foxes fucking in a forest fire."

"Yessir."

"Knew him for a few years after the war, before I reconnected with Cade. I guess you could say he was my right-hand man for a while. He liked to fight, and there was always somebody out to whip my ass. Instead, they'd try to whip Harlen. Usually didn't go too well. He wasn't quite the specimen ole Cade is, but he got the job done more often than not."

"What happened to him?"

"How do you mean?"

"Where is he now?"

"Now? Oh, he's buried out back, below that little ridge. Got a hole in his head you could put your arm through."

"He got shot?"

"He did indeed."

"Aryans?"

"No, nothing like that. It was before all them days. I shot him myself."

Dustin's throat was closing up on him.

"How come?" he asked, the words shivering out.

"He withheld information."

The tears were coming and Dustin didn't think he could stop them.

"What about?"

"A goddamn dog. You believe that?"

John Curtis shook his head and spit.

"I was just starting out as a dogman. Working my way through the mud circuits and everything. Back then it was the Wild West, let me tell you. Weren't no special task forces or anything like that. Hell, one of the top dogmen in East Texas was a sheriff's deputy over in Calhoun County.

"Anyway, I had this one mean sumbitch named Gito. He was a ferocious damn animal, I shit you not. Harlen took care of the dogs for me. This is before I met old Claude, of course. And I could tell just by the way he was that he didn't like it. Not the caretaking, but the fighting. Saw something of himself in those dogs, I think. Felt bad for them. Whether he let Gito run off or not, I'll never know. He said he didn't, and I tend to believe him. The man wasn't a liar."

"But you shot him."

"A week or so later, somebody spotted Gito out along the highway. Word got around to gay Jerry out at the bar that one of John Curtis's dogs was loose. So Jerry told Harlen, thinking he'd either tell me or get the dog himself."

"But he didn't."

"No, he didn't. It wasn't a lie. Unless you believe in lying by omission. Harlen just figured whatever came of Gito out there in the wild would probably be better than the fighting pits. And I don't doubt that he was right about that. But when you can't trust a man to be forthcoming, even about the smallest thing, you got no use for him. You understand?"

"Are you gonna kill me?"

John Curtis leaned back and crossed his arms.

"That's not really a fair question, is it? You're asking me to make a determination without having all the facts. And I sure wouldn't want to mislead you, one way or the other. Especially not when it comes to some-thing so . . . permanent. Frank says you're holding out on us. Maybe he's wrong. Maybe he's not. Now's your chance to set things straight. Did you help her run off, or do you just think she's better off on her own?"

Dustin was shaking. He nodded his head.

"Well," John Curtis said. "Go on."

The boy told him everything, and when he was finished John Curtis stood and walked to the edge of the porch and was a long time standing.

"I'm so sorry," Dustin said, whimpering, unable to withstand such silence.

John Curtis walked over to the boy and stood above him. He looked down into his sunken eyes and saw there the fear and uncertainty of a child awaiting punishment. He put his hand on the boy's back and felt his spine.

"Dustin."

"Yes, sir?"

"How does a vacation sound?"

"What?"

"I've got something I need sent to Houston. I can't rightly mail it. I was hoping you'd take it for me. I'll pay for your gas, your hotel, even a steak dinner if the mood so strikes you."

The boy hesitated.

"What am I running?"

"Oh, nothing like that. Just some money and a message. You'll take it to our bean-eating friend there."

Dustin nodded. He had begun shaking again.

"It's alright, bud," John Curtis said. "Don't be scared."

"Yessir, I'm sorry."

He was crying.

"It'll be in a public place. Somewhere sacred to Mexicans and Americans alike."

"A church?"

"A ballpark."

John Curtis opened the door to the cabin and stood with his hand on the knob.

"I'll have Frank get with you on the details. Keep your phone on."

Dustin nodded.

"What you told me, that stays between us. Not a word to anyone. You got me?"

John Curtis went inside and closed the door. Dustin walked on weak legs through the rain to his truck and climbed inside. He put his head on the steering wheel and sobbed.

17

When the boy returned the girl was asleep and he boiled the water and set the pot in the fridge to cool and then poured it back into the jug and set it on the mattress beside her. Then went into the living room, took off his clothes, and collapsed onto the couch.

When his eyes opened next, she was standing in the den in his mother's T-shirt and a pair of his own blue jean shorts which she had been unable to button. Her hair fell across her face and shoulders and she held the half-empty jug, and he was in awe at how beautiful she appeared.

"You don't got any food," she said, and the boy nodded and pulled the blanket up to cover his bare chest and bony shoulders.

"Well," the girl looked around. "The hell are we supposed to eat?"

The boy opened his mouth, but the girl didn't let him speak.

"Don't say eggs. I swear to god, you better not say eggs."

The boy's shoulders slumped.

"You got any money?"

The boy shook his head.

"How 'bout a phone? Or a charger?"

"No."

"No food, no phone. I guess you have a Corvette out back that you drive around to get whatever you need?"

"No, I don't have a car."

The girl shook her head.

"How far are we from the highway?"

"Ten, maybe fifteen miles."

"That's not impossible to walk."

"Closer to twenty if you use the roads."

"Goddamn it."

The girl paced the room. The boy watched her scrunch her face and push back her hair. He watched her legs flex with each step and saw the veins in her neck as she threw her head back and sighed.

"It's hot as shit in here," she said at last. "Let's go down to the water so I can think."

The boy nodded and scrambled from the couch and kept himself wrapped in the blanket until he was in his room with the door shut. When he emerged again he wore light-colored blue jeans and a T-shirt with a polar bear drinking from a Coke bottle. The girl was gone and the door was left open.

He found her at the river. She'd taken the largest of the trails leading away from the trailer and she sat on the stunted beach with her knees pulled to her chest and her feet half in the water.

"Feeding the minnows," the boy said.

"What?"

He pointed to the two-inch-deep water and the girl saw the tiny creatures swarming around her toes.

"At least somebody's eating," she said.

"I can find us some food."

"Why the hell do you live out here alone?"

"I don't. My dad works the pipelines. Two weeks on, two weeks off."

"And he's there now?"

"No. He's off, but he's at Shawna's."

"Who's Shawna?"

"His friend."

"Mmhm. How long has he been gone?" she asked.

"Since the day you came."

"He stay gone like that a lot?"

The boy shrugged.

"I guess."

"How come you helped me?"

He shrugged again.

"You don't know?" she asked.

"What should I have done?"

"I don't know. Left me there. Threw me in the fucking river."

"You didn't want me to help you?" he asked.

The girl softened.

"No, I did. I do. Thank you. I just . . . wasn't expecting it."

"Do you have a name?"

"We all got a name."

"What's yours?" the boy asked.

The girl looked down and then out at the water.

"Call me River."

"Is that your name?"

"It's what I want you to call me."

"Okay, River."

"You know what I am, right?" she asked him.

"A girl."

"I'm a meth addict. Do you know what meth is?"

The boy nodded.

"Well. I use it. Or I did. That's why I been acting so weird. That and a bunch of other stuff."

"What other stuff?"

"Do you know what depression is?"

"Yes."

"What about psychosis?"

The boy shook his head.

"It basically means I hear and see shit that ain't really there."

"Like what?"

"I don't know—voices, whispers, fucking jolly green giants."

"You see giants?"

"God, no, it's just an example. Listen, I'm in a world of shit, and as much as I appreciate what you did for me, I gotta get out of here. I lost something really important, and there's bad men who are gonna kill me stone dead because of it."

The boy dropped his eyes.

"What'd you lose?" he asked.

"A backpack. Had something in it worth a lot of money."

"Oh. Well, what if you stayed here?"

"Why would I do that?"

The boy looked around, not sure of an answer.

"You came from upriver," he said, pointing. "So you probably lost your backpack somewhere in the woods. You can stay here, and we can go out looking for it every day until we find it. Plus, the people looking for you aren't going to think you're here with me."

The girl ground her teeth in contemplation.

"What about when your old man comes home?"

"I don't know. Maybe we'll find your backpack before he gets here."

They stood, the boy staring at the girl, her arms folded in front of her.

"I'm going in," she said, and began to undress. The boy looked away.

"You gonna make me go alone?" the girl asked, and the boy found himself removing his shoes out of some thoughtless instinct.

The sun shone even as it rained and the world around them was humid and airless. They stripped their outer layers and spilled into the swollen brown river, and the chattering of squirrels and the grousing of sparrows filled the country. And somewhere in the beyond, a single fate was selected from a row of fates, no one more certain than the other, yet each bound to the world by threads of choice and circumstance.

The girl ran her hand across the water's surface and the smallest wake left trailing, and she stood there, waist deep, and stared down at her stomach as it moved with each breath. She walked further into the river until her stomach was submerged, then back to the shallows. *Amen,* she whispered.

The boy saw her hair pinned up in flashes of purple and blond, a few rogue strands hanging wet on her neck. He saw her shoulder blades, her spine, the indented small of her back. He saw the curve of her hips as they disappeared into the water. She moved toward the shore, her legs rising from the river, her panties clinging to her skin. She was skinny, but she was a woman. And as the boy watched her, a great weight of inadequacy pressed down on him. With each step she took, he felt more naked, more exposed. It was as if he were seeing himself for the first time. As if he'd ate of the forbidden fruit and was at once awash in the shame of his own being. His bony chest, his thin arms and knobby knees. He was a head shorter than the girl. He sunk down in the river until only his face was above the water.

The girl turned.

"Quit staring," she said.

He went under. He held his breath and closed his eyes and let the pull of the river pass by him. The pressure in his ears was comforting, the low hum of a world submerged. He always wished he could stay under longer, but it was impossible to breathe; above the surface it was only hard.

The girl sloshed to the shore and pulled the shorts on wet and leaned up against a cypress trunk. Whatever the boy had done to her feet, they felt better. But a twenty-mile walk seemed like a tall order. And where would she go, anyway? John Curtis had eyes and ears all over the county. She had to get far away from this place, and that was going to take money. She needed cash, and that bag was the only way to get it. She crossed her arms and looked out at the boy and shook her head.

"C'mon," she said. "Let's go eat some goddamn eggs."

18

The sheriff's office was run for the most part out of a series of portable buildings behind the county jail. The largest of these structures had a handicap-accessible ramp up to the door and the words "Neches County Law Enforcement" in two lines of block lettering on the outward-facing wall. Just inside the door was a low ceiling, vertical wood paneling, and the smell of day-old coffee. Behind a desk with only a phone and computer atop it sat an aging woman with gray-streaked hair and glasses. She worried with the keyboard in front of her, but was trying her best to hear the conversation in the other room.

"Look, Mr. Curtis, we both know I could have you sent away for the rest of your goddamn life. So don't come in here making demands. We have a relationship, and despite what you river-rat rednecks might think, relationships aren't supposed to be abusive. Now, if there's something I can help you with, you're welcome to ask nicely and let me see what I can do."

John Curtis grinned without disturbing the lit cigarette in his mouth.

"I'm hurt, Sheriff, I truly am. And of course I apologize sincerely. It's just, I didn't realize you had those sort of feelings for me. But since you're painting me as the bad guy in our arrangement, let me go ahead and finish out the picture for you. You arrest me, you shoot me, you do anything to take me away from my position atop this little shitpile we have here, well, you're gonna have scumbag cooks and pushers and everybody else flocking to these bottoms. And guess what? They ain't gonna be as nice as me. They ain't gonna be willing to give you the little gifts that I do. Your name and picture in the paper every couple of months for making a meth bust, for keeping these streets clean. We both know the truth. I'm the law, not you. You take me out, this place turns into a goddamn bloodbath. No more freebies just handed to you. You might actually have to work to catch criminals."

"Now hold on just a—"

"Then come reelection, I'm not around to make sure my boys, along with every other tweaker in Neches County, are turning up to vote your fat ass back into office. 'Course, that's all politics, and you're smarter than you look, so I imagine you already knew most of that. But there's something matters to me more than politics, Sheriff, it's principle. And if you ever threaten me again, or talk down about me and my people, I'll have a couple chalk heads go down to the elementary where your daughter's in Miss Lacy's class, and I'll get 'em to snatch her up by her pretty blond hair and slit her fucking throat. And they'll do it too. They'll do it for a baggie of crank and a pat on the fucking head. See, you have deputies, Sheriff, but I have soldiers. And there ain't no law, god's or man's, gonna stop my boys."

The sheriff swallowed.

John Curtis shook his head.

"There will forever be those who stand in judgment with no knowledge, no true understanding of what it is before them. These conjectures are inevitable, of course. Nuance is too complicated for the masses. It further confuses an already muddled world. They look at us and they see trash. Sketchers with bad teeth and worse manners. They believe, because our trade is outside the boundary of law, that we can never have true power. That's where they're mistaken. It is precisely our lawlessness which makes us dangerous. Which makes us feared. And fear, above all else, is the root of power.

"My father taught me that. He didn't mean to of course. He didn't mean to teach me anything. But as soon as I shed my fear of him, he lost his power over me. The moment I realized he was just a man, no different than me, that's the moment I unsheathed my blade and took the power from him."

"Jesus Christ, John, you just admitted to murder in the goddamn sheriff's office."

John Curtis laughed.

"So arrest me."

The sheriff frowned.

"Yeah, I didn't think so," John Curtis said. "You see, the world is full up with bad men. Folks don't like to admit that, or even think about it; but what good does lying do? I guess people will lie about anything to make themselves feel a little better. I never found the use in it. I'd rather see the truth of the matter, then set about with meeting it head-on, trying to conquer it outright. And how do you conquer bad men? You become one. Even bad men are scared of someone. Scared of worse men. And let me tell you, there are none worse than me.

"So, you're gonna help me find that girl, or every speed freak in the county is gonna come crawling out of these bottoms with a mind to burn your whole world to the ground.

"And as a thank-you, since I don't want your hard work to go unappreciated, I'll give you Dakota Cade."

"My ass." The sheriff scoffed.

"You calling me a liar?"

"Even if you wanted to do something like that, how in the hell would you go about it? You'd end up dead, and I'd be in the same spot as if I didn't help you. Maybe worse if that big bastard started running things."

"I can handle him."

"I'll repeat: my ass. I saw what he did to that Nazi boy out in Redtown, back when you all had trouble up that way. I've never been scared a single day doing this job. But that day, the way we found that boy, I was terrified. Not just for my own life either. I was scared for the world entire, that something that evil was out there, with that sort of capacity for violence. And now here you set, telling me you're going to throw a rope over it. I don't think so, son."

"You leave that to me, Sheriff," John Curtis said, rising from his chair. "And don't be afraid. This is my world, and nobody gets hurts unless I say so."

"Well."

The sheriff stood, doubtful, then another thought came to him.

"Since you're here," he said. "You ought to know them USDA boys have been up my ass about the goddamn dog fights. They been calling every other day, and now they're getting ready to send a couple agents down here to look into things."

"So?"

"So I need you to cool it with that shit for a while. Let the feds poke around, see there ain't nothing going on, then you can start up again after they're gone."

John Curtis rubbed the back of his neck.

"No."

"No?"

"If they're coming down here, they won't be satisfied to leave empty-handed. We're gonna have to throw 'em a bone, so to speak."

"How's that?"

"Keep your phone on."

The sheriff sighed.

"I just work for you, is that it? I'm to be ready whenever you call?"

John Curtis flashed a yellow-toothed grin.

He left the office and walked into the small lobby, such as it was, and the woman behind the desk stared up at him, her eyes a mix of fear and curiosity and, maybe, something more. He nodded and winked at her and opened the door and walked out.

John Curtis had made the bottom of the ramp when the sheriff opened the door. He took off his hat and held it just below his chest, as if in reverence to some unspoken tradition. He looked out at the pines and up at the storm clouds and, finally, at John Curtis.

"There'll always be someone worse," he said. "You ought to keep that in mind."

He put his hat back on and turned and went inside and closed the door.

19

The hacienda outstretched in the foothills above the Chihuahuan desert where grew plants of creosote and sotol and yucca. The main house was surrounded by sumac and prickly pear and great adobe walls higher than the head of a horse. A stone patio ran the length of the house on its east side and there sat tables and chairs and chimineas, all of them empty.

In the courtyard bloomed aster, dahlia, and Mexican hat flowers. And at its center, a concrete fountain stood, with water surrounding a statue of the Virgin, her arms at her sides with both palms facing forward. She looked down at the water beneath her feet where splashed three yellow-eyed juncos, drinking and shaking the water from their feathers.

The house was connected to various smaller structures, a garage, a kitchen, guest lodging, and several storage buildings, and the wind whistled through the breezeways between each one.

Inside the main house three men sat in a parlor adorned with great bookcases and desks carved from mahogany. The ceiling stood twenty feet and on it was painted a battle scene from a hundred-year-old revolution. The men were attended by two middle-aged women in matching dresses who brought coffee and tea and a tray of fruits and cheese, pan de colotes and Mexican sweet bread.

The thin man sat on the leather sofa, his legs crossed at the knees, one brown ostrich boot hovering above the cherrywood coffee table. He sipped his coffee from an ivory cup and made notes in a small book and nodded occasionally when he felt the time was right.

The men across from him were his elders and they spoke slowly and he did not rush them. He wanted every detail. Some of what was said were facts, others opinions, and the thin man would hear them all. Would piece one to the other.

In the end, the men shook hands. More refreshment was offered, but declined. The thin man was handed an envelope and a cell phone, each of which he tucked away inside his jacket pocket.

"Vas a pasar la noche?" one of the older men asked.

"No. No te conozco."

20

The plague of methamphetamine waxing and waning in correlation to the ease of supply, the vigilance of law, the economic markers of hope, the discovery and abandonment and rediscovery of god, the political relevance, the quality of the shit, the price of the shit, the cartel alliances, the ability to cross the border with a truckload of hominy cans full of product. And Frank and Lonnie, driving in the rain, the penultimate caretakers, making their rounds.

"Who you voting for?" Lonnie asked.

"Whoever John Curtis tells me to vote for," Frank answered.

"Mighty American of you."

"I suppose you got other ideas."

"You know I do."

"And I also suppose, to my own detriment, you'll be wanting to share those ideas."

"What sort of citizen would I be if I didn't enlighten my fellow voters?" Lonnie asked.

"The less annoying kind, for starters."

"Fine. Make your fun. But when the government sends duck boats full of soldiers down the river, I doubt you'll be laughing."

"I can't believe I'm gonna ask this, but I'm gonna ask it anyway. Why would the government send soldiers to the bottoms?"

"Power move. Population control. Experiments and such."

"Horse shit," Frank said.

"That's what they said in Germany."

"And what soldiers are they gonna send? Every shit kicker who ain't in the oil fields is in the damn military. You think a bunch of good ole boys are gonna turn on their own people?"

"Two possibilities. The first is that they'll use foreign troops. Why do you think we're so interested in training other countries' militaries?"

"What's the second?"

"Mind control."

"Jesus Christ."

"Fine. Don't listen."

"I'm not."

"Don't."

"I won't. But, just out of curiosity, with the understanding that everything you're saying is utter nonsense, who are you voting for in order to avoid this great Battle of the Neches?"

Lonnie looked down and shook his head.

"You've got a lot to learn," he said.

"What?" Frank asked. "Why are you shaking your damn head?"

"I'm not voting for anybody," Lonnie told him. "That's how they get you. First it's your information, then it's jury duty, next thing you know there's a bag over your head and somebody's speaking Russian. And what's worse, you're understanding it."

"It must be nice, being able to slide that needle in without worrying about having a brain to rot."

"Fuck you very much," Lonnie said. "Speaking of, let's find a place to get high, all this rain is depressing me."

"We're supposed to be looking for the girl."

"She'll come crawling back sooner or later. That's too much of a load to carry."

"I imagine she's trying to get rid of it."

"Shit. Who around here would do that? Word's done got out. She ain't got nowhere to go."

"Well, I guess let's go over to Fox Run and find us an empty apartment."

"Now you're talking."

"And, hey, nothing about mind control or foreign invaders," Frank said.

"Not a word."

"I'm serious. I don't want to think about that shit when I'm high."

"That's exactly what they want you to say."

21

The dawn broke and brought forth a red fire sky and the trees rose up near black against its coming. A single barn owl stood sentry over the dying of the night, its heart-shaped face in motionless contemplation, its yellow glowing eyes overseeing the sunrise as if the creature itself needed some confirmation of the world's return before it could take its leave. Finally, its fears momentarily quelled, the owl set off on pale white wings and swept low across the water and disappeared into the forested bottomlands to set about the resolution of some other inevitable worry.

"Where do you think he's going?" the girl asked.

"Probably hunting a place to stay dry."

"You think it'll rain?"

"Red sky at night, sailor's delight. Red sky at morning, sailor's warning." He looked at the girl.

"Means it's gonna come a proper storm this afternoon," he said.

"Well, then, we'd better get after it."

The two of them spread apart ten yards and traipsed through the woods, sticking brass tacks into trees every twenty minutes or so to mark their progress. They said very little for the first two hours, and by nine o'clock it was hot and they made for the banks of the brown river where the trees grew wild and overtop one another, as if the water, through some mystic agency all its own, had called out to them the very secret whereby they might live forever. Each cycled season a revisiting of a promise long kept.

The sound of the falling rain had become such a part of the world that its absence was unsettling. The forest came alive in the interim, with red-throated lizards scurrying along through the mud, zipper spiders hanging new webs between trees, and katydids and crickets launching themselves through the high grass as if they'd been attached to a dozen hidden springboards.

The bears and cougars and wolves all gone from these lands, and races of men come thereafter and most of them gone as well, and the boy wondered about such things, and thought perhaps his people would be the next to disappear.

The boy closed one eye and squinted at the sky through the holes in a great canopy made up of shade oak and cypress leaves, and there hung a host of glow worms, suspended by a silk too fine to see. Further skyward, a redtail hawk screamed out some ancient and piercing cry of war, and the honeysuckle mixed with the smell of mud, and the water moved one way and the palmettos bent another, and the boy found a dry tract of sand and sat looking out at all these things and more. He looked out at the bale of Mississippi map turtles as they filed one after the other on a half-submerged log, and at the fox squirrels as they clung wayward to bending branches, and at a world too green to understand. A world full up with maidencane and switchgrass, and the sound of birds and the sound of water, and the wind came down to tousle the soft stem rush, and the Indian blanket flowers bloomed red and orange and bobbed heavy atop their thin stalks. The barnyard and brownseed grasses crawling ashore from amid the wading willow reeds, and all of the bottomlands mantled in such a state, and the boy gave thought to how any place else would not be this place, not be this color and this smell and this last bit of truthfulness.

The respite from the rain was short-lived as soon the clouds were full up again and looking to unload on the earth below. The plants and trees of the wetlands were heavy and saturated and overburdened, but still the rain came. The boy could hear it falling in the western woods, and it fell in rabble and swarm, and the boy put his hand in his pocket and touched his fingertips to the arrowhead. He listened to the sound of the rain as it closed the distance between, and he imagined a horde of warriors sweeping down into the river valley, riding their painted Spanish ponies and crying out in falsettoed voices that carried across the water and across the very piece of country he'd been born unto. And he thought about the people of this river, in those times and the times since, and he wondered if he'd been alive during any of them, could he have survived. Or maybe, could he have been something more than what he was.

They left out from the water on a different path than what they'd come, trekking up a shaded draw littered with pecans and pine needles, and climbing on all fours and grabbing branches for support. They stopped under the biggest tree, and the boy cracked a fallen nut and offered it up.

"You could like, be a nature guide or something," the girl said.

"Guide for what?"

"I don't know, just like, a fucking nature guide."

"Alright."

The pines rose up on either side of the tired mud path, like loyal sentries guarding a treasure too long lost. There, amid the short-leaf and loblollies, they followed the thin line of trail until it grew thinner still and gave way to a mangled thicket of greenbriar and thorns. The boy used a dull, rusted machete to cut a lead, but it was slow going. His shirt caught and tore and slowed him down. He took it off. The briars cut across his arms and chest in all directions. The girl stood at a distance with her arms crossed, doubtful.

"It wouldn't be in there," she said.

"Could be."

"How would I have made it through there?"

"You were pretty tore up."

"You're wasting time."

"I'm not the one complaining. Besides, if you know where it's at, go on and get it for us."

The girl shook her head, but followed the boy through the underbrush. They continued as straight as the nature of things would allow, until finally the thicket softened, opening into a natural ravine.

"Could've got washed down in this ditch," the boy said.

"And swept away to the river," the girl replied.

"Maybe."

They slid down the mud slope and poked around near stagnant pools of mousy water. The rain began to fall harder.

"I guess we're stuck in this shit," she said.

"Maybe not. Look yonder."

The car sat above the ditch, thirty yards further inland through the thicket, and it had long turned from its original color into a mesh of brown and coral corrosion, rust collecting in layers to mark the passage of time and oxidation.

It was a Plymouth, manufactured sometime soon after the Second World War, though neither of them knew such details—only that it was old. There were no tires and no headlights and only the back windows remained, and never had the boy seen something so out of place in the bottoms. The car looked as if it were waiting for some event which had never come to pass, and never would. As if the car had been there first, and it was the world what grew up around it.

"How in the hell did an old car end up this far back in the woods?"

"Couldn't say. Maybe there used to be a road down here."

"There hadn't never been a road through here." The girl scoffed. "Where the hell would it be going?"

"Where any road goes, I guess. From one place to another."

"There's probably a mess of snakes or wasps or something in there."

"Maybe there's a briefcase full of money."

The girl shook her head.

"Right. Somebody went through all the trouble of pulling off the tires, but they left the million dollars in the back seat."

The boy frowned.

"I'm just telling you right now," the girl said, "I ain't getting in that thing. I'd rather stay out here and drown."

The girl pursed her lips and climbed across the molded seats and into the back. The boy had checked for reptiles and insects alike and found nothing save a spiderweb, which he took down with the machete. The girl sat awkward in the back seat, trying to touch as little as possible. She could hear the boy behind her trying to get the trunk open.

"It won't open," he said, spilling into the back seat, the girl shifting away from him as the rain peppered the roof and hood and the exposed front dash.

"That must be where the money is," the girl chided him.

"We saw a video in school about how there was a car pulled up out of a lake somewhere, and it had a bunch of human bones still in the trunk."

The girl cocked an eyebrow.

"It was in science class." The boy shrugged.

"You like school?"

"It's alright."

"What's your favorite class?"

"I don't know. History, I guess."

"You got a good teacher?"

"Not really. He coaches the baseball team. I don't think he cares too much about the class."

"They don't have a real history teacher?"

"I like reading the textbook. Hearing about how things happened back then. It's like, well, it's like we're connected to all of it. The people, the wars, everything. If any one of them had gone different, we wouldn't be here."

"Too bad it didn't."

"Maybe."

"I hated school. Or I guess I hated the other kids at school. It seemed like they were all so happy or normal or, I don't know. Something. Maybe I just never got over all the Donuts with Dad days where I was the only one sitting by myself."

The girl looked off.

"What about you," she asked. "What's your old man like?"

"I don't know. He's not here a lot."

"Shit, I wish my mom had stayed away more. She used to whip the shit out of me. I deserved it about the half the time, but still."

"Did you really?"

"No. Nobody really deserves that."

She looked at him.

"Your daddy beats on you, too, huh?"

The boy was quiet and when he spoke again he asked the girl about her own father.

"Why wasn't he at the donuts days?" he said.

"Don't know him. Don't even know who he is. What about your mom?"

"I know her. Or I did. She left when I was little."

"You still remember her?"

"I remember she was picking me up. We were walking somewhere and I think I must have got tired or something, so she picked me up. Carried me. I don't even know if it's real. It may be a dream. I'm not sure I care, though. I just like thinking about it. I guess we got to carry ourselves, now."

The girl nodded and the boy looked off and into the past and for a while she watched him and when he returned to her there were tears in his eyes and she reached out and took his hand and he let her.

"You know, it's crazy to me," she said, "there's kids—kids who aren't kids anymore—they grew up their whole entire lives and never found out the truth."

"What's the truth?"

"That their parents are stupid pieces of shit."

"Maybe they aren't."

"They are."

"You think all parents are bad?"

"I think all people are bad."

"What about you?" he asked.

"Shit, I'm worse than most."

"Not worse than them hunting you, though?"

"No. Not that bad." The girl sighed. "God, I'm an idiot."

"No you're not."

"Well, then I've been acting real convincingly like I am," she said. "When I left home, I headed west. It always seemed like the thing to do, at least in the songs. I thought maybe I'd go to California or something, but I didn't get very far."

"What happened?"

"Ran out of money. What little I had. Ended up at a casino in Livingston, had to turn a couple of tricks just to—"

The boy's face had changed.

"Sorry," she said. "You don't need to hear all that. Cade took me in. Took care of me. Made me feel safe."

"And made you take drugs."

"No. He didn't make me. I wanted to."

The boy looked upset.

"Hey, you asked."

"I know."

"Well."

The boy moved his hand away. The girl looked out at the rain.

"I'm from Louisiana," she said, and the boy wasn't sure if she was talking to him or herself. "Place called Leesville. Military base there. Plenty of customers. We lived at Sun Inn for a time. I remember Momma would stick me and my sister in the bathtub and tell us to shut up, don't make a sound."

"You have a sister?"

"Sadie." The girl tried to smile, but she couldn't. "Younger than me by a couple years. Prettiest blond hair and blue eyes. We used to have a lemonade stand, the way little kids do. We set it up in the motel parking lot. The way we figured it, our daddy might still be in Leesville, and if he was, he might get thirsty at some point, come by our stand. We had it all planned out in our heads. He would come by and get some lemonade, he'd see us and immediately fall in love and take us to live with him in a nice house somewhere. I don't know why we thought he'd know who we were. I don't even know that we have the same daddy in the first place. I guess it didn't matter, in our little kid minds.

"We did move away from the motel, but it was with Momma. Got us a trailer on the south side of town. Me and Sadie shared a room. She'd lock us in there when she had a customer. We didn't mind all that much. It was better than a bathtub. I left when I was fifteen."

"You ran away?"

The girl nodded.

"I was about your age when she realized I'd fetch a higher price. I think it made her mad at first, you know? Like jealous or something. She used to put makeup on me, real thick and everything. Then she'd tell me I was nothing but an ugly whore. That never made sense to me. She was the one who'd done the makeup. She would slap me until I cried and the mascara ran down my face. She said I wasn't any better than her, and I better not think that I was. 'I don't think that, Momma,' I'd tell her. Then she'd say, 'Good. They only want you because your snatch is still tight.'

"But the money and the meth came in faster than it had before, and that kept her happy enough. She'd still slap me around, if somebody complained about me crying or something like that. 'I'll give you a reason to cry,' she used to say. But I already had too many reasons to count."

"I'm sorry."

"Why?"

"What?"

"Why are you sorry? You didn't do anything."

"I'm sorry those things happened to you."

The girl shook her head, disapproving.

"You can't think like that. If you start being sorry for everyone else, for every little thing in the whole damn world, it'll cripple you. You won't be able to put one foot in front of the other and keep moving forward."

"Okay. But I'm still sorry."

The girl shook her head again. This time she fought tears.

"I left her there. Just left her."

"Your sister?" the boy asked.

"I knew what was gonna happen and I left her anyway."

She cried. The boy patted her back.

"Maybe she ran away, too," he said.

The girl shook her head.

"I had Cade send a letter a little while back. Asking after her. It was my Momma who wrote back. Said Sadie"—the girl began to sob into her hands—"said she killed herself two months after I left. One of the soldiers had brought a gun with him. He wasn't looking or paying attention or something, and she got a hold of it. Put it right up to her head. That was it."

"I'm sorry."

"Stop with your fucking sorries. I don't deserve it. I'm the one that killed her."

"It's not your fault."

"Like hell. I abandoned her."

"You had to leave."

"I could've took her with me. I told myself that if I left, maybe Momma would appreciate what she had. Be nicer to Sadie than she'd been to me. But that was bullshit, and I knew it. I just didn't want to have to take care of her, look out for her. Didn't want her slowing me down."

"You were just a kid."

"I was older than you are now. What would you have done?"

The boy was quiet.

"That's what I thought. Anyway, I've been waiting for my reckoning ever since."

"What do you mean?"

"I don't know. It's just a feeling I get. Like, there's a man, or something like a man, and he's out there in the world, and he knows about me. He knows about everyone. But, but he really knows about me."

"Is he gonna kill you?"

"Not kill me. Just be there, out in the world, and me knowing he's there. Me feeling him, almost like he's watching, following. Just waiting."

"What's he waiting for?"

"I don't know. But whatever it is, I think I'm waiting on it, too."

"I'll wait with you," the boy said and he put his arm around her as the rain weakened.

The sunlight fought through the branches above them and sent scattering its rays and the forest floor appeared as a never-ending stage covered in rogue spotlights, and they looked out across it and held onto the other, both thinking of things far away and out of reach.

22

The two of them sat the porch and watched as lightning danced and parried upon the hill, appearing in frozen flashes against the gray sky and expiring into such a sky as if being called to some accounting by each thunderclap come after it.

The big man was coming down from an eight-hour high and he hated the rain. He loaded a half-can of Skoal between his pinched fingers and lodged it into the dugout space inside his lower lip. A gust of wind blew a misting of rain onto the porch and onto Cade's boots and he spit tobacco juice out into the storm in what might have been retaliation. He rose and drug his chair backward and sat again.

"Some raggedy crew of Mexicans been working out at the mill in Corrigan County," he said. "Joe T says they been bothering him since they got there about setting up a show."

"He figure them to be proper dogmen?" John Curtis asked.

"He didn't say. But I surely do doubt it. I know one of the old boys from work overtop the Eagle Ford. He's was too dumb to be a proper rig hand, let alone a dog handler."

"Illegals?"

"Can't say that neither. Good chance."

John Curtis nodded.

"Well. Alright then. Set it up."

"You gotta purse in mind?"

"What are they asking for?"

"Five thousand a side."

John Curtis looked up.

"Don't sound so raggedy."

The big man shrugged and spit again.

John Curtis waved his hand.

"Fine," he said.

Cade nodded.

"Any weight qualifiers?" Cade asked.

"No. Let's just see what happens. I've been wanting to put Rose in the box, see what kind of game she has in her."

Cade's face upturned.

"Something don't set well with you?" John Curtis asked him.

"Rose ain't even two yet. Not to mention she's on the small side. Don't seem smart to put her in a show without qualifiers. They're liable to bring a dog weighs fifty or sixty pounds."

"Good. Then we'll learn how she does when she's outmatched. Hell, everybody can win when they're supposed to. What is it with you big, soft types?"

"Claude ain't gonna be too happy. He ends up falling in love with every one of them bitches we send out there."

John Curtis cocked his head.

"I know it."

"I can't figure out why he still does it. Throws a fit every time we go to pick one up. Seems like he'd just quit training 'em."

"They say it's better to have loved and lost than never loved at all. Plus, that old cajun needs the money."

"Well. He sure is good at it."

John Curtis nodded.

"Still," Cade said, "he ain't gonna be too happy."

"I'll ride out there first thing in the morning. You wanna come?"

"Naw. I'm crashing hard. Need to sleep it off."

"Suit yourself."

That night Cade dreamt of the girl and in his dream she sat atop a horse like the one he'd ridden as a child at the state fair. A man in a straw hat led the horse at a walk and the horse went in circles and each time it passed by Cade the girl laughed at him.

John Curtis drove his truck out of the bloodred sunrise and across the county line into Lansdale. He turned off the highway and onto a gravel road and followed it eight miles and turned again and navigated down an old logging road where at the end sat the makeshift kennel. The main house was itself not much more than a lean-to and it was surrounded by all manner of chain-link fence and wooden walls. The yard was scattered with what looked to be a series of junk steel and discarded machine parts, but most every item had some purpose known only to the kennel master who hurried himself through the morning to meet John Curtis.

"What do you say, Claude?"

"Mr. John Curtis," the man said, with an accent caught somewhere between French and fried frog. "How is you dis mo'ning?"

"Oh, I'm doing just fine. Better question is, how's my dog?"

"Come own see fuh yo'self."

Behind the house, the dog was on a homemade treadmill, pieced together with welded brackets and precision cuts of wood. Her brindled skin was pulled taut over her muscles and each striation flexed as she moved.

The two men folded their arms and watched her run.

"How's her conditioning been?" John Curtis asked.

"She onnuh slatmill three, four time a day. Done run her all down through the mud like how you ast. Watch here, now."

The old cajun stepped forward and pulled a lever on the machine and the track under the dog pitched backward, forcing her to work harder as if she were running uphill. But the dog took the change in stride and continued pumping forward with little to no panting.

Claude laughed and smiled.

"Conditionin' won't be no problem," he said. "She a little undersized. I got some injections might fill her out a little mo'."

John Curtis shook his head.

"No time. How's her neck?"

"Shit. I 'magine she hang from dat sprangpole days atta time, if'n I let her."

"Good. Very good, Claude." John Curtis clapped him on the back.

"You want I should roll her with a mo' seasoned bitch? See how she do?"

"No, that's alright. We'll see what she's got soon enough."

"She fighting?"

John Curtis nodded.

"Well, hold on now," Claude protested. "I don't know she's ready fo' all dat."

Now it was John Curtis who laughed.

"The big man said you'd be that way."

Claude looked offended.

"I ain't being no way. Just think she could do with a little more time. Look bad on me if she get out there and lose."

"Oh, come on now, Claude. I know you better than all that. You're worried about her getting hurt, not your damn pride. You had any pride, you wouldn't live out here in such a shithole. You wouldn't let me pay you such a low price to train these dogs, and you damn sure wouldn't let me come take them from you whenever I want. You love these dogs, Claude. And that's okay. I understand."

The man put his head down.

John Curtis put his hand on the man's shoulder.

"As men, we are aware of our own mortality. Aware of it in a way no other creature can claim. We quarrel with finality because we are unwilling to accept such a painful existence, void of the promise of better things to come.

"And in our foreboding we cast aside the discernible, ignoring our unique ability to employ adaptive reasoning; in short, we lie to ourselves, to our children, to each other. But there is no dishonesty in these dogs. They have too much nobility. A dog can't soothe itself with stories of hope or redemption. It won't call for mercy or curse its circumstance. Instead, a dog slowly and eventually succumbs to its fate—fate as decided not by the world or by god or by the dog itself. But a destiny of which the animal has no knowledge. Can never have. An existence, purposed or not, which is not confined to the limits of concept. There is honor in that. Honor in these dogs that we'll never have, because we'll never see things that simple, never be that pure. It's okay that you love 'em. You ought to."

Claude looked up. There were tears in his eyes.

"Whatchyou want me to do?" he asked.

"Have her ready this evening, or I'll end whatever lies you've been telling yourself about death."

23

The boy and the girl mapped a search grid in the woods and when they ran out of push pins and thumbtacks they took to using rusted nails and torn magazine pages. And so they went, walking the forest and leaving their marks as if it were all part of some long-ago pagan rite.

They found a rusted necklace made of fool's silver, a cooler with the sides eaten away, and enough empty beer cans to build a sanctuary. They did not find the backpack.

On the afternoon of the third day, they followed a deer trail through the swamp lilies and powdery thalia. The spiraled blooms of navasota tresses shuddered on their stalks at the thunder upcoming from the southwest. The boy looked in that direction. The sky had long been dark, but the storm clouds were darker still, relieved of their crawling shadow only through the pale violet bursts of lightning that gave shape to the clouds, the clouds in their backlit outline appearing as some great barrier, straining to hold back the galvanic wrath of a vengeful god.

The boy, hands on his hips and arched forward, watched the sky in its bright fracturing. He'd insisted the girl continue to sleep in his room and he on the couch, its sagging playing havoc on his bony spine.

"That'll be twenty-two days in a row that its rained."

He turned toward the girl, and she had her back to him and her hands covering her face. When she pulled them away they were wet with tears.

"I can't do it," she cried. "I've heard people talk about it. But I've never seen anyone do it. Hell, I don't even know anyone that's done it."

"Do what?"

"Get clean. Stay that way. Not completely lose their shit."

"You're going to do it."

"You don't know shit."

"I'm gonna help you."

"I don't want your fucking help," she snapped, then softened. "I'm sorry, goddamnit, I just, I can't control anything right now. I'm fucked up. Everything's so fucked up."

The girl began to cry in earnest.

"Why don't you tell me all the bad things about it?" the boy asked.

The girl rolled her eyes and put her head in her hands again.

The boy waited, and they stood for a long time without a sound.

"Meth chips away at a person," she said finally. "Hollows them out. Body, soul, even the teeth. Until they're not anything but a living ghost. Or maybe not a ghost. Maybe something worse. Ghosts at least keep something, you know? They keep some part of whoever they were when they were alive. Meth takes everything from you. Makes you something less than a ghost of your old self. Makes you something else altogether."

"It can kill people too," the boy added.

The girl shrugged. "So? Folks live and they die and who can tell the difference?" she said, shaking her head. "If I died, or you, who notices people like us? Who even cares?"

"God might care."

"Do you believe in god?"

"I don't know. Maybe. I think my dad does."

"Yeah? What does he have to say about it?"

"He said there was a man who threw him off a deer lease, and then that man got cancer."

"So he thinks god gave the man cancer for kicking him out?"

"He says everything happens for a reason."

"What about babies dying? Or people starving or getting killed in wars?"

"I guess he reckons there's a reason for that, too." The boy shrugged again. "Do you believe in god?"

The girl wiped at her face. It was red and swollen around her eyes.

"When I was little, before my sister was born, my momma used to sit me in front of the TV set and turn the sound up real loud so I couldn't hear what she was doing in the back. Don't get me wrong, I knew what she was doing. Maybe not exactly, on account of I wasn't very old, but I knew something. I saw the men come and go and I knew once they left she was different. She'd talk different, but it was really just her eyes. They were so sad and empty, like they were there, but they weren't. Like they were watching everything happen, but from a place far away."

The girl stopped and sighed and shook her head.

"Anyway, this one time she sat me down and there was this show on. I guess it wasn't really a show. More like a speech or something. And there was this old man with big glasses and he was in a brown suit and he was yelling into the camera about how god only helps the people that are willing to help themselves. He was a preacher. The TV kind. And he said god only answers prayers if you show him you're serious about whatever it is you're praying for. Well, my grandma had taken me to a Sunday School class or two, and I knew some about Jesus and god and how they loved you no matter what and would take care of you always, and it didn't sound like this preacher was talking about the same god they talked about in my grandma's church. And to tell you the truth, I liked it. I thought this god sounded legit."

The boy let out a half laugh.

"I did," the girl continued. "I swear, I thought that shit made more sense than anything I'd heard before about some all-loving god. This man said you gotta pay for god's promises, and that sounded a hell of a lot more like the world I knew about. So then the preacher man, he said, 'If you're watching this, I want you to send ten dollars to the address on the screen.' And sure enough an address came across the television where you could mail your money."

"Did you send ten dollars?" the boy asked.

"I was just a little kid, I didn't have any money. But my momma was back in the bedroom with some old boy, so I found her purse and took out ten dollars—there probably wasn't but fifteen or twenty in there to begin with. I wrote down that address in my little girl handwriting and I called my grandma to come pick me up and take me to the post office so I could mail some money to god."

"Did you?"

"Sure as shit."

"And?"

"And what?"

"Did he answer your prayer?"

"No."

"What did you pray for?"

"Doesn't matter. I didn't get it. That man on the TV kept my stolen ten dollars, and when my momma found out what happened she beat me black and blue and wouldn't let me see my grandma anymore."

"So you don't believe in god?"

"Oh, who knows. Maybe god was busy that day, or maybe he pissed off the postman. Truth is, I don't know. I don't know what I believe about god or anything else. I do know one thing though."

"What?"

"I believe in you."

"What?"

"That's right. Why not? You helped me more than god ever has."

He pushed the wet hair out of his face and stared off and it seemed he was considering this new information with great care.

"Well don't be weird," she said. "I ain't gonna worship you or nothing."

The boy nodded.

"But it would be nice if you could conjure up some food and wine like how Jesus did for them hungry folks in the Bible."

"Alright then. I will."

"What? I was just playing."

"I will. I'll do some conjuring."

The boy smiled, and it occurred to the girl she had never seen him do so and this in turn brought a smile of her own and they sat, the two of them, grinning, until the boy slapped his knees and stood and started down the trail toward the river. He stopped a few feet from the cypress grove and turned.

"You just gonna stand there?"

"And miss you partin' the Neches? Not a chance," she said. "I'm right behind you."

The boy slipped soft into the water and the water came over his feet and turned them brown. The boy closed his eyes and dipped his hands into the murk and the girl stood some feet behind him and shook her head.

"I knew you were a river rat but I didn't know how long a tail you had."

"You want supper or not?"

"Whenever you're ready."

He felt above the small holes and hallowed wood near the shore, then spotted a near-black driftwood log three-quarters submerged along the bank. He waded over to it and studied it and turned and grinned at the girl, then plunged his arms into the water and came up splashing and struggling with a river cat the length of his own torso.

"Holy shit," the girl said as the boy launched the fish onto land where it flopped and thrashed in the tall grass. The boy was right behind it and soon he was on the fish and holding it still.

"How did you do that?"

"It's pretty easy. You just have to find where they're nesting and then grab their mouth before they can get away. They'll usually fight instead of run, 'cause they're guarding eggs."

"Wait, you catch them when they're trying to protect their babies?"

The boy frowned.

"Yeah. I guess so."

"That seems messed up."

The boy looked down at the fish, then back at the log.

"Yeah. I guess it does."

"I'm not really hungry anymore."

"Me neither."

The boy took the fish by the mouth again and tried to get it back to the water but it fought back and tore a chunk of flesh from the boy's hand. He dropped it, grabbed it again and this time made it to the log and let it go.

"Do you think it'll go back to its nest?"

"I don't know," the boy said breathing heavy.

The girl grabbed the bottle of hydrogen peroxide from the boy and motioned for him to sit on the couch.

"I can do it myself."

"I'm sure you can, but you took care of me plenty, and now I get to give a little something back. Plus, I've gotten pretty good at stopping folks from bleeding or getting infected after they make a piss-poor needle play."

The boy looked uncomfortable with such information.

River tipped the bottle over his hand and began dabbing up the excess liquid with a paper towel.

"I wonder if the fish are drawn to you because of your name. You know, Jonah, from the Bible?"

The boy winced.

"That bullheaded little bastard sure didn't think too much of me. Besides, that's not how it goes. I mean, there's a whale or a big fish or whatever, but there's a bunch more. I used to read it a lot. Daddy told me my momma named me Jonah like from the Bible and so I thought maybe I could find out something about her if I learned the story."

"Did you?"

"I don't know. I don't think so. I just found out the real story ain't how it is in the little kid books about the Bible."

"Tell me."

"Well, in the story, Jonah is supposed to preach god's word to enemies of Israel, but he doesn't want to because they are evil people. He tries to run from god by sailing in the other direction, but god sends a storm that's going to sink the boat he's on. Jonah know it's his fault, so he sacrifices himself by having the other men throw him into the sea. He would've drowned, but god sent a big fish to swallow him. He lived inside the fish for three days, and the whole time he prayed to god and asked for forgiveness. God did forgive him. He had the fish spit Jonah on the shore of the place he was supposed to preach. So he walked through this city and told the people there that god was going to destroy them if they didn't repent. The people were scared and they listened to Jonah and they did repent, so god spared them.

"But in the end, Jonah is mad at god for not destroying these people. He thinks they are bad people and they don't deserve forgiveness. That's why he didn't want to go in the first place. It's not because he thought they wouldn't listen, it's because he knew they would. He didn't want them to ask forgiveness, because he was afraid god would grant it."

The girl thought about it, then nodded.

"I like that story better," she said.

"How come?"

"Because some people don't deserve forgiveness."

"Even from god?"

"Especially from god. I bet it doesn't say what happens to those people after Jonah leaves. I bet their goody-two-shoes act didn't last no longer than a knife fight in a phone booth. Shit, soon as Jonah was rowing his boat back to Israel or wherever, they started up with all the same things they'd always done. I'd bet anything."

"Maybe."

"That's how people are, kid, they're assholes. They're liars. They're all out for themselves. They get caught doing something and sure as shit they're so sorry about it; but turn your head for two seconds and they'll be at it again. Now hold still and let me finish my doctoring."

24

The box was built on-site in the early morning when there was the least chance of rain, yet the rain still fell and the men felt it mix with their sweat and one of them killed a snake with a power drill. They worked quickly and didn't talk. Twelve by twelve, two feet high.

"Here," one of the men said, handing out shovels. "Dig the grass up, the muddier the better. John Curtis's been mud-training Miss Rose."

The men nodded. Any advantage they could get.

When they quit and left out from the place, the box was a framed mud pit, the rain adding to it. And there it would sit, untouched and unassuming until it was called to blood, and blood there would be.

The gray day slipped unnoticed into night without so much as a dying breath. The mosquitoes swarmed the wetlands and the frog songs echoed through the bottoms in a ghastly collective, and the procession of truck lights came crawling through the red mud, shaping out the trees and tall grass on the far side of the field. The first truck circled the box then stopped, idling, while the others parked in haphazard rows. When all had arrived, the first truck pulled back onto the mud path and followed it to the gravel, then the blacktop, and eventually out to the highway.

A man stood in the dark near the box, his silhouette just visible in the early night. He stood like a man purposed, waiting for something. Everything around him was dark and still.

After a short time, his radio gave static and the driver of the missing truck gave the all clear. No law had followed, nor did any lay in wait for an ambush.

The man nodded, as if such a confirmation could be seen through the airwaves. He walked to the parked vehicles and banged his hand on the back of one and men began to file out, hoisting generators and lighting equipment from the beds of their trucks. Some greeted one another in Spanish, others in broken English. Cade spoke quietly with a man he'd known in the oil fields south of San Antonio.

The set up took less than ten minutes. The generators revved and hummed and powered the lights as they were placed and angled down at each corner of the box.

"Bring in the dogs," the man said.

John Curtis stepped down from the front of the black four-door Ford pickup and opened up the back. The dog leapt down and landed firm and started to pull toward the box, John Curtis doubling the end of the leash around his wrist.

"Look at that hard-mouthed bitch," Frank said. He crossed his arms and spit.

Rose looked every bit the specimen of a gaming dog. She stood high-chested and ears pinned, waiting to follow her owner's lead. Her brindled coat moved up and down with each breath, and the russet and tawny markings gave the dog the look of some exotic beast from the jungles of the eastern world.

"You sure that little ole chihuahua's ready for this?" one of the white men said, heckling the Mexican contingency.

A short Mexican called Jay stepped forward to shake John Curtis's hand. "Where's your dog?"

"Luto," the man called, and both dog and handler stepped forward out of the darkness. John Curtis gave no reaction, but the others in his party frowned. Luto was jet black with yellow eyes, and looked to outweigh his opponent by ten pounds. He crept forward with his shoulders up and head down, as if he'd come from some ancient breed of panther.

Jay grinned at John Curtis who still betrayed no emotion.

Cade shook his head.

"Alright then," John Curtis said, "let's get after it."

They mixed milk and vinegar and soap into the buckets and a man from each group was sent to wash the opposing dog. The other spectators drank beer and smoked cigarettes and heckled the opposition.

"Wash 'em good, José. Y'all gonna need all the help you can get."

"Frank, what do you reckon John Curtis is gonna spend that five thousand on?"

"I imagine he'll buy a night with the most expensive Mexican whore there is. But I don't know what he'll do with the other four thousand nine hundred and ninety-five."

"Seguir hablando, gringo. Ya veremos."

"Hey, Cheech, how do you say ass-whoopin' in Mexican?"

"Perro pequeño," the Mexicans laughed, pointing at the brindle dog and holding their thumb and forefinger close together in a pinching motion.

"We'll see who's laughing when it comes to the nut cuttin'. We'll see."

"Si. Ya veremos," the Mexicans answered.

John Curtis and the Mexican handler cradled their respective dogs behind a white, painted scratch line on either side of the box.

The dogs faced away from one another. John Curtis whispered in Rose's ear and ran his hand along her neck, trailing a thin liquid gel along her fur.

The referee took position, and the dogs were turned. Rose bared her teeth and pulled against John Curtis's grasp. The big black dog crouched and snarled.

"Release," the referee said.

The dogs barreled forward. Rose feinted sidewards from Luto's first strike and locked into his left leg, but the dog was too strong. He pulled away, flinging blood from the fresh gash. Luto moved forward again and this time overpowered the smaller dog. He bit Rose's neck, but just as quickly let go and shook his head. The brindle dog took advantage, launching at Luto's throat and latching. The Mexican handler and his compatriots immediately went into hysterics. The referee called a stop and the men did their best to unlock Rose's jaws. When John Curtis finally pulled her away, the male dog's neck was wet and matted with blood.

"Puto tramposo," Jay accused, running forward, then being held back by his own men.

John Curtis gave him the same grin Jay had shown earlier.

Cade stepped in.

"This was a no qualification show," he said. "You all agreed to it. You brought a goddamn dog looks like it's been pumped full of every Mexican steroid you could get your hands on. Now if there's a problem, you're free to walk away and forfeit your money."

The Mexicans argued angry amongst themselves. They weren't handing over any money, but if they walked out on the show, they'd likely never get another one in East Texas. They pointed at the black dog, at John Curtis, at the pitch-black heavens.

Finally, a lanky man stepped forward from among them.

"We stay," he said.

Jay threw his hands up and cursed in Spanish and walked into the darkness.

John Curtis looked over at Luto. The dog was taking ragged breaths and bleeding unobstructed from the neck.

He looked back to the man and nodded.

On the restart, Luto turned his back and cowered behind the scratch line. There would be no more fighting.

There was no handshake afterward. The men on both sides were silent as they tore down the box and loaded the equipment. The only evidence left would be tire tracks and the still-wet blood that seeped into the muddy ground and was there mixed and become part of the bottoms for all of time.

"Y'all hang back a second," John Curtis told his boys. "Let them go on. We gotta talk some business."

The Mexican caravan came up from the river road and turned out onto the highway and the night went from black to red and blue. Squad cars and SUVs blockaded the southbound stretch of pavement. The lead truck turned and sped away in the opposite direction. It was going ninety miles per hour when it hit the spike strip and went airborne and turned over and slid into a ditch. More lights came up from the north and there was nowhere left to go.

"You think they'll know it was a setup?" Cade asked.

He and John Curtis sat on the porch, back at the hill, and listened to the twilight chorus of crickets and cicadas and somewhere, to the west, a lone coyote calling out.

"They'd be damn fools not to," John Curtis said.

"How's Miss Rose doing?"

"She's just fine. Claude come and picked her up. You should've seen him fawning all over her."

"Lord, I can't imagine."

"You know I think that ole boy might be part dog hisself."

"Wouldn't even raise my eyebrow at it," Cade said.

John Curtis produced a flask from his boot.

"You want a nip?"

The big man didn't answer but reached across and took the flask and pulled from it and passed it back.

In an hour's time they were half drunk and both had determined that dogs were as near a perfect animal as could be.

"If animals could conceive of god, what do you think they'd come up with?" John Curtis asked.

"How do you mean?"

"If a cat were given the ability to describe to you, or even draw for you, what god looked like, what would they draw?"

"I imagine they'd draw some sort of cat," Cade said.

"Exactly. Just as we think of god in our own image, so too would animals."

"But not dogs."

"No. Not dogs. Ask a dog to describe god, and it would describe its owner."

"I could see that."

"A trained dog is nothing more than a religious extremist, willing to do anything and everything for its god," John Curtis said.

"A true believer."

"Yes, sir."

"How come that is, I wonder."

"Guilt. Shame. These are things that dogs have and other creatures don't. It's what makes them like men. It's why we can manipulate them."

"What about apes? Ain't they like men?" Cade asked.

"They're too much like us. Too aware. They can't be controlled as easily. You try telling a monkey to fight his brother, he's liable to turn on you. Rip your arm off."

"Yeah. That's what I'd do."

John Curtis studied the big man, then nodded.

"I know it."

25

The stunted cliffsides rose up from the river in uneven lines of red and pink. The water sat brown and so nearly still but for the sticks and needles bestrewn upon its surface, being pulled onward, signaling to those ashore that the calm river was not as stagnant as it appeared. The boy led and the girl followed and together they slid down a short ravine, and in its gullet there was water still standing from the last rain and they slogged through it. The ferns and horsetails, the hornworts and mosses, all of them growing thick near the water.

Along the Neches the horizons were few, with great shade trees and always another bend in the river, and in this way the bottomlands did mirror the futility of progression for those who were left to dwell there all these years since.

The path of the river narrowed and widened, a muddy lung for the green earth, stretching and constricting, breathing life into the pine forests and tangled underbrush that grew out from the river's bank. Breeding, as it went, this shadowed world of branch and thorn, a canopy where fed those plants and living things born to the darkness of the bottoms, reaching up from the wet ground like a scourge upon the earth.

The buzzards circled the air around some dying thing, like ghastly morticians awaiting their charge. The breeze played against the treetops.

"Shut your eyes," the girl told him, closing her own. The boy watched her as she tilted her head back and brought her arms outstretched on either side.

"Are they shut?" she asked.

"Yes."

"Alright, now listen to the noise the leaves make when the wind blows them."

The boy stood with his eyes closed. He listened.

A breath of wind rose above him, the sound of the trees growing like static, then falling away as the gust faded.

"Do you hear it?"

"I guess."

"It's like the ocean," she said.

"I've never been to the ocean."

"Me neither."

"How do you know what it sounds like?" he asked, opening his eyes.

"You're ruining it."

"Sorry."

The boy closed his eyes again and this time he imagined the sea. The swells building and crashing and dying out. He listened.

"I hear it," he said. "The waves."

"See."

He opened his eyes, and the girl was standing in front of him. She bent and kissed his cheek.

"We'll go there, one day, to the ocean," she said.

"Okay."

"Promise?"

"I promise."

So many times over the years the boy had waited to hear that very sound. He'd prayed for it. But now the truck's exhaust and the clatter that followed as it rumbled down the river road filled the boy with dread.

"Wait by the water," he told the girl. "Let me talk to him."

"That's a bad idea. He'll turn me in."

"He doesn't know those men."

"Everybody knows them. Everybody's scared of them."

"Let me talk to him."

"Fine. But if you don't come back in ten minutes, I'm gone."

"Okay."

The headlights topped the last ridge and their beams cut the darkness and exposed the bottoms of the trees in a great sweeping arch as the truck turned toward the trailer. The engine took a last gasp as it cut, and the lights were gone and the boy's father stepped into the darkness.

"The hell you doing out here this late?" Dwayne scowled.

"Nothing."

"Well. C'mon. I got a grocery or two."

They climbed into the trailer. The boy's father carried two plastic bags into the kitchen and crouched and began unloading them into the cupboard under the microwave.

"You were gone a long time," the boy said.

"Jesus Christ, are you gonna start whining right off the bat?"

"No, sir."

"Good. I want some peace and quiet until I go back to the pipeline. Then you can run around and cry about anything you want."

"Yes, sir."

The boy stood staring at his father's back. The man could feel the eyes on him. He turned his head and looked over his shoulder.

"What?" he asked.

"Well, I was wondering. I have a friend. And I was wondering, hoping, you would let her stay with us. Just for a little while."

The man stood and put his hands on his hips.

"A friend?"

"Yes, sir."

"A girlfriend? You know, I half figured you for a faggot."

"Well, she's older than me."

His father's brow raised.

"An older girl."

"Yes, sir. She's seventeen. She needs a place to stay for a little while."

"Why can't she stay at her own place? She hiding from the law or something?" The boy's father laughed as he opened the fridge.

The boy didn't answer. He watched his father. The man straightened and turned.

"This wouldn't happen to be the girl run off from Splithorn Hill?"

The boy froze. His every output betraying him.

"You stupid little sonofabitch," his father said. "She's been staying here already, hasn't she?"

"Yes, sir."

The man's head swung around on a swivel, and him wide-eyed and arched up like a surprised cat.

"Where is she? Is she in here?"

Dwayne slung the door to the trailer open and called into the darkness.

"Do you know the likes of who's hunting her?" He turned back to the boy. "Do you know what you done? They'll be after us now. After me."

"Nobody knows she was here."

"I've heard stories, about what they do to folks," the man said, ignoring the boy. "Stories it's hard to even believe."

"They're true," the girl said, walking up out of the darkness. "But Jonah's right, nobody knows I'm here."

She made the furthest stretch of ground lit by the porch light and stood.

The boy looked to her and then to his father and they were silent the three of them and each waiting on the other to make some discernment.

"You," Dwayne said. And the boy watched as something strange and familiar passed between the girl and his father. But there was no time to assess, as his father was on the ground and moving toward River at a hurried pace.

"You trying to drag me and my son into whatever jackpot you're caught up in?"

"No," she said, without giving an inch. "The boy just gave me some water."

"You'd better get the hell outta here and not say a damn word to anybody about this place or my son."

"I was just leaving," she said, calm. "I've got a car parked a few miles upriver."

She looked at the boy.

"I don't give a good goddamn what you got or where," Dwayne said. "Just get out from here and don't come back."

The girl turned and disappeared down the trail, and when she was out of sight the man climbed back into the trailer and slammed the door.

"We could've help—" the boy started, but the man backhanded him and sent him sprawling onto the ground.

"I've got to get out from here, too," his father said to no one. "Go down to the reservation and hide out."

"At the casino?" the boy asked, pushing himself up on his elbows.

"What?"

"That's where the casino is, right? At the reservation."

"Yeah, that's where the casino is. But that ain't why I'm going. I'm going because you just put my name at the top of the most-wanted list belonging to a pack of savage sumbitches. So now I gotta get out."

The boy stood, chest out, fists balled. "But I guess you don't want me to go with you. I guess you're not worried about me."

"You're just a kid. They ain't gonna do nothing to you. It's me they'll really put a hurtin' on. That's why I'd better make Livingston before daybreak."

The man threw a change of clothes in a duffel.

The boy stared at him, his chest rising and falling, his teeth grinding.

"What'd you bring me?"

"Huh?"

"For my birthday. You said you'd bring me back a present. What did you bring?"

The man lit a cigarette, then waved the smoke out of his eyes.

"I had you a good present, but there ain't no way you're getting it now, after the shit you just pulled."

"You're a liar."

"What'd you just call me?"

"You're a liar, and you're going to gamble away all our money, and you don't care anything about me."

"Our money? You got a job you ain't told me about? What's this 'our money' shit?"

"I'm your son. You're supposed to take care of me."

"You're a goddamned pain in my ass, is what you are. You got in your head you love that little tweaker bitch, huh?"

"Don't call her that."

"I'll call her what she is."

"She ain't that."

"You stupid little bastard. You gone and got cuntstruck by a goddamn meth head."

"I said don't call her that."

"Or what, boy?"

The boy charged at his father and the man easily threw him to the side and jumped on top of him. The boy squirmed and fought to no avail, and the man laughed and slapped him once and then again, and the boy's ears set to ringing and he could see two of everything.

"I hate you," the boy screamed.

The man continued to laugh.

"You made her leave! You made Momma leave and now you're making River leave and I fucking hate you!"

The man let the boy up and the two of them stood there, the boy crying and the man breathing heavy.

"You think your momma left because of me? Is that it?"

The boy didn't answer.

"You think I run her off? Well, guess what? It was you she left, not me. Your momma, the selfish bitch that she is, couldn't stand taking care of your whiny little ass. Didn't have it in her to put anyone before her own self."

"You're a liar."

"Believe what you want. But I'm the one that's here. I'm the one that stayed. Made sure you had clothes, food, a place to sleep. You ungrateful fucking brat."

The boy wiped his eyes.

"And I'll tell you something else. You ever raise a hand to me again, I'll put your ass out on the street. Let you see how good you really got it."

The boy wept.

The man was breathing heavy. His hands on his hips. He sat in the recliner and opened a beer and turned up the volume on the television.

"I'm too tired to drive to Livingston tonight. I'll go at daybreak. Now get the fuck out of here and go to your room. I don't wanna hear jack shit from you the rest of the night."

At 4:00 a.m. the boy had estimated the man was deep into a drunken sleep. He'd been listening to the snoring for an hour. He came out from his room and passed by the sleeping man in the recliner.

The boy opened the cabinet under the microwave and scanned the meager selection within. There were six cans of Vienna sausages, a package of saltine crackers, two cans of refried beans, a four-pack of peach cups, and a bag of off-brand potato chips.

He looked over his shoulder at his father and then emptied the cabinet into his bag, all save the potato chips which he left not out of kindness, but because he feared the bag would make too much noise in transit. He also opened the refrigerator and took from it the jug of water and two cans of RC Cola.

With his backpack full, the jug in one hand and his flashlight in the other, the boy stood at the door of the trailer and tried to steady his breath. He watched his father sleeping, mouth open and body slunked down in the recliner as if he were some ballooned puppet whose air had been let out. The boy thought about what his father had told him and decided it was lie. It had to be a lie.

He opened the door and eased himself down to the ground. He looked up at his father, then slowly brought the door to its frame. He readied himself, then gave the door a strong push so that it would shut completely, and as soon as it did the boy was off and running across the yard and down the trail. He ran without looking back until he reached the river where the bank trail intersected his own. He turned northwest and followed along the bank, the water sloshing in the jug and the beam from his flashlight erratic across ground and sky alike, jerking as he ran.

Miles later, the boy reached the ravine and shined his light down and tracked the creekbed up the ridge and across. He spotted the car as the last hour of darkness was waning and the pale light breaking beyond the trees.

To the east, the dawn was hard at work pushing a sanguine sky overtop the vestiges of the falling black, and when at last the glowing corona of the sun did emerge, it looked as if the earth were sacrificing its very heart to some ancient luminary. As if the sunrise was not but an extraction of the world's soul, or the thing most liken to a soul, and it was being uprooted from the horizon and trawled through the great firmament what separates the waters below from the waters above.

The boy made the car and whispered the girl's name and peered inside and his heart sank with her absence.

"Jonah," she hissed from the underbrush.

"It's me," he replied.

She stood from her crouch and walked forward and he dropped the light and ran to meet her. They stood in front of one another and what sentiment or inclination held within their eyes would not be spoken, and the girl looked at his bag and at his face and she knew the truth of things and what he'd done for her, and what he might yet do.

She put her arms around the boy and kissed his cheek.

"I'm so sorry, Jonah," she told him. Soft. "So so sorry."

She loosened the black cord she wore as a necklace and put it over his head.

"What's that for?"

"I don't know. For you."

26

The morning sun didn't hold, and soon the rain fell and gathered on the ground and in the trees, and the leaves weighed down and dripping, and the branches and plants sloped over like some great melting of the world. The squirrels looked out from their hiding holes, and the birds shook their wet feathers, and the deer moved silent toward higher ground. They moved in groups of threes and fours, like untrusting survivors of the apocalypse, stopping to lift their heads skyward and blow, trying their best to discern the true measure of their own safety in the storm.

John Curtis stood atop Splithorn Hill and pissed off the porch and looked west, the road to the cabin winding and falling away into a sea of green trees and gray mist, the fresh tire tracks deepening the ruts like mud-carved trenches from some studied war. Far to the south, some twenty miles, the highway ran hidden by the foliage, and to the north and east there was nothing save river and wilderness and, eventually, Redtown.

"You know," he said. "I do believe I'm a hungover son of a gun."

Cade stood on the far side of the porch, watching the steam from his coffee rise and swirl in no particular pattern, as if it wasn't sure of its own place in the world.

"I ain't too far behind you myself," he said.

"I think the last time I drunk that much rot gut was right after we put an end to them Hitler-worshipping cocksuckers. Well, I guess I should say, after you put an end to 'em."

Cade slurped his coffee and said nothing.

"You know, you killed that old boy, what's his name?" John Curtis said.

"Donaldson."

"Yeah, that old boy, Donaldson. And then that was it. That ended the whole damn thing."

The big man shrugged.

"He was their boss," Cade said. "Or grand wizard or führer or whatever the hell."

John Curtis laughed.

"He was. He sure was. But there was something else about it. Reminded me of how folks talked about dropping the bomb on Japan. Something that savage, that inhumane—just seeing it, breaks a man."

The big man shifted his weight and sighed.

"Alright, fine," John Curtis said. "I know you don't like talking about it. But you saved lives that day."

"Ole Donaldson might see it different."

"I don't believe he sees anything but hellfire and brimstone these days." John Curtis laughed and shook his head. "I never have understood that," he said.

"What's that?" Cade asked.

"How come they want to dress up like Germans and worship some dumb sumbitch who got his ass kicked by the USA."

"I don't understand it neither."

"Well, I'd expect you not to understand it, you're from the North."

The big man frowned.

"Dakota ain't the north, it's just the cold South."

John Curtis was about to laugh again when something caught his eye.

"Look there," he said, motioning with his head toward the tree line, where the land sloped sharp from under them.

Below, the deer were fleeing to higher ground, leaping as they went, over the fallen fences and scattered debris from long abandoned hovels, and they moved with the ease of a morning.

The two men watched as the herd climbed up at an angle.

"Graceful," John Curtis said, "like a flock of birds on the clear sky. Fish in open water."

"Old man used to call 'em timber ghosts," Cade said.

"I like that. Of course, they aren't ghosts. They're as alive as you and me, and fighting just as hard to survive. Harder, I'd say. The river rises and up they come, leading the fawns to the safety of a higher ground they've never before set eyes on. It's a pretty picture, wouldn't you say? Good parenting, at least."

John Curtis reached inside the doorway and brought forth a 30.6 rifle and leveled it against his shoulder and Cade plugged his ears.

"Good parenting," John Curtis repeated as he pulled the trigger.

The men walked together to retrieve the kill, the rest of the deer scattering at the sound of the gunshot. They tucked their jeans into the top of their boots and Cade carried a rope and John Curtis the rifle.

"I hate this fucking weather," Cade mumbled.

"Can't say man and nature aren't connected to each other, somehow. Like when the skies go gray and can't stop raining, makes folks like you sull up and get ornery. It's a funny thing, if you ask me. But I wonder, if you was in a house without no windows, but the outside world was coming a proper flood, would you still feel ill-tempered about things?"

"I imagine I would."

"'Cause of how we're impacted by the weather?"

"No, because I'm in a house with no goddamn windows."

This made John Curtis laugh too hard to walk, and Cade spit and wiped the rain from his eyes and water fell from his hat brim as he stood and waited for his companion to continue on.

"You are one surly son of a bitch, you know that?" John Curtis said.

"Heard it a time or two."

The big man seldom slept. When he did, he dreamed the story of his life, played out under an always dark sky. The war. The oilfields in Dakota. The drugs. The girl.

But long before any of that, he was a child. There was a blue ball resting on the hardwood floor of a cabin somewhere deep in the Black Hills near the Wyoming state line. His mother was in the kitchen, he could see her through the doorway of the den. She stood over the sink, working at the dishes with a torn and tattered rag.

She sang a song so sad it hurt. It filled him up with pain and sorrow and he was too young, far too young, to understand. The smell of rich, burning pine escaped the stove pipe and mixed with the sadness and it was all too beautiful, too overwhelming. He didn't know what to do, what sounds to make to make it all stop. He looked at the blue ball and reached for it, out of some instinct, and grabbed it and sent it bouncing into the kitchen and against the back of his mother's foot.

She looked down, then wiped her hands on the rag and laid it to rest on her shoulder. She knelt, delicate, and retrieved the ball. She smiled at him, and he knew he'd done well. He knew he'd fixed things somehow.

His brother, Rory, was born the following year. His father was laid off from the factory in Great Falls. His mother's songs grew sad again.

His father was a proud man. Proud of what, Cade did not know. His abuse was unpredictable. The slightest, often strangest thing would set him off. The whole world seemed crudely balanced on an uneven plain.

And so it went, his life for a dozen years, until his brother whispered to him, "We gotta stop that sonofabitch."

"You're dead if you try," Cade told him.

He did try. And he was dead. And Cade's father in prison. And Cade's mother never spoke again.

When he was sixteen he hit a second growth spurt. He wasn't small to begin with, but by his seventeenth birthday he'd gone from five ten to six six. And it wasn't just his height. His arms filled out, his chest barreled, and his thighs grew so fast he had to buy jeans three sizes too large and cinch them at the waist with his belt.

As his body grew, so too did his rage. The things long suppressed from his childhood began to surface. He found that violence came natural, and that most everyone was afraid of him. He relished that. Thinking of his own fear of his father, and how he'd left Rory to confront him alone, Cade promised himself he would never back down from anyone again.

He fought in Afghanistan and Iraq, not out of some patriotic calling, but because he wanted to get as far away as possible. And also he imagined the army was the best place to unleash the rage that had swelled inside him.

After the explosion, he never lost consciousness. He remembered every second of turning silently through the air, seeing what was left of the Humvee below him. The sand seemed far away, then closer, then he was laying on it, watching the fighting unfold sideways, as if the soldiers were running up the brown edges of some anti-earth.

"C'mon, you big sumbitch," a man said, and Cade felt himself being dragged across the desert.

The man grunted and strained and cussed.

"I hate to tell you this, bud, but there ain't a purple heart in the world gonna make up for what they done to you."

"Hey," Cade said in a sleepy voice. "Hey."

The man let go of Cade's shoulders and pulled his handgun and fired it twice. The two men running toward them both crumpled to the ground like puppets with cut strings, limbs bending and sprawling in ways unnatural, as if they were tied to one another and tied to death.

The man bent down again and grabbed Cade under his arms and tried to keep pulling.

"I can walk," Cade whispered.

The man helped him to his feet and they staggered a few yards before the big man collapsed again.

"Might just be me and you, brother," the man said. "Your boys look to have been cleaned out. They'll send in the big guns here pretty soon. You just stay with me."

The man managed to drag Cade some forty yards and into a sand bunker and there stood guard over him for four hours until a medical evac came. As he was loaded into the copter, Cade looked over at the man and his dark eyes and boyish face. Then, finally, he closed his eyes and slept.

When the military was done with him, the oilfields came calling. Money and drugs. A reckless life. A distraction from those things buried deep. The things lived and the things lost.

He started out taking pills to stay awake during his shifts. Then he started using on his off days. Pills to powder to crystal. He was a quick study. He followed the gas leaks and the drug trade from the Bakken formation up north to the Eagle Ford in Texas. When he hit the barracks in the Lone Star State, he whispered to the nearest hand about the availability of the drug.

"Hey, y'all," the old boy called out to any and everyone within earshot. "The new guy wants to know if anybody's got that Tina."

Dozens of hands rose slowly, then the entire room filled with laughter.

Slam sessions weren't exactly secrets in the Dakotas, but they hadn't been broadcast over the same frequencies he found in Texas. Then again, Texans were like that, he learned. Loud, brash, unapologetic. He liked it. They would laugh in the face of company officials—"the suits," they called them—when they'd hold press conferences and announce zero-tolerance policies on meth and the like.

Every time some kid would get his head stoved in or split in half by a motorized cable spool, they'd talk about making a big push on drugs. Ten percent of the workers tested positive for meth, but they laughed at that number, too. The drug only stayed in your system for a few days, and most everybody had a heads-up about the piss man coming around. Even then, they usually just picked the boys they figured would be clean anyway.

The truth of it was, the state was getting rich and nothing was gonna get in the way of that. Nothing covers up cronyism, corruption, and failed economic policies like a never-ending flow of taxes from oil and gas revenue. A mainline injection into the state coffers. Cade took his share and would've kept on doing it if his past hadn't come back to find him.

Cade dreamed about him, the man who'd saved him in Iraq. Out there in the desert, the wind blowing cold, and he saw the man's face, looked into his eyes.

When he woke up the man was staring at him. The same boyish face and crooked teeth and the same black eyes. Dark and wild.

"Hello, Cade," he said. "You about ready to quit working for a living?"

In the hours to come, John Curtis never asked what Cade had been doing in the years since Iraq, he never offered up his own past, or even told Cade how he'd come to find him in the first place. Instead, he laid out grand plans for a meth empire in East Texas that sounded too wild and farfetched to be real.

"Be my general. My right hand. My brother," he'd said, and Cade accepted.

And, in time, all the crazy things John Curtis said had come true. They controlled everything. The land, the people, the law. He could walk into the courthouse, a known murderer, and no one would touch him. John Curtis was right, they were gods.

Still, there was something missing, and he didn't know what it was until he found the girl. She didn't love him. He knew that. But it didn't matter. She was scared and alone and he became her protector and it made him feel wanted, desired. She didn't flinch when she touched it, and she didn't care when he said he'd never be able to have a family. She never asked what happened and he never told her. Instead, she curled up into his arms every night and there they would sleep. Together. Until she ran out on him. Left him humiliated. Probably shacked up with somebody else. She said she didn't mind, but he'd also wondered if she was lying. Of course she was, he thought. She's only human.

27

In the years before he died, my father would complain about a great many things. Politicians, union busters, atheists, immigrants, gays, the heat, the cold, and the antenna reception. But what he complained about more than anything was breakfast.

You can't get a proper breakfast nowadays, he'd insist. Powdered eggs, microwaved bacon, biscuits that come in a can. Metaphor for the times, you ask me. I know you didn't. Still. Everybody wants things fast. Somewhere along the way folks mistook "fast" for "good."

I know it's every new generation that's said to be ushering in the end times. I know it to be true in the eyes of my father. And who could argue? Man lived through the Great War, the height of the Depression, only to see two sons die fighting the Nazis, a daughter lost to polio before she was six years on earth, and a wife taken by the grief of it all. What does Armageddon look like, if not the stealing away and destruction of all we have?

Of course, we won the war, cured the diseases, even went and put a man on the moon. Straightforward tasks, straightforward thinking. I try not to allow myself to become the angry old man my father turned into. But I can't figure how to go about approaching the things that's out there nowadays. Can't find a soul to tell me what a war on drugs even looks like.

I heard the state representative for Neches County—man by the name of Chalmers—say that we needed to stop the drug supply at its source. Said it was corrupting our youth and whatnot, and we needed to pull it up by the roots.

It was a pretty speech and all, but he didn't never say what the source was. Raiding cook trailers and throwing folks in jail? Maybe. Marching into Mexico and going to war with the cartels? I kindly doubt it. And there's something else old Chalmers didn't account for, and that's men like John Curtis. What's the source of a man like that?

What I do know is that we do terrible things to our children, then wonder why it all turns out like it does. There's talk of evil in the world, as if it were a lone thing come into being by no other means than fate. As if it were something we were owed without having worked for.

But I don't believe I can abide by that prescribing of evil or anything else. What we name evil is in truth just consequence, the result of things long connected, spooled out over the histories of men in ways we're like to never understand. But that doesn't mean we get to wash our hands of the blame. When it comes to the way the world turns, we ought not be allowed to claim ignorance as an alibi.

I read about a boy who killed his own sister. Called the police and told them he'd killed her. They asked him how come he done it, and he said he had to. Said he'd been a drug mule for one of the cartels, and some money went missing. His handlers told him if he couldn't come up with money, they were going to kidnap his sister, do all sorts of things to her. I guess he knew them to be men of their word, 'cause he drove straight to that poor girl's house and shot her in the head.

When the police asked him how come he didn't just give back the money, the boy said he didn't have it. Said he wasn't the one who'd took it.

Wasn't long after that, I quit reading the paper.

I think maybe the country has the same problem I do. Half of it just wanting to believe everything's fine, the other half knowing it's not. I've studied on it a great deal. In the end, it's my estimation that the psychology of man has more to do with the world than anything else. It's not politics or policy, or what's best for the rich or best for the poor. It's the ongoing battle between hope and fear. And it's not near as simple as some might think. Like everything else that gets whittled down to black and white, it's neither. It's gray and nuanced and delicately balanced. But there's no place for such things anymore. Makes a poor headline, and an even worse campaign slogan.

Sometimes, I think if this is all there is, all that we're working toward as a species, then there's a not-all-together insignificant part of me wishing we'd gone the way of the dinosaurs. What creatures, dinosaurs. Gets a man to thinking, or at least it should. I don't know what about. But something. The dinosaurs ought to make a man think about something.

28

"You sure as shit don't learn your lesson the first time, do you?" the girl asked.

They were walking through the rain, holding palmetto leaves overtop their heads.

"Mr. Carson's not like that. He's a good man."

"No such thing as a good man."

"What about me?"

"You're still young," she said. "Give it time."

It was late afternoon when they spilled out of the woods on the northwest side of Carson's keep. The old man was in his always overalls and fussing with his cats over some grievance he believed called for redress.

"I swear on my daddy's grave I'll skin these little bastards and use 'em as bait," he said to the two of them, without offering a greeting.

"You ought to quit feeding them," the boy said. "I mean, if you don't want them around."

"Who's this?" the old man asked, pushing his head forward and squinting down at the girl.

"This is my friend, River. We need a place to stay. Just for a few days."

The old man rocked back in the chair and nodded.

"Mmhm. And I'm guessing your own house ain't an option?"

"Nossir."

The old man nodded, again.

"Well. C'mon in, get out of this rain. I'll make us a pot."

The three of them sat around the table and a number of cats stood outside the screen door yeowing until the old man shooed them away. They scattered off the porch and by the time he was back in his chair they'd reformed by the door and there appeared to be more of them than had started out.

"Your daddy know where you're at?" Mr. Carson asked.

"Nossir."

"But he knows you're gone?"

"I imagine he'll figure it out after a while."

"What about you, young lady?"

"What about me?" the girl said.

"Your people know you run off?"

"I don't have any people."

"I see."

"It's just for a few days," the boy repeated.

"And then what?" the old man asked.

"Then we'll leave."

"And go where?"

The boy opened his mouth but didn't say anything.

"That's enough questions," the girl said. "If you need to know every little thing, we can just as soon find another place to hole up. Jonah, I told you this was a bad idea."

The old man furrowed his brow.

"I didn't mean to offend, darling. Your business is your own. And I trust the boy."

"But not me, huh?"

"All due respect, I don't know you."

"No. You don't."

The three of them were quiet, until Carson set down his coffee.

"What have y'all been a'hunting, out there in the woods?" the old man asked.

The girl and the boy looked at one another.

"What?" Carson continued. "It ain't like y'all been slipping through the trees real quiet."

"You been watching us?" the girl asked, rising from her seat.

"Naw. Just hearing you."

"A backpack," Jonah said. "We're looking for a backpack. You seen one around?"

"Can't say that I have. What's in it?"

"I thought we already talked about what business belonged to you, and what didn't," the girl snapped.

"River," the boy said.

"No, to hell with this."

She walked out, and the cats again disbanded and again reformed their ranks.

The boy stood and looked toward the door and looked at the old man.

"You want to tell me exactly what all's going on here, son?" Carson asked.

The boy looked pained.

"I can't, Mr. Carson. I'm real sorry. I gotta go. I'll come back as soon as I can."

The old man watched him go and shook his head and drank his coffee. After a while he stood up and opened a can of tuna and opened the screen door and let the cats into the cabin.

He caught up with the girl under an old pecan tree where she was trying to find a nut that hadn't already rotted away. It had stopped raining, but the trees were still shaking free of the water with each small breath of wind.

"I can't do this shit anymore," she said, throwing down a black shell. "It's too hot, too wet, and I'm too hungry. I'm gonna go to China to be a doorman."

"You're gonna do what?" the boy asked.

"I saw it on TV a few months back. The rich Chinamen try to show off to one another by having white folks as their housekeepers and whatnot."

"Really?"

"The taller the better is what they said on TV. I'm five seven, which is pretty tall for a girl. Especially a Chinese girl, I imagine."

"Would you have to become Chinese?"

"How the hell would I become Chinese?"

"No, I mean like, be a citizen of China."

"I don't know, Jonah, it's a joke. I'm not really going to go live somewhere they eat dogs."

"Oh. Okay. What *do* you want to do?"

"Well, I'm not shacking up with some old man. I'll tell you that much."

She expected him to protest, but he didn't.

"C'mon, then," the boy said.

He led her away from the river banks and through a muddy sink and up a draw to an overlook dotted with maple trees.

"You better not be dragging me up here for the view. I've seen about as much of this river as I can stand."

"I'm not. But it is pretty here in the fall, all these leaves turn red."

"You're not one of those fall people are you? Pumpkin spiced scarves and all that?"

The boy looked confused. "I like the fall," he said, hoping that was answer enough.

He let his backpack drop to the dirt and he knelt and unzipped it and pulled the bright-blue tarpaulin from the main pouch and unfolded it threadbare across the ground. He spread it out, running his hands meticulous over each crease, then placing rocks on each corner to hold it down.

The girl stood with her arms crossed.

"This isn't you trying to be romantic, is it?"

The boy shook his head.

"Here," he said, pulling a can of Vienna sausage from the backpack. He tossed it to her.

"I take it back," she told him. "You're a natural Don Juan."

They sat cross-legged on the tarp, and the boy used his pocket knife to peel thin slices of cheese from a block of cheddar. He opened a sleeve of saltine crackers and set it in between them. They ate in their own silence, but there was no silence to the world.

Woodpeckers echoed their work through the forest and ruby-throated hummingbirds passed by with the low thrum of their always motion. Insects called, seemingly from every blade of grass, and below them the river continued to expand, to spread across the land like slow-leaking ink, staining the earth with brown umber streams and brindled pools.

The girl leaned back onto her elbows.

"It is a nice view, though."

Just before dusk, the storm clouds gathered again, and whatever agreement the sun was beholden to saw it sent away. The boy and the girl in river, cooling, cleaning, neither willing to talk about what might come next.

She splashed water onto him. He wiped at his eyes and stared her down. Her look was of defiance, mischief. His eyes narrowed. She took off and him behind her, both splashing and laughing. He lunged toward her and wrapped his arm around her waist as he fell, dragging her with him into the shallow water. Their skin touched in a half-dozen places and he felt them all. She slipped his grip and spun to face him, the boy on his bottom in the river, the girl crouched above him. Both smiling.

Water dripped into one of his eyes and he squinted it closed. They were both breathing heavy. She offered her hand and he took it. She pulled him halfway up, then grinned and shoved him back down. He recovered and kicked his foot out, spraying her with water. The chase was on again, and in that moment they were the children they were supposed to be.

They lay in each other's arms in the back seat of the old Plymouth and listened to the sound of the rain and the sound of the river at night.

"Well, what now?" the girl asked. "You planning on living in this back seat?"

"Let's go to the ocean, like you said."

The girl smiled but it was a thin smile, defeated.

"Without that backpack, there's no way to get there. The world costs money, kid. Without money, you can't do shit."

She sat up.

"You ever feel like, like there's just too much?" she said. "Like maybe, if you only had one or two things to worry about, then maybe things would be alright?"

The boy nodded.

"I don't know," she continued. "I just . . . my momma. I always hated her. I used to think every bad situation she was in was her own fault, because she was a bad person. Or maybe not bad, but stupid. Like she just always made the wrong choices. But now, I . . . she was so young and with a baby and . . . everything's just so goddamn hard, you know?

"People like us, we get reminded of who we are, every day. We're the trash messing up somebody else's pretty picture. The ones putting back toothpaste at the grocery store because we don't have enough cash and we're out of food stamps. The ones stuffing their panties with public toilet paper because they can't afford tampons. I've stolen. I've begged. I've gone without. I've hated myself and my family and the place I come from.

"But when I found meth, it took me in. It told me it didn't matter about all the other shit. Didn't matter I was poor white trash. Didn't matter what my momma was and how folks talked about her. Didn't matter about what I'd done, or even what I'd do later. The meth told me I could do anything, and I believed it. But then the high passed and I wasn't ready for it to end, wasn't ready to let that feeling go. I kept using, kept chasing that euphoric dream of feeling like someone. The peace it brought, even for five minutes, I can't tell you how good it was.

"Of course, whatever plans I made, they'd fade away as soon as I was coming down. And then it's like, it's like everything just stops. Your heart. Your breath. The whole world around you. You're like a bay dog, just a hundred percent locked in on one thing. Shit, it's hard to even think about those moments in between.

"It's all just so fucking pointless," she said. "The backpack's gone. It got caught up in the river and is probably halfway to Houston by now."

"Beaumont," the boy said.

"What?"

"The river goes to Beaumont."

"Jesus Christ. I don't care."

The boy shrugged.

"What was in it, anyway? The backpack."

The girl looked at him.

"You know what was in it. You've known the whole time. Even a kid as weird as you wouldn't spend this long looking for something without asking what it is."

"You could probably make a lot of money if you sold it, huh?"

She nodded.

"It might even be enough for us to go to the ocean."

"Sure. It could be."

"But let's say it suddenly turned up. Wouldn't you be scared that you might want to keep it for yourself? Do the drugs, I mean."

The girl cocked her head.

"Jonah."

"Promise me you wouldn't."

Her eyes narrowed.

"Did you take my fucking backpack?"

"Promise."

"Where is it?"

"I ain't gonna tell you unless you promise."

"I swear to fucking god, if you don't tell me where it is I will drown you in a pool of mosquito water."

The boy thought he might be making a mistake, but he led her to the shallow grave anyway. They walked through the dark, the boy apologizing, the girl not saying a word. They were a long time walking and when they finally stopped they could make out the false moonlight from the boy's own trailer.

"You've got to be fucking kidding me," the girl said.

He pointed at the ground and she dropped to her hands and knees and tore at the soft dirt. She uncovered first a strap and used that to pull up the rest and she clutched the bag across her chest and closed her eyes.

"I'm not going to use," she told him. Her voice slow and calm and steady. "I promise."

She stood and hugged him.

"You're not mad?" he asked.

She pulled away and smiled, then swung the backpack hard against the side of his head.

"What the actual fuck, Jonah? You lied to me this whole time. You acted like, I mean—you asked questions about where it was. You made me look like an asshole."

"You don't look like an asshole."

"Shut up. Oh my god, shut up. You don't get to talk right now. I trusted you and you lied to me. Why did you do that?"

The boy was silent.

"Well?"

"You said not to talk."

"Fucking talk. Answer me."

"I was afraid you'd leave."

The girl scoffed and shook her head.

"Well, congratulations, kid. You got to play make-believe that you had a girlfriend. Or any friend. But now, guess what? I *am* leaving."

"I'm coming with you."

"Like hell you are."

"You don't have a light. And you don't know where you're going."

"I'm pretty sure I can figure out how to stay on the roads."

"There's snakes," the boy said, desperate.

"Rather get bit by a real snake than a fake friend."

The boy's face had gone beet red and the tears began to come and he turned away from her and said nothing else.

She stood there watching his back rise and fall and she was a long time standing. Then she took a deep breath.

"Fine," she said. "Come on."

29

"What if it never stops raining?" Lonnie asked. "Like, what if, everything just floods?"

"I imagine we'd evacuate up toward Dallas or something," Frank said.

"But I mean, like, what if there was nowhere to evacuate to? What if everything was flooding?"

"That's not possible. Even if the whole world were under water, we're Americans. We would just find the highest spots on earth and take them over. Like, in the Himalayan mountains or something. Mountains don't flood."

"I like the mountains. It's cold though. I don't like being cold."

"Better than being drowned."

Lonnie nodded and looked out the truck window.

"Mount America," he whispered.

They turned south and headed toward the lake.

"You ever worry about getting robbed on these drops?" Lonnie asked, running his fingertips along the length of his forearm.

"Nobody would rob us," Frank told him.

"Shit, I would absolutely rob us."

Frank sighed.

"I don't mean you and me specifically. I mean, nobody would rob us because that would mean they robbed John Curtis. Would you do that?"

"Why would I rob John Curtis?" Lonnie asked. "I work for him."

Frank shook his head.

"Oh, hey," Lonnie said, opening the glove box in front of him, "did you see where them good old boys from out in Kender beat up on that Mexican fella?"

"Yea, I heard about it. What are you doing digging through my glove box for. Quit that shit."

"I don't see what the big deal is," Lonnie said, taking out a pistol and turning it in his hand. "I hadn't never had no Mexican take a job from me."

"You've never had a job in the first place. Now put that back and close it up."

"That's not true. I used to work at the Pizza Shack. I don't imagine a Mexican even knows how to cook no pizza."

"Mexicans know how to cook everything. You've never eaten anything a Mexican can't cook. I said, put it back."

Lonnie did as he was told.

"Well, still, I don't have no problem with them being here."

"I don't have a problem with them being here. I have a problem with them coming here without going through the proper channels. We can't just let anybody in."

"I don't know. It just don't seem very nice. What if Indians had built them a wall, to keep white folks out?"

"They damn well should have. Look what happened."

"I never thought of it that way," Lonnie said.

He was quiet for a few seconds, then he opened the middle console and began rummaging through old packs of gum, cigarettes, and receipts.

"You ever heard of it flooding and being this goddamn hot at the same time?" he asked.

"I heard of lots of things," Frank answered. "What the hell are you doing now?"

"I'm just looking."

"Can't you just sit and be still until we get there?"

"Where we headed?" Lonnie asked, then plucked a small canister from the console and held it up.

"New guy. Out near Rayburn."

"I hate new guys."

"He put in a big order. John Curtis said he's alright. Put that back."

"What is it?"

"It's an air freshener spray."

"Ozium," Lonnie read the side of the canister. "I don't know, you just can't trust these tweakers, man. I want to sell to the professionals."

"Professionals?"

"Yea, doctors and lawyers and shit. What's it smell like?"

"They don't do meth. Cocaine, maybe. But not meth. It doesn't smell like anything, it just gets out other smells."

"Can I spray it?"

"No."

"What about that one old boy? The radio guy? He did meth."

"Yeah, and he was the talk of the goddamn town when it all come out. Lost his job and just about everything else. That's why them sorts of people don't do meth."

Lonnie held the nozzle out in front of him and sprayed it and then began coughing.

"Goddamn it, I told you not to spray it."

"Holy shit, that's strong," Lonnie said, rolling his window down. "I thought you said it didn't smell like nothing."

"It's chemicals and whatnot."

Lonnie stuck his head out the window and took a breath and brought it back in.

"Man," he said. "Why didn't you just say it smelled like chemicals?"

Frank stared at him and then shook his head.

"You ever think about what you might have done?" Lonnie asked. "I mean if you didn't get into all this in the first place."

"No."

"You never even thought about it?"

"No."

"I think maybe I could've been an accountant or something. Wear a suit to work and everything. Have a nice office with a nameplate."

"Accountant?"

"Sure. Why not?"

"You know this fella's buying fifteen grams?" Frank said.

"What?"

"That's right. Having some sort of lake party I'd imagine."

"You're telling me we got fifteen Gs in the goddamn car?"

"Calm down. Nobody's pulling us over out here. And if they do, they'll be the sheriff's boys. He and the boss got an arrangement."

Lonnie breathed out.

"Fifteen grams," he repeated.

"I shit you not," Frank looked over at him. "Got a little accounting test for you."

"What?"

"Yeah, come on. Fifteen Gs at eighty-five dollars a pop. What's this old boy gonna owe us?"

The car was silent for several miles.

"That's why not," Frank said.

30

All night it rained. They walked the road for a short while and then took shelter, such as it was, in a grove of cedar elm. When the rain gave out at long last, the river was brown and marbled and heavy in its running, the reach of the water expanding further into the woods and wetlands around it.

The boy led them off the road and onto a trail that would cut the distance to the highway. They hiked up into the hills and the forest dripping around them and the humidity a part of them and the boy's glasses fogged and slipping down his nose. They walked one behind the other, each taking a turn at the lead, as if they were tethered together in some solemn march, the girl clinging to the backpack as if it were the last relic of a forgotten world.

"You're still mad?" the boy asked.

"I don't know, did you still lie to me?"

"I'm sorry, River."

"I guess it doesn't matter now. We'll get to a phone and then figure it out from there."

"Figure what out?"

"What I'm going to do with you."

The boy stopped walking. The girl turned around, and they stood staring at one another under a canopy of hardwood.

"I ran away for you."

"No, no, no. Don't put that shit on me. Your old man likes to drink and play whack-a-Jonah, that's got nothing to do with me. You can call CPS or something. Or call an aunt in Shreveport."

"I don't have an aunt in Shreveport."

"Jesus Christ, I know. I just mean, call someone to let you live with them."

"I want to live with you."

"You're killing me, kid."

"You owe me."

"Yes, I did owe you. And that's why I didn't drown you for stealing my backpack. But now we're even."

"You know what, you *are* an asshole."

"Ouch, tough talk from a thief."

"I didn't steal it. I hid it. I was protecting you."

"You were lying to me. You let me stumble through the woods every day looking for something you had the whole time. You don't get to choose what's best for me. You think you're being different, treating me nice, being my protector or some shit. But that's the same as all the rest. Besides, you already told me the real truth. You just wanted to keep me around because you're a lonely, pathetic kid."

The boy put his head down and moved past her. She followed.

They walked in silence.

It took just over four hours to hit the highway, and another forty minutes before the boy and the girl came to the gravel lot outside of the bar.

"Hey, Jonah. I'm sorry. I know you did a lot for me. I shouldn't have said those things."

"But you believe them."

"I don't."

"You do. Because they're true."

"Jonah—"

"Just leave me alone."

"Fine."

They walked into the bar and stood and took in their surroundings as if they were, the two of them, itinerants from a world lost to mud and sand, vagrants with no further direction upon their wayward souls. The barman frowned.

"You ain't old enough to be in here," he said, not unkind, to the girl. "And if you are, he damn sure ain't."

"I been in here before. I'm a friend of Cade's. Y'all still got a payphone on the deck out back?"

"It's back there. I got no idea if it works."

"It works," the girl assured him. "Give me some quarters."

"Excuse me?"

"Maybe you didn't hear me. I said I'm a friend of Cade's. Now give me some goddamn quarters."

"Fussy little thing," the man said, but nonetheless produced a stack of quarters and slid it across the bar.

"Stay here," she said to the boy.

He nodded.

The boy had never before seen the inside of a bar and decided then that he felt oddly comforted by its lifelessness—the desperation of the neon signs and the veneer of stale smoke long bonded with the air. There were several round tables offset from the far end of the bar itself, spotlit by rectangled fixtures each with a different beer's branding. Two pool tables stood back center on a slightly slanted wood platform. The middle of the space was open for dancing and a small stage was pushed back on the wall opposite the bar. Four people, two to a table, sat in the back, and a single bar stool was occupied by a middle-aged man in a flannel shirt with a mesh-back cap and a graying beard.

"That your sister?" the man asked.

"No, sir."

"Christ, it ain't your momma is it?"

The boy shook his head.

"Well, alright then."

The boy lingered near the front door.

"You want something to drink?" the man asked.

"Leave him alone, Carl, he ain't even supposed to be in here," the barman said.

"We can't set him up with a Coke or something? Hell, look at the boy. Say, son, you been wrestling gators or something?"

"No, sir."

"Well, how come you to be in such a state?"

"Texas?"

"I mean the disheveled look about you. My god, you're dirty as a politician."

"We been in the woods."

"For some time, by the looks of it," the man said. "For the love of Christ, Jerry, get the boy a Coke."

The boy climbed atop a stool next to the man.

"What's your name, son?"

"Jonah."

"Jonah, I'm Carl. That sour sumbitch behind the bar is Jerry. Don't let his prickly demeanor fool you, he's as sweet a man as ever there was."

"Okay."

"So, tell me then, how is it you come to be living in the woods?"

"I don't live in the woods. I live in a trailer with my dad, Dwayne Hargrove. I just been helping my friend."

"And she lives in the woods?"

The boy pursed his lips.

"I don't know where she lives."

The two men exchanged unsettled looks.

"Dwayne Hargrove?" Carl asked. "That's your daddy?"

"Yessir."

"You know him?" the barman said.

"I do," Carl said. "Spent some time offshore with him, maybe ten or fifteen years ago. Degenerate gambler these days, I hear. No offense, kid."

"So what's the story with the girl?" Jerry asked. "Why are you helping her? What are you up to?"

"I don't think I should say."

"I don't believe he wants to talk to us, Carl," Jerry said, then turned back to the boy. "Kid, we know who she is, and we know who's looking for her. However it is that you come into this, you ought to see your way out of it."

"Did your old man get you into this mess?" Carl asked.

"No," the boy answered, and the men waited for more but it never came.

"Well, okay then," Carl said and turned back to Jerry. "The quiet, understated type."

"You could take a lesson or two from him."

The two men took a shot of whiskey, and the girl returned with a dejected look.

"Did you call?" the boy whispered.

She nodded.

"And?"

"They don't want it."

"What now?"

"I don't know."

Truck tires tore at the gravel outside. A rumbling exhaust. The girl's eyes widened.

"He's here."

31

Cade had been stewing for the better part of the morning, and John Curtis knew it. The big man sat in the den of the cabin tying a hoop fishing net, threading nylon back and forth on itself and burning the ends and tightening the throat and webbing of what would become an underwater trap.

"You ought not let yourself get so worked up, big fella," John Curtis told him.

Cade stared up at him with dead eyes.

"Been damn near a week," he said. "I thought you said you were taking care of it."

"I am," John Curtis said, crossing his arms. "Listen, I know you want your girl back. I know she's gone and embarrassed you. But sitting here yanking on these knots ain't helping nothing. Why don't you do me a favor and make a run out to the Dark Horse. Jerry owes a couple grand."

"You asking me or telling me?"

"What do you think?"

Cade grunted and stood from his chair.

"Don't look so sour," John Curtis said, clapping him on the back. "You get back, and I'll have a hit measured up for you. Help you relax."

Cade slid his bowie knife in its sheath and pulled the sheath along his belt until it was at his back, then covered it with his shirt tail.

"And, Cade," John Curtis said as the big man walked out the door, "don't ever question me again. If I say I'm handling something, it's handled."

Cade stopped, clenched his jaw, then closed the door.

Two men stood from their table at the back of the room and walked toward the bar. The girl with purple hair rushed past them and out the back door.

"What I wouldn't do," one of the men said, turning to watch.

"Too skinny."

"Shit."

"I like me a big girl."

"Plenty of 'em. Speaking of big," the man said as Cade walked in the front door, "you ever see an old boy bigger than Dakota Cade?"

"Can we get two Rolling Rocks and two shots of Old Grandad, Jerry," the second man asked, then turned back to his buddy. "I sure hadn't. I seen some big'uns, but he's about as large as they come."

"Like a goddamned tree."

"Yessir, tough as bark too, I reckon."

"Killed a man for accidentally drinking out of his beer."

The men took their shots.

"Horse shit."

"I swear. Happened out at Tommy's Place."

"That ain't true."

"Go on, ask him."

"You'd like that, huh? That big sumbitch would knock me into next week."

"You could tell me how the weather is on Tuesday. I'm thinking about goin' fishing."

"Aw, shit, he's coming over here."

"Cade. How are you?"

The big man nodded and said nothing.

"Bud," he told the bartender.

The man closest to Cade tried to think of something clever to say but couldn't. Instead he said the only thing that came to mind.

"Heard a banker got stabbed to death in Neches."

The man's drinking companion looked away. Cade turned toward the man.

"So?"

"Nothing, I just . . . did you hear about it?"

"No."

"Oh, okay. It was in the paper."

"Don't read the paper."

Cade leaned in close.

"Paper's just a bunch of folks talking about things they don't really know about," he said. "Things they're lucky they don't know about. You're not like that though, are you?"

"No. Nossir. Not me. I realize what all there is that I don't know about. It's a lot. Hell, I'm basically a goddamned moron."

The big man moved down the bar.

"Jerry," he said.

"Cade."

"You owe."

"What?"

"John Curtis says you're behind two grand."

"Well, I don't know what to say, other than he's mistaken."

"That what you want me to tell him?"

"I don't care what you tell him. He's already stole half my profits this year."

"Stole?"

"Raising the rent when nothing justifies it. Adding more money to what I owe, calling it renovation taxes. Look around, big boy, anything in this shithole look renovated to you?"

"You wanna watch that mouth."

All conversation had stopped.

"Peckerwoods," Cade announced to the room. "Put down those peckerwood drinks and exit the establishment. Your tabs are covered."

No one moved. Frozen at the onset by the fear of the moment, the threat of what was to come. Then all acted at once, clamoring for the door.

Only the barkeep and a man on a stool remained.

"I'd get up," Carl said, placing his hands over his ears, "but the arthritis in my back says it won't listen to whatever private matter may be discussed."

"You see a girl come in here?" Cade asked the barkeep.

"Well, Cade, girls come in here all the time. Maybe you could be a little more specific."

"I've done decided to take it easy on you. Don't make me change my mind."

"What'd she look like?"

"Skinny. Purple hair. You remember her?"

Jerry shook his head.

The big man nodded.

"Alright, then."

He turned to leave, then stopped. There was a boy sitting alone at a table near the door. He hadn't seen him earlier. He seemed to manifest from dirt and bone and unkempt hair.

"What's a kid doing in here?"

Carl spoke up.

"That's Dwayne Hargrove's boy. I'm just looking after him for a spell. You know ole Dwayne, can't stay away from the damn Indian casino. He'll give them enough to buy back their land and then some."

Cade bent down and put his face in front of the boy's. His breath smelled of tobacco and beer.

"You see that girl I was asking about?"

The boy shook his head.

"You speak?" Cade asked.

"Yessir."

"Good. Then maybe you'll tell me why you're wearing her necklace."

The big man jerked the black cord around the boy's neck and the boy flew forward onto the floor and the necklace snapped off.

The barman hollered something that no one heard.

The boy scrambled up. He clenched his fist and gritted his teeth and threw a flailing right cross full of awkwardness and bone. The man moved to the side and the boy went sprawling again but was quickly back to his feet and lunging at the man. This time Cade caught the boy's wrist and turned it.

The boy screamed. Him on the floor, holding his arm and crying, and the big man standing over him, a conqueror, a warrior, a god.

"I'll tell you," Carl said. "Just stop. I'll tell you where the girl is."

Cade kicked the boy hard in the ribs and the boy whimpered then curled into a ball and sobbed.

"That one was for you, Carl," Cade said. "For your first lie. It better be your last."

"I'll tell you where the girl is. I swear."

The boy tried to protest but the words were muffled with pain and tears.

"Let's hear it," the big man said.

"She's out back, probably hiding. She made your truck when you pulled in. Ran out the back door."

Cade strode through the bar with only a handful of steps. He swung the backdoor open and stood, filling its entire frame.

"She might have made for the creek," Carl called from the bar.

Cade shut the door and the light vanished and the room was dark again.

"I'm taking the boy," he said.

"You can't," Carl said. "I'm responsible for him."

"Another lie."

"He's just a kid."

"And I'm taking him."

The big man bent down to collect the moaning boy. He stiffened at the shotgun blast, then stood and turned back toward the bar.

Jerry pumped the scatter gun and leveled it.

"Walk away, Cade."

"Or what?"

"I'd say you been around guns a time or two. Enough to know what. I'd even bet you can tell when somebody's ready to pull the trigger just by looking in their eyes. Well, go on and look into mine. Tell me what you see."

The big man nodded, a grin spreading across his face.

"You know what this means, don't you?" he asked.

"I know what it means, and I don't care. You tell John Curtis I'm done with all this shit. If you want to kill me, that's fine, but you'll have to cover a lot of ground to do it. I'm leaving here and I don't aim on coming back in this lifetime."

Cade laughed.

"There's not a place you can go where I won't find you."

"We'll see. Now go on and get in your truck. Go on."

Cade looked down at the boy.

"I'll be seeing you real soon."

Jerry kept the shotgun against his shoulder until the sound of the truck had faded down the highway.

"So much for retiring," he said.

"What the hell did you just do?" Carl asked.

"I'm not sure. But I think it's best if you found another bartender to annoy."

The girl came through the back door and ran straight to the front door and looked out after the truck. There was nothing to see.

"He'll kill you. He'll come back here and kill you."

"I know he will," Jerry sighed.

"What are you gonna do?"

"I'm gonna leave. John Curtis has been robbing me blind for years, but I've managed to put a little away here and there. I was getting tired of this place, anyway."

"You just—I don't know how to thank you."

"Well. For starters, if you do find yourself face-to-face with that big sumbitch, tell him I'm headed to El Paso."

"Where are you headed?"

"Not El Paso."

32

They watched the rain, the two of them, and they could see it coming down upon the road and veiling the landscape in a haze, and moving closer and growing louder as if it was the culmination of some long set in motion plan, bringing with it a future both yet determined and as certain as the dawn. The falling curtain enveloped the light of the world around them and they did not flee but rather stood their ground and were at once awash in the downpour and whatever fate was held therein.

The girl walked always forward. The pickups and big rigs would start out as toy cars on the faraway plain and the boy would watch them as they came closer and life-sized and he would turn and wave at the drivers with both arms and shout "Hey!" as they passed by and sprayed water and the girl never turned or looked or seemed to notice. She stuck out her thumb and nothing else. Her wet hair hung heavy across her shoulders and the rain ran down her face and the whole of the world around her made no matter as she walked forward, thumb out.

"Don't look like anybody's gonna stop," Jonah said.

"They think you're my son."

"Huh?"

"That's why nobody's stopping. They figure they aren't getting a blow job if my kid's with me."

"Maybe they think I'm your boyfriend."

The girl didn't respond for a while. When she did, she tried to keep herself from crying.

"I'm sorry for what happened," she said. "I didn't mean for you to get hurt."

"It's okay. I broke my wrist when I was nine, and this doesn't feel like that. I bet it's just sprained."

"How are your ribs?"

"I'm fine," the boy insisted.

"Let me see," the girl said, pulling up the boy's shirt.

He jerked away and winced.

"I said I'm fine."

The girl rolled her eyes.

With an unnoticed swiftness, the sun was again shining. Steam rose from the wet pavement. The humidity and sweat and rain mixed on the girl's neck and the borrowed shirt clung to her frame.

"Quit staring," she said.

"I wasn't."

"Quit lying."

"Alright."

They could see the roadkill from thirty yards out. It had been drug onto the shoulder just outside the nearest highway lane. A committee of buzzards hopped along the wet ground and through pools of standing water. The two fiercest of the bunch ate from either end of the dead animal. It was a deer. Its head kicked back unnatural, neck exposed, the two buzzards snapping and pulling at the fly-covered flesh. The others made challenges, wings spread, squawking. Eventually enough of the outliers banded together to mount a successful coup, running off the larger birds and then squabbling amongst themselves as to who was entitled to what. One of the buzzards buried its face in the exposed entrails of the animal and emerged from its feasting covered in dark blood and bits of viscera. Upon the approach of the two humans the birds bounded away in stunted flight, reforming near the tree line and waiting.

The girl held her nose and gagged and hurried past the deer, the flies rising in unison and then touching back down as if their every movement was magnetized. The boy stopped and stared down at the animal. It was a doe. She stunk something fierce. The buzzards hopped, impatient. Further down the tree line the boy caught movement. He squinted into the shadowed underbrush and there saw a glimpse of brown fur, spotted white.

He couldn't know for sure it was the same deer he'd been feeding. But he knew, all the same.

"Come on," the girl said, her shirt now covering her nose and mouth. "Let the damn birds finish eating."

A sheriff's car passed and made a U-turn and pulled alongside them near the shoulder of the highway. A deputy rolled down the window.

"Deputy." The girl nodded.

"What are y'all doing out here on the side of the highway?" the man asked.

"Just getting a little fresh air, sir."

"What's in the satchel, there?"

"Oh, just some water and snacks and bug spray and whatnot."

The man nodded.

"I'm headed right up here to the Dark Horse, y'all come from that way?"

"Nossir," the girl said. "We live right off the county road, yonder. Just came up to the highway to see if the blackberries were still ripe."

"Uh-huh. Well, I don't buy that country-cooked story even a little bit. Y'all need to get off the damn road before somebody sees you."

The deputy saw their confused glance.

"You know John Curtis has got the whole damn force out looking for you, girl."

"You ain't gonna take us in?"

"Are you not listening to me? I'm trying to help. There ain't but one or two of us that still believe in right and wrong, but we're out here. Now get off the damn highway and, if you can, get somewhere far away from this place."

"We're working on it."

"Well, work faster."

The deputy pulled back onto the roadway, and the boy shifted uncomfortably.

"They even got the cops looking for us?"

"Looking for me. Not you. Why don't you go on home?"

"After what happened back at the bar, if they ain't looking for me yet, they will be soon enough."

"So what are we then, Bonnie and Clyde?"

The boy frowned. "Bonnie and Clyde ended up dead," he said.

"Yeah, well, everybody ends up dead."

The boy begrudgingly agreed to hide behind a tree while the girl tried to flag down a ride. It took less than three minutes for a truck to stop.

"Howdy, ma'am," a younger man said from behind the wheel. "Where you headed?"

"Greenwood Apartments."

The man's face scrunched up.

"The projects?"

"That's right. Gotta buy some weed."

"Alright then, I guess I can drop you."

"Great," the girl smiled, then turned to the woods. "C'mon, Jonah."

The boy emerged with his head down, and the man in the truck looked confused.

"Who the hell is that?"

"Oh, he's just my little brother."

"You're taking your little brother to buy pot?"

"Yeah. He's real discreet," the girl said and winked at the man. "Get in the back, Jonah."

They rode in silence, the driver glancing over at the girl a handful of times per minute. By the time they hit the first traffic light in the town of Neches, the man realized none of this was going to be how he thought. He dropped them at Greenwood without saying a word.

"Why is you here? I told you on the phone we ain't want that shit."

"I need to talk to Trina," the girl begged.

"Who the fuck is this?" the man asked, looking to the boy.

"He's a friend. He's cool."

"Cool, my ass. This little motherfucker look ten years old."

"I'm thirteen."

"The fuck you doing running with this bitch?"

"She's my friend." Jonah shrugged.

The man shook his head.

"You gonna let us in or what?" the girl asked.

The man motioned for them to come inside, then he looked out at the parking lot and the road and shut the door.

"I'll get Trina out the back," he said.

The girl had called the apartment a shithole but the boy liked that there were stairs. In his estimation, only rich people could afford a second story. The carpet was worn and stained, but still it felt softer than what was in the boy's trailer. The television was the biggest he'd ever seen. He imagined it was likely the biggest in the world and that there was a certificate somewhere saying as much. There was a man in the small kitchen off the living room, peering through the open space above the bar. Several others were lounged on leather chairs and a couch. In a tiled space where the living room met the kitchen, two men sat at a small circular table of glass, whispering to one another.

The boy watched the men in the room, each of them aware of every movement, their own and those of the others. There was a forced calm in the room, and it made the boy uneasy. The skunked smell of marijuana mixed with sweet cigarillos and lingered in the air and in the apartment and would for many years to come. On the television, men with machine guns wearing various masks were shooting at one another in the desert.

"Hey, boo boo," a woman said, coming down the stairs.

"Hey, T," River said.

"What are you doing here, baby girl? I ain't talked to you in a minute."

"You got a phone charger?" the girl asked weakly, trying not to cry.

The woman's face grew stern. She eyeballed the girl.

"That motherfucker Cade do something to you? He hit you?"

"No, no. I mean, it's not that. Can we talk alone?"

"Yeah, girl. C'mon upstairs to the salon."

A man laughed.

"What the fuck is funny, Julius?"

"Man, just 'cause you be up there tying nasty weaves on ugly bitches don't make your bedroom a salon."

"Mind your business, nigga. I'm working for a motherfucking living. Police come up in here, whatchyou think they care more about? My legitimate business or your punk ass surrounded by a bunch of fucking weed and coke."

"Alright, I was just playing."

"Piece of shit."

"Alright, I said. Damn. Sensitive ass."

"What?"

"Nothing."

"What the fuck I thought."

River told him to stay and the boy stood near the foot of the stairs and looked into the kitchen and the big man holding court looked back at him.

"What's up, little man?"

"Hey."

"Already."

The man looked away, and the boy assumed this was the end of the interaction.

"Say, man, lemme line you up."

The boy was caught off guard.

He looked behind him on the stairs and a young boy who looked to be the same age stood in a red-and-navy striped T-shirt and khaki shorts.

"What?" Jonah asked.

"Lemme line you up in the back, dawg. When's the last time you got a haircut?"

The boy could not recall.

"Whatever, man, come on," the other boy said.

Jonah followed his counterpart up the stairs and into a hallway. He could hear the girl talking on the other side of a closed door. He paused outside of it and tried to listen.

"Come on, man," the other boy urged, and Jonah followed him to the bathroom at the end of the hall.

There were cigarettes in the sink and a variety of pipes, body sprays, and pill bottles on the counter.

"Right here, my man."

The boy sat on the stool provided.

"I'm Terrance," the other boy said. "But everybody call me Lil' T. Trina, my sister, she already Big T. That dude down there fucking with her is my older brother, Julius."

"I'm Jonah."

"What's up, Jonah."

"Nothing."

"Alright, I'm gonna clean you up, dawg. Make your shit look good."

Lil' T flicked on the clippers and Jonah heard a muted hum and felt the dull tickling sensation on the back of his neck. The boy watched in the mirror as Lil' T focused and took great care in every pass, occasionally backing away to study his progress.

"You're good at this," the boy said.

"I'm the shit. I'm gonna have you looking fresh as fuck. Your girl gonna love this shit."

"She's my friend."

"Friend? Shit. That's about to change, I get through with you. Believe that."

"Okay."

Lil' T laughed.

"You don't talk much, huh?"

"I guess not."

"I hear you, Jonah. I'm like that shit, too. All serious and everything. Don't worry, that just means we're wise. You feel me?"

"I feel you."

"Ha ha, hell yeah. You cool as shit, Jonah."

"Thank you."

"Thank you," Lil' T said in a playful, mocking voice. "You cracking me up, dawg."

He again studied the boy's hair and made delicate and deliberate adjustments, attending every detail of his work. When he finished, he used his hands to wipe the hair from the boy's neck and shoulders.

"You good, bruh."

The boy looked at himself in the mirror.

"You like that shit, right?"

"Yeah, I do."

"Alright, gimmie ten."

"Ten what?"

"Ten what? Dollars, nigga, what you think?"

"Oh, I don't—"

"You don't have any money? What you think this is free? You think my time don't mean shit, huh?"

"No, it's not that, I just—"

"Ayyyy, I'm just messing with you, Jonah. Damn. We cool, bruh."

The boy exhaled.

"Whatchyou think about all this rain, anyway?"

"I don't know. The bottoms are flooding. But it's not too bad here yet."

"Yeah, 'yet,' is the key word."

"You think it will get worse?"

"Hell yeah, bruh. We all gonna be under water."

"You think it's god?"

"Huh? Naw naw naw, it ain't god. It's the government."

"The government?"

"Shit. It's always the government. Trying to get rid of black people."

"But there aren't many black people in the bottoms."

"True. But y'all poor as shit down there, right? So to the government, that makes you black. Welcome to the club."

Lil' T shook his head and continued.

"It's just like Katrina, bruh, and that Bradley Cooper motherfucker."

"Who?"

"The sniper dude, not Bradley Cooper for real, but the dude he played in the movie. He was out there talking about shooting black folks during the hurricane. Government denied it. Of course. Then that motherfucker end up dead? Nah. That's some shady shit, and so is this. Bet."

"Okay."

"Say, you wanna see some real shit? Follow me."

The boy followed Lil' T to a darkened bedroom and the latter switched on the light then pulled a cardboard box from a closet and dumped its contents onto the bed.

"Check this shit out," Lil' T said, and the boy looked and saw several handguns of varying shapes and sizes.

"Whoa."

"Right?"

"Do you know what they all are?"

"Shit no, I'm trying to be a barber not a gangbanger. Still looks badass, though."

The boy agreed.

There was a pounding on the door of the room next to them. Lil' T scrambled to put the weapons back in the box.

"Come on, Jonah, help me with this shit. Julius'll kill my ass."

They replaced the guns and the box and turned out the light and stood in the hallway and listened to the voices in the next room.

"This bitch gotta go, Trina," Julius said. "She mixed up in some bull-shit I don't want no part of."

"This my girl, Julius. I ain't about to be like that."

"I'm not asking. I just talked to a nigga who knows what's up. This bitch stole a bunch of crystal from John fucking Curtis. You remember that motherfucker? The one who went all Scarface on them Nazi-ass white boys up in Redtown? I gave that crazy fool my word we wouldn't mess with the meth game no more. Everybody know cocaine about to comeback hard, anyway. The Weeknd singing about that shit. So we gonna let that dude have the meth heads, and what we damn sure *not* gonna do is play babysit-ter for some bitch who stole from him."

Trina stood, ready to continue the argument, but the girl stepped in.

"It's okay, Trina," she said. "We'll go. I don't want to cause problems. But please, Julius, don't tell anyone we were here."

"Shit, I ain't trying to have nobody find out you was in my house."

The girl came out first and saw the two boys and motioned for Jonah to follow her.

"Sounds like you in some shit, bruh," Lil' T told him. "Keep your head on a swivel out there."

"Huh?"

The other boy laughed and shook his head.

"Just stay safe, Jonah."

"Oh, okay. Thanks."

33

The thin man sat at the bar and sipped his tequila from the glass as if it were something hot, something to be consumed delicately.

He listened to the sound of the planes taking off and the cry of children and the distorted announcements being made over the speaker. He hated airports, grocery stores, public places in general.

"Hey, cowboy."

The woman was tall and blond and drunk.

"Hola," said the thin man.

"You speak English?"

"Yes."

"Well, you gonna buy me a drink?"

The thin man held up two fingers and circled the air in the barkeep's direction.

"Where you headed, handsome?"

The man shifted on the barstool to face the girl. He looked her up and down and smiled.

"I am headed toward a destiny, senorita."

"I'll drink to that," she said.

"And you?"

"Conference in Dallas. Corporate wants us to go up there and promote the new environmentally conscience side of the industry."

"Which industry?"

"Oil and gas."

"I see."

"What do you see?"

"I think you know."

"Tell me," she said.

"It is unpleasant. You know this. I know this. This tequila is too fine for such unpleasantness."

"It's alright, go on and tell me about it. I promise I've heard it all before, and worse."

"All I see is . . . a beautiful woman."

The man raised his glass and swirled it and downed the contents just as the bartender arrived with the bottle.

"Fine, I'll let you off the hook. This time. What do you think about all this rain?"

"What do you think?"

"I don't know. Some people say it's climate change. Some people say it's god."

"What do you say?" he asked.

"I say what they pay me to say."

"Ah. Perhaps like a prostitute."

"Well, aren't you a charmer."

"Maybe."

"I think you are. In fact, I'd say you're an actor. Maybe on one of those Mexican soap operas. What are they called?"

"Telenovela."

"That's it."

The man smiled.

"It is a creative guess."

"What are you really?"

"Just a man."

"Just a man, huh?"

"That's right."

"Just a man with thousand-dollar boots, a gold watch, and a ring that could pay for a house in some places."

"Not any place someone would want to live."

"Still. You're somebody," she said.

"We're all somebody. Until we're not."

"Games. Games. You are a charmer. I'm Jennifer."

"Hola, Jennifer."

"And you? Tu nombre?"

"Raul."

"Hola, Raul."

They sat in silence for a short time until the woman laughed and touched the thin man's shoulder.

"You're really not gonna tell me are you?" she asked.

"Tell you what?"

"Who you are. What it is you do."

"Do you believe this to be the same, who a man is and what he does?"

"Depends, I guess."

"On what?"

"On," she laughed again, "on who you are and what you do."

"I am a man of consequence. Do you believe in consequence?"

"Sure, I do."

"If you drink too much, you might feel unwell the next day. If you do not pay your electricity bill, you may have your lights shut off. These are consequences."

"Okay."

"That is me. I am the unwell feeling. I am the darkness."

The girl smiled.

"Sounds pretty scary."

"And yet you are not afraid. This is very American of you. Your whole country is unafraid of consequences, because it has so rarely faced any. You play loosely about the world, impacting forever the history of others, but never facing your own."

"Oh god, are we really gonna talk politics? What are you, some kind of a diplomat?"

"No. What brings me to your country is not diplomacy. As I said, I am only a consequence. Nothing more."

34

Night had fallen. Mounted on metal posts and lining the sidewalk outside the townhouses were dozens of timed lights which had come on. There was a low electric hum from each of them and winged insects of every kind were drawn into their glow. The rain was hours gone, but the world still felt wet. The boy's shoes sunk in the grass along the roadway.

"Why'd we go to that place?" the boy asked.

"I had to ask my friend about something."

"About what?"

"About a bunch of stuff. Anyway, she said there's somebody else who might be interested."

"Who?"

"Guy named Wild Bill. Lives right across the street from the old church on Lawrence Street. Used to work for John Curtis."

"The man you're hiding from?"

"One of them, yeah. But Bill and him had a falling out. They don't have nothing to do with each other no more."

The boy twisted his lips together.

"What? You got some people you know who wanna buy twenty-five grand worth of ice?"

He shook his head.

"Alright then, let's go. It's only a couple miles from here."

They cut through the downtown corridor, the street lights at play on the wet black pavement, casting upturned simulations of the untenanted shopfronts. The buildings sat in straight rows, one and two stories, and the streets made perfect crosses. There was a tile shop, a police department, and a hair salon. There was a feed store which also served coffee, and a post office open half the day. There was a volunteer fire station, a pharmacy doubling as a diner, and a low-ceilinged brick building that was used as a courthouse, city hall, and holding jail, all in one.

There had been a time when this town, and many like it, were a part of the world's progression, but such a time had long passed and those who could leave had done so and those who remained had little choice else.

They walked, the two of them, and they did not speak, and the only sound was the occasional passing of an eighteen-wheeler in the distance—beginning and ending in some other place. A bell rang above a shop door and they both turned to look and saw an old woman locking an antique store called Tammy's Treasures. When she felt their presence, the old woman put her head down and hurried to her car. They continued on.

The humidity hung thick, a heavy heat independent of the sun, and the boy felt sweat on the back of his legs. It was a moonless, starless night, a black portiere draped overtop the world as if to signal the end of some stage play, with the heavens and the earth left guessing at which side of the curtain they might be on.

A truck turned onto the road behind them, and they were framed for a moment in its headlights. The truck crept alongside them, and they both looked up but could see nothing through the dark tinted windows. The girl stopped walking and turned to face the side of the truck. Likewise the boy. There they stood in some silent defiance as the truck's exhaust throttled in metered sequence familiar to such a place. Then, without cause, the truck's engine revved and it lurched forward and sped away before them.

"Somebody you know?" the boy asked.

"I don't think so."

"Think it was them who's hunting you?"

"No. If it was them, we'd know it."

"You reckon them to snatch you off the street?"

"I'd reckon them to drag me out of the middle of a Sunday service if that's where they found me."

"Well."

"Let's just get up to Bill's and unload this shit."

"Then we leave for good?"

The boy looked worried. She smiled at him.

"You got it, kid," she said. "I can smell the ocean now."

"What's it smell like?"

"Different than here, and that's all that matters."

35

Dustin squirmed in his seat. A worm on a hook, dangling at the end of the line. Drowning. His hands were shaking. The loudspeaker startled him each time the booming voice came across. It was already the sixth inning and he was worried. No one was there. No one had met him.

He was in the highest section. The furthest away from the game, the crowd, the world of the living. T-shirt cannons launched souvenirs into the stands below him. He checked his seat number again. How many times had he checked it? A dozen? *More.* There was something wrong. The crack of the bat. He flinched. Cheering.

Breathe.

He could smell the beer and popcorn and the meat cooking.

He looked at his veins, followed them up his wrist, his forearm, his bicep. Bruises. He looked up at the sky. He was so close to it. Could he reach for it? Could he touch it?

There's nothing wrong. Stop thinking it. What am I supposed to say? "John Curtis sent me. He said he looks forward to a productive partnership. A productive partnership. He said he looks forward to a productive partnership."

He needed to piss. He'd needed to piss since the game started. He was afraid to leave his seat. What if he left and the Mexican came and he wasn't there and everything went to shit. He could have already pissed by now. *Could've pissed and been back and pissed again. Stay fucking still. Breathe.*

A man. How long has he been sitting there? Is he real? Sometimes they aren't real. Like the voices.

"You are the messenger," the man said without looking at him. The man wore sunglasses and a ballcap, his face all but covered. He smoked a thin cigar with a plastic filter.

"Yes. John Curtis sent me. He said he looks forward to a, to a, a—"

The words were catching. Something's not right. This isn't right.

"Save it," the man said. "You have something for me."

Dustin nodded. He pushed the envelope toward the man who took it and slipped it into his shirt pocket.

"You are the messenger," the man repeated. "So I will send with you a message."

"I don't do so good at remembering. C-can you write it down? I have a pen."

"That will not be necessary."

The blade went in six inches, then came out.

Dustin didn't see the man pull anything from his pocket. He didn't even see him move.

Warm in my ribs. Warm inside. Is this what the sky feels like? Like floating. Like pissing.

36

They made Lawrence Street and stood motionless in what had once been the church parking lot. Weeds sprung up through the cracks in the concrete and some grew horizontal and the boy thought they looked like earthen arms coming out from some underworld buried alive by the pavement. Coming out to claim vengeance and all else.

The church was limestone and mortar and most all of it stained in some way by the century of weather and the decade or so of disrepair. The front steps were full of fissures and breaks and a faded yellow tape hung from the arched wood doors.

The boy's eyes tracked up from the doors and there he saw a stained glass Christ dressed as a shepherd with robe and staff. Behind him a white sun hovered above a green-hilled horizon, and the boy could not discern if the sun was rising or setting. The Christ figure's unstaffed hand was raised and pointing to the hills, and his face was turned opposite to look at his flock. Whether it was men or sheep, the boy also could not discern, as sometime in the past a vandalous rock had found its mark, and now the shepherd led only some broken mix of darkness and glass.

Higher still, each side of the church roof pitched upward and there met and gave way to a thick wooden cross erect with iron bolts and a metal plating at its base.

"It's a nice church," the girl said, as if only just remembering. She too was staring up at the cross. The two of them, heads back as if in preparation for some great happening in the skies.

The girl navigated the broken steps and tried the doors. They did not open. She put a foot up against the left door and used the leverage to pull at the right.

"Well, shit," she said, when the door remained closed. "I would've liked to see the inside."

"How come?"

"I don't know. Just a feeling I couldn't shake. Like, trying to find something you know ain't there; but looking anyway, hoping it might turn up in the last place you remembered seeing it."

The girl descended the steps.

"Doesn't matter," she said. "Let's go."

Cars and trucks were lined up and down the street's edge, half in the roadway, half in the ditch alongside it, as if the vehicles themselves were somehow undecided as to which surface presented the better path forward.

The boy spotted the truck they'd seen previously and he nudged the girl and pointed. She nodded, and they went on past the cars in the driveway and passed by the front door on their way to a side gate leading into the backyard. The boy heard the last fiddle note of a country song he didn't recognize, then the opening bass of a hip-hop track and the accompanying roar of approval from the partygoers.

Texas where we live, nigga, Texas where we stay,
Go on talk that weak shit, we Texas every day. Ay.

The boy closed the gate and took in the scene. There were a dozen or so people gathered under a converted tin-roof carport. Red Solo cups were lifted high into the air as the all-white crowd twisted its collective body in rhythmic gyrations, screaming the lyrics and creating a low-hanging cloud of tobacco and marijuana smoke.

Houston niggas put it on, Dallas that's my shit,
Corpus up to San Antone, Austin keep it lit.

"Come on," the girl said. "He'll be on the back porch."

The boy watched a dark-haired girl dance in a tube top made to look like a rebel flag. She wore red-and-brown boots and a jean skirt and jewelry hung from her belly button. Three men closed the space around her, and she smiled, playing first to one and then another. The third man slapped her bottom and she squealed and laughed and put her body backward into his and continued to move to the beat.

"Hey, let's go," River repeated.

The boy nodded and followed her across the outskirt of the makeshift dance floor and onto a screened back porch.

"Well, hello, darling," Wild Bill said.

The boy looked toward the voice and the only light was on the man's jeans and brown ostrich quill boots. The rest of his body sat back in the shadow that fell across the outdoor sofa.

"Bill," the girl said.

"Who's this with you?"

"A friend."

"I like friends," the man said. "Are you here as a friend?"

The girl nodded.

"Do Cade and John Curtis know you're here?"

She shook her head.

"Well. Hot damn. Did you finally come to give me a taste?"

"Not that kind of taste."

"Oh, the plot thickens," the man hissed.

"I brought you something."

"A present?" The man feigned excitement, then leaned forward over a round patio table and ashed his cigarette in a plastic cup. The light shone on his face and he flashed a smile at the boy. His teeth were rotting, save the two top cuspids made of silver. His dark hair hung across the sides of his face, come down from under a stunted-looking top hat. He had the look of a vampire made homeless.

The boy took a step back.

"It's not a present. It's product," the girl said.

The man considered this. He brought his hands together as if in prayer, tapping his fingers against one another in procession.

"Not interested," he announced and leaned back on the couch.

"You haven't heard the proposal."

"Whatever it is, it isn't worth getting strung up and gutted alive by Dakota Cade."

The man stood. He was average height, skinny for the most part, but carrying a sizeable stomach beneath his pearl snap shirt.

"I heard what you did," he said. "And I know the penalty for helping you."

The man laughed and shook his head.

"What made you think you could steal damn near thirty grand worth of crystal and get away with it?"

"I don't have to tell you shit."

"Fair enough." The man raised his hand in front of his face and stared at it as if it held something, then brought it slowly toward himself and with one finger began to tap at the point on his own chin.

"A thought," he said, and sank back into his seat, crossing his legs. "If the meth disappeared, and you along with it, my old friends on Splithorn Hill would just assume it was still with you. Then, if say, it were to be offloaded in Lake Charles, a man could make a pretty penny on that."

"He could," the girl said.

"Still," the man frowned, "there's a lot of risk involved."

"I expect that man would want a discount."

"I expect he would."

"I'll give you everything for twenty, we'll be gone before the sun comes up."

"No deal," the man said, removing his hat and brushing at his hair with his cigarette hand.

"You break that into eight balls and grams and you could make almost fifty thousand dollars."

"Ah, but I won't be breaking it. I'd be looking to get rid of it quickly, just like you. I have a guy in Lake Charles who'd be willing, but he'd want the whole show, including distribution rights. So if I sell to him at cost, somewhere around twenty-six grand, then I'm only making six thousand dollars."

"Six thousand bucks for not doing a damn thing."

"Other than sticking my neck out so John Curtis can have his boys cut it off."

"What's your price, Bill?"

"Half."

"Half? That's thirteen."

"That's my price."

"Goddamnit."

The girl hung her head, and for a time all was quiet and still, and the boy watched the lights from the party below them as they danced across the back wall of the house. His heart began to pound. This could be it. They could get the money, even if it wasn't enough, and they could go somewhere, anywhere.

"Fine," the girl said. "You got the money?"

"I'll go get it. I gotta make a call."

Bill stood and went inside.

"You think there's a bathroom in there?" the boy asked.

"It'd be fucking weird if there wasn't."

"Are you okay by yourself?"

"I'll survive," she said. "Go on."

When Bill returned, he sat down in front of the girl and smiled. He took out a sack of weed trimmings and shook a clump onto the table and pulled a knife and a cigarillo from his pocket and set them next to the weed, all in a row.

"You got the money?"

He just stared at her, then smiled again and cut the cigarillo in half and began to scrape out the tobacco from inside it.

"You know how all this came about?"

"All what?"

"Our law enforcement set out to stop people like me from cooking crystal, and all they did was push it into other places that knew how to make it cheaper and better. There's more meth than there's ever been, but the coppers run around beating their chests like they actually accomplished something by busting up some old boy's homemade kitchen. He'll do his time, get paroled, then end up with a more pure version of the drug than he's ever had. Plus, now he can get spun without the risk of blowing his pecker off."

"Great story. What's the point?"

"It's all bullshit, anyway. Some politician or police chief pushing a tough-on-meth stance to get votes from the church secretary whose perfect little angel held up a gas station while he was tweaked out of his mind. Meanwhile the government's been giving it to our troops in some form or fashion since we had to go kick Hitler's ass. Artists, housewives, even those same politicians calling for harsher penalties—they all do it. And don't even get me started on these oilfield hands. There's enough of them to keep me in business without John Curtis even noticing I'm undercutting him. Let's face it, everybody likes to fight and fuck. And meth lets you do both while feeling like a million bucks."

Wild Bill licked his lips.

The girl rolled her eyes.

"I don't need to feel like a million bucks. I just need to feel like thirteen thousand. So are we doing this or what?"

"Patience, darling. I'm almost done.

"See," he continued, "meth's more powerful than god. Hell, you include money, and I imagine god's sitting in third place. I remember growing up, when them boys shot up that high school in Colorado. There was a girl got killed, but they ask her, before they shot her, did she believe in god. She said she did and they went on and shot her. Probably would've shot her anyway, but you never can tell. Anyway, I had this one old boy, came from somewhere up near Alto. Used to be a preacher or a deacon or some such position in a little church up there. He had a son overdose a few years back. Guess he couldn't handle it, or maybe he just wanted to see firsthand what his son had seen, but he came asking for a taste and we gave it to him. Came back a few days later, then a few days after that. Finally, one day, he says he needs more but he don't have no money. Well, that's alright, John Curtis tells him, just say there's no such thing as god, and I'll give you a free pass. He even took the baggie out and pitched it to the poor fucker.

"So here's this man, or what's left of him, and he's having to decide right then and there between god and crystal and it didn't take him five seconds, a former something or another, to say god don't exist."

"Maybe he was just saying it to get the drugs," the girl said. "Maybe he prayed about it later and asked forgiveness."

"Maybe. But there's a lot of Christian folks around these parts. To say out loud that there ain't no god, that means something to them. Something might be beyond forgiveness. Not from god, you understand, but from themselves."

"I understand. I get it. You're so wise. Whatever you want to hear. You got the money or what?"

"It's on the way."

"On the way?"

"I have some here. The rest is on the way. What kind of fool keeps that much cash in his own house? Just relax, darling. Have a drink."

"I'm fine."

"You sure I can't interest you in anything while you wait."

Bill grabbed at his crotch and smirked.

The boy burst through the door and onto the porch.

"Jonah?"

The boy closed the bathroom door behind him and stepped into the living room.

"Katie."

The girl was wearing the same blue jean shorts and tank top as when they'd met. She ran toward him and draped herself around his shoulders.

"Jonah," she said, giggling, and he could smell the liquor.

"What are you doing here?" he asked.

"Devin's my older brother."

"Who's Devin?"

"This is his house."

"I thought this was Bill's house."

"They split the rent. What are you doing?"

"Uh, I know Bill."

"Really?"

The boy cleared his throat.

"Yeah, Wild Bill. I know him."

"Whoa. That's crazy," the girl looked at him and nodded. "I told those guys you were cool. Down by the river, I mean. Sorry about all that."

"It's okay. They're assholes."

"Yeah, they really are. Let's go get a drink."

Katie grabbed his hand and led him through the house and into the kitchen.

"Whiskey or tequila?" she asked.

"Whiskey," the boy said, looking around the empty room as if he might be denied permission.

"You're more hardcore than me," she said, tipping a Jameson bottle into a red cup and sliding it toward him, then pouring herself a cup of the clear liquor. "Tequila for the lady."

She stared at him. Smiling. He smiled back.

"What should we cheers to?" she asked.

The boy shrugged.

"Devin taught me this one," the girl said. She cleared her throat and lifted her chin along with her cup. The boy likewise. "Here's to hell. May our stay there be as much fun as our way there."

The girl laughed and knocked her cup into his, then drank. The boy put his own drink to his lips and it stung them, and stung his tongue, and stung his throat, and he grimaced, but kept drinking. The girl slammed her cup on the table and her body shivered. They poured and drank again, then she refilled their cups and took his hand and led him out the front door and onto the short porch.

The porch light had long been burned out and they sat in the darkness in a groaning swing with rusted chains. The boy's stomach was warm and he was smiling and he liked the girl's hand touching his, and he liked the way she smelled, like jasmine and cigarettes.

There was a horned moon hung pale behind a bank of storm clouds and the muted light turning the night sky into dark layers of gray. The world was separated from the stars by the coming rain, and neither knowing when they might meet again. Droplets began to clatter on the roof above them.

"This might be the one," the boy said, his voice lazy.

"What one?"

"The one that doesn't stop. The rain that just keeps falling."

"That's impossible. Everything stops sooner or later."

The boy was quiet. The girl frowned.

"Besides," she continued, "my daddy says if anything happens, god will take care of the Christians. It's the terrorists who need to worry."

The boy didn't understand, but he nodded anyway, then took a drink.

"So, Jonah, what's your favorite song?"

"I don't know. I like all of them."

"You like every song?"

"Sure. Why not."

"Well, my favorite is 'Drop and Get It.' Do you want me to play it for you?"

"Okay."

The girl stood and downed the rest of her cup and then took out a cell phone covered in stick-on jewels. She laid it on the swing next to the boy as the small speakers began to vibrate. The boy looked down at the phone and the girl touched his face and directed it back to herself. She began to dance in front of him, smiling and giggling. She put his hands on her hips and the world was swimming. She bent down and kissed him. Her lips wet and hot and he felt her tongue inside his mouth. He stood and pushed her away.

She scowled at him.

"What the hell?"

"Sorry."

"What are you gay or something?"

"No, I—I'm in love with someone else."

"What? You have a girlfriend?"

"No, she's not my girlfriend. But I love her."

"You're an asshole."

"I'm sorry. You're really pretty. And I liked your dance."

"Oh my god, shut up, Jonah. Just shut up."

The girl crossed her arms and walked into the house, slamming the door behind her. She reemerged moments later and snatched her phone from the swing, the music still playing.

"And you better not tell anybody about this."

"Okay."

The boy sat for a time on the front porch swing. He could hear the party in the back, the pulsating bass. The swing moved gently under his weight. His cup was empty and he could smell the rain, somewhere out in the still night, coming back to drown them all.

Out on the road a truck slowed and killed its lights. The boy watched. The truck turned into the church parking lot and stopped. Three men got out. The boy strained his eyes. A fourth man, the driver, climbed down from the cab and the boy's stomach rose into his throat.

The boy raced through the house and spilled out onto the back porch.

"It's the big man, from the bar. He's across the street with a bunch of other guys. They're coming around back."

"What? How did—" The girl turned back and looked at Wild Bill. "You sonofabitch."

"Sorry, darling," the man said. "But I've been trying to figure out a way to stop John Curtis from coming after me for a long while now. Then you showed up and did the work for me."

"We gotta get out of here," she said to the boy.

Bill moved to block the door.

The boy reached into the back of his pants and pulled out the gun. He clicked the safety off.

"That's a bold move, little man," Bill said. "But you're not about to shoot anybody."

The man stepped forward and grabbed the gun and wrenched it free from the boy's grip, then backhanded him with the steel handle. The boy crumpled.

"Now," the man said, looking at the girl, "let's go talk to that big boyfriend of yours."

He slid the gun halfway into the front of his jeans and the girl watched him. She lunged forward and was able to get to the trigger just as Bill caught her wrist. She squeezed twice. He released his grip and fell to the floor, screaming.

"You shot my dick," he moaned. "You shot my fucking dick."

"Next time turn the safety back on."

She kept the gun in her right hand and used her left to pull the boy to his feet. Blood ran from a cut on his head.

"Come on, we have to go."

She led him inside and down the hall and into a laundry room with a screen door that opened to the side of the house. The music in the back stopped.

"Come on," she whispered, and the two of them moved, crouched, toward the road.

"Did they come in a big truck?" she whispered.

The boy nodded weakly. His head was spinning.

"That stupid bastard," the girl said, fishing in one of the backpack pockets and producing a set of keys with a pink rabbit's foot. "Come on."

They continued at a crouch toward the church.

"Hey," someone called. "There they are."

"Shit," the girl said. "Run."

They sprinted toward the truck, the men closing fast.

"Get in," she screamed. The girl started the truck and threw it in drive without turning on the lights and slammed the gas pedal to the floor. They lurched forward through a ditch and out onto the road. In the rearview mirror, Cade stood, staring after them.

"Where the hell did you get a gun?"

"Terrance gave it to me. Or, not gave it. I stole it. I think I'm drunk," the boy said, leaning over in the passenger seat.

"Hey," the girl told him. "Sit up. Focus. Can you get me upriver?"

"How far?"

"Redtown."

"What's in Redtown?"

"Can you do it?"

"Why can't we just drive?"

"You heard that deputy earlier. The whole sheriff's department is hunting us. Not to mention we're in Cade's truck."

"Well, we're gonna need a boat."

"Can you get one?"

"I think so."

"Alright, then. Let's go."

"River?"

"What is it?"

"Have you ever heard the song 'Drop and Get It?'"

The boy fell in and out of sleep in the passenger seat, and he heard the girl talking on the phone, and when she was done she turned it off and looked at him and smiled.

"They're in," she said.

They left the truck in a thicket hidden from the road and nearest they could get to Hog Creek headwater and followed a mostly overgrown path to the river. They turned northwest and made Old Man Carson's cabin just before dawn.

The girl beat on the door, and the boy shot her a look.

"We're sorry for waking you, sir," he said when the old man pulled back the screen.

"Bah, I hadn't slept proper in twenty-some-odd years. I'll put on a pot."

The old man stepped heavy into his overalls and pulled the straps over his slumped shoulders. He looked for a long while at the cut on the boy's head, the bruising on his face.

"You all look like you're only one step ahead of some trouble."

"If that," the boy said.

"Well, son, what can I do for ye?"

"I was hoping we could borrow your canoe."

Carson looked at the boy and smacked his lips.

"The canoe? Yeah, you can, you can borrow the canoe. Why not just take the flat-bottom? It's got a twelve-horse motor on it."

"Yessir, I thought about that. But we're going north of the spillway and the boat would be too heavy to haul on land."

"The spillway?"

"Yes sir. We got business in Redtown."

"If'n you all are going to Redtown, you're not running from trouble, you're gone looking for it."

"It's a long story," the girl said. "But this is our last chance at a different life. At any life. I know you and me ain't been friendly, but I know you care about Jonah. And this is the best thing for him."

The old man thought for a while, then nodded his head.

"Alright, well, let me get some food to send with you. It's a long trip by canoe."

The old man shuffled to the cupboard, muttering to himself.

"Redtown," he said. "Here, take these."

He took down two tins of diced pears, a can of corned beef, and an expired MoonPie.

"Ye know how to make a cookfire?"

The boy nodded.

The man tossed him a package of cornmeal.

"I reckon you'll be needing a pan for that. Go look in the feed shed. Pick out whichever cast iron you like."

They started for the door.

"Hold on, darling. You stay here with me for a minute."

The boy looked at her, and she nodded for him to go.

"How'd you get caught up in this mess in the first place?" the old man asked her.

"Made a wrong turn or two. Ended up with the wrong people."

"They running meth?"

"Yessir."

"Oilfield?"

"Used to be. Some of them. Army too."

The old man nodded.

"I was army. Still am, I suppose, in my nightmares."

The girl stayed quiet.

"It just seems like things ought to go better for these boys," Carson said. "A generation in full, swept off like autumn leaves, scattered to the very same winds of change what brought us here in the first place."

"You feel bad for them?"

"I do. Yes."

"They're the ones choosing to do it, though."

"Are they?"

"Why, hell yeah. Nobody's got a gun to their head. Least not the majority."

"I disagree. It's my belief they were born, all of them, with a gun to their head. They are, by their very existence, predisposed to every choice they'll ever make."

The girl scoffed.

"You don't see it that way," Carson said. "But I'll ask you, what alternative is there? What option is given to these children of the pines? Raised by parents of a likemind, worshipping in great, towering churches but sent to decaying schools. Raised to use the land but not to respect it. No, the choice is little and less and I pity every last one of them as they disappear down the same well-worn path, believing they are living free. Rebels, all of them, in their own caged minds."

"You think there's no helping it, huh."

"There's always helping. But it's never enough. You got a herd of cattle dying of thirst, and one jug of water in your hand. You can help, sure. Maybe it'll ease your own mind about things, but it won't change the outcome."

"Well. What happens now?"

"The cycle continues. Those who can make it out rarely turn back, and those who can't are left to perpetuate the endless poverty passed down as some accursed birthright by men who see in the eyes of their sons a mournful playback of their own half-lived lives."

"What's the truth?"

"That they didn't choose any of this. That they aren't free. That they're merely products of their environment."

"Nossir. I don't think that's the truth at all."

"No?"

She shook her head.

"People are who they are, Mr. Carson, and I don't believe it matters whether their spoons are polished silver or filled with dope."

"That's a sad way to look at things," Carson said.

"Don't mean it's wrong."

"No. It certainly does not."

The old man touched the tips of all his fingers together, moving them back and forth like a spider on a mirror.

"He's a good boy," he said. "You're right, I do care about him. And we both know this ain't what's best for him."

"Yessir."

"Do you understand what I'm telling you? Jonah is a good boy. He loves you, I think."

"He's too young to understand all that."

"Is he? In your estimation, who loves more pure, a child or some sour old bastard like me? You think love is more understood with age? Hell, you think love is something to be understood at all? No matter, girl. You know the right thing to do. It'll hurt him, but it'll be best in the long run."

"He ain't gonna listen."

"He will, if you say what needs to be said."

37

John Curtis stood contrary his reflection in the bathroom mirror, his skin vibrating in the sanguine glow of the red bulbs above, his eyes dilated to total darkness, like sabled spheres inked out of a great black lake. He stared at the glass and the figure within and he saw there some antipode of his own existence, an obversion of himself come forward from this walled-off counterworld to take measure of the calamity without.

He took a breath in and held it. He opened his mouth and flexed his jaw muscles and leaned closer to the mirror and looked doubtful, as if he were unsure which iteration of himself was the mimic and which was the truly begotten. He breathed out.

He crushed the crystal between the counter and the blunt end of his knife handle and snorted it and felt in his pocket for the tuft of hair.

"How is it, Mac, that one donkey-fucking cartel can chop the heads off another, then turn around and decide I'm the enemy. As if my seeking out a business partnership has broken some sacred rule of the Virgin. He was a good boy. A nervous boy, but good. I sent him off to his death. To be slaughtered by the bean eaters as my proxy. Send me a fucking message. Fine. Message fucking received. But now, Mac, they'll get to see what horrors I might unleash. Were that you were here to tell them, eh? Were that you were fucking here."

He moved the powder closer together with his blade and snorted the rest.

"And the feds," he banged the counter with his fist, "dissatisfied with my gift. They want dogmen, I give them dogmen, but they ask for more. No." He shook his head. "They don't ask. They demand more. They come after me and my operation. My dogs. Poor Claude. They overstep their bounds at every turn. I could burn their government to the ground if I so chose. But I don't, Mac. I choose something else altogether.

"Mexicans on one front, feds on the other. Two wars. And in between it all, the girl. And the girl has become my only concern."

John Curtis and Cade stood over the kitchen table and both staring at the flickering candle like generals of some long-entrenched war, hoping for a mystic sign in whatever portents lay before them.

"The boys know about Dustin?"

Cade nodded.

"They read about it in the paper."

"Since when do they take the fucking paper?"

"Copy laying out on the counter at the pawn shop."

"You get the guns?"

"Yessir."

"Boys to shoot 'em?"

"Working on it."

"Work faster. Send word to the oilfields. I'll double their pay."

"You expecting that much trouble?"

"The Mexicans won't come up here and get their hands dirty. They can't afford it. Start coming this far into the country and leaving bodies, every deal they've ever made with the feds will be worthless. One of two things will happen. They'll either start a proxy war, maybe partner up with somebody else looking to take us out."

"Redtown?"

"That'd be my bet."

"What's the other thing?"

"They'll just kill me and get it over with."

"Is that likely?"

"Can't say. It took some balls to do that to Dustin. Leave him to be found by a fucking janitor like that. It gives me pause."

"You ought to hole up on the Hill for a while. Let me and the boys handle things on the ground."

"You're a good man, Cade. Or a good soldier, at least. But there's something more important than all of this."

"The girl?"

"Word gets out that I let that much product disappear, nobody south of the border will want to have anything to do with us."

"Maybe that ain't such a bad thing."

John Curtis spit.

"You know how ancient kings would stop rebellions?"

Cade was quiet.

"They'd never let 'em start," John Curtis said. "They'd always have some of their own people infiltrate whatever groups they thought might be a threat."

"Spies?"

"Something like that."

"Alright."

"You know Jim Haskins?"

"One of the new players out in Redtown, ain't he?"

"That's right." John Curtis grinned.

"He's ours?"

"Been keeping an eye on things for me. Had a little news he figured we'd be interested in. Said the crew he runs with is setting up for a big buy in a couple days."

"Is it her?"

John Curtis nodded.

"You get the troops together, we'll go up there and preempt the Mexicans, get our meth back, and make a quick twenty thousand in the process."

"They'll be a good bit of blood," the big man said. "Would've been nice to have the dogs with us."

John Curtis nodded again.

"You know what they do with the dogs in raids like that?"

Cade shook his head.

"They kill 'em. Just put them all down. Threat to the public or something, they say."

"Save a dog, just to kill it on your own terms?"

"That's right."

"Don't make much sense."

"Never does."

38

He stared out at the morning as if he'd been asked in that moment to take measure of the world and all that it held. As if one day god would wipe clean the earth's surface and the boy alone might be tasked with putting everything back in its place.

He'd heard the ice was melting at the North Pole. And that it was making the oceans rise, like a body in a bathtub. His science teacher had rigged up a demonstration at the school. He'd brought in an old soak tub and filled it with water, then he'd give each of the kids an ice cube. One by one they'd dropped the ice in the tub, but wasn't hardly nothing happening. To really make a difference it takes something big, the teacher told them; and then he jumped in, clothes and all, and sent the water spilling over the sides. The kids got a kick out of it, making learning fun and all that.

The boy thought about it. About how everybody had laughed, and about how the teacher dried off with a towel and had himself a change of clothes for after class. He also thought about all that water that had come over the side and onto the floor, and about how somebody had to come clean it up.

The same teacher showed the class a video on the computer of a satellite image of the earth during each season, showed the green parts expand in the spring and summer, then shrink in the fall and winter. It was all sped up and digitized, but the boy could see what was happening. The world was breathing.

In and out and in again, as if drawing to it a scarce strength, summoning from the frailty of the universe a life force from which we all might be fed or starved or, perhaps, divided—cleaved and quartered and partitioned by some arcane appraisal wherein one existence holds more value than another.

He stood and walked toward a grove of trees, the dogwood flowers withered on their branches, the white and pink petals giving way to green shade leaves in the summer. He looked upon the tree and all its mythos. The blossoms mirroring the same holy cross whereon Christ did meet his preordained death. And the cross itself constructed of the very wood from which the flowers grew.

The boy ran his hand along the bark. He felt the girl behind him.

"You alright?" she asked.

He nodded.

"I like your haircut. Terrance did a good job."

The boy blushed.

"You ready?" he asked.

"For our big river adventure? You bet."

He turned away from her. She put her hand on his shoulder.

"Hey. What's wrong?"

"I'm scared," he said.

"Of what?"

"Of what might happen."

"I won't let anything happen to you. And who knows, the way things are going, the flood might get us all anyway."

"That supposed to make me feel better?"

"I don't know. It might be nice to die with other people, instead of alone," she said.

"I think everyone dies alone, even if they're with other people."

The rains had oversaturated the earth and the already green flora was turning a sickly, drowning yellow. The forest stank of a wet dying, mosquitos and gnats and water bugs swarmed entire acres. The algae was thick upriver and it seemed to hold position even as the water moved beneath it.

The boy sat the rear, the girl up front. They paddled through the scum water, against the low current.

"You ever wonder how it is fish came to be in the river?" the girl asked.

"What do you mean?"

"Like, how did the first fish get in this river? They don't have channel cats in the ocean, so how'd they get here?"

The boy considered the question, his mind full of reckonings, but none to his liking.

"I guess I don't know."

"Seems like we ought to have an answer for that one."

"Seems like."

"Maybe it's god, after all."

"Maybe."

"You never answered."

"I did. I said I don't know how they got here."

"Not that. You never told me if you believe in god," she said.

"Oh."

"Well?"

"I think . . ." The boy's mouth twisted. "I think it doesn't make any sense for there to be a god. But it doesn't make any sense for there to not be."

"That's not much of an answer."

"I guess I'm still deciding."

"Fair enough. But if I die before you, I'm gonna come back and tell you the truth."

"You'd haunt me?"

"Hell yeah. I'd haunt the shit out of you. Make sure you don't turn into just another asshole."

"I'll already be old by then," the boy laughed. "By the time you die."

Further upriver the soil turned to deep sandy loams, then hard red clay, the elevation growing, the world rising up away from the sea. Far to the west, the earth stretched and the timber thinned and the prairie land was green and plenty, fed by the Brazos River Valley. Further still sat the Edwards Plateau, its mesquite-covered hills reaching hundreds of miles before giving way to the high desert of the Trans-Pecos. Toward the dawn the land stayed thick with pine, crossing all the way to the Sabine and into the low swamplands and deltas of Louisiana.

The boy had seen neither expanse, east nor west, and the spillway marked the furthest upriver he'd ever traveled. The waters were calmer here and the forest somehow quieter as the pounding of the spillway faded into the once before.

They docked the canoe along the bank near a grove of yaupon hollies sprung up in a sunlit clearing, and the girl sighed and bent forward to touch her toes and then stretched to either side. The boy watched her.

"Quit staring," she said, but she smiled and the boy blushed and walked from the clearing into the woods to check the area around them.

He came first to a small stand of cottonwoods and slipped through the unmanicured vegetation below and emerged into a field of alamo switchgrass that had grown in time to reach the same height as the boy. He stepped out among it, wary of snakes, and walked until he reached the center of the clearing where rested a great stone altar, unmoved these last ten thousand years.

The boy ran his hand along the shale rock, formed by the deposition of mud and clay and born to an arcane planet whereon no one and nothing could foretell what violence would result from man's inability to understand—understand one another, understand purpose, understand himself.

The rock was made warm by the sun and by the ancient soul still within it, and the boy felt there the spirit of the place, the dark ritual more time-worn than even the rock itself. The sacrifice of blood and body to some long-forgotten god of war, the clashing of tribes, the ebb and flow of an eternal tide, pushing and pulling at the very existence of these cousined creatures, forcing evolution with the merciless hand of death.

The boy withdrew his hand and shuddered and even in the absence of wind the top grass surrounding him began to move back and forth, and he could hear the drumbeat heavy and slow as it kept the march for some ghostly army of almost men, spectered soldiers making their way through a buried past.

They made camp with no fire and the rain fell and the boy counted the days in his head and wondered if the world was stuck in some infinite loop, a scratched record, the needle wobbling back and forth inside a gash, playing the days over in cosmic repetition. Or. Perhaps. The earth readying itself for the next great cleansing.

The boy imagined a future where gardens were grown on boats, houses built floating, and those left living cared for one another as if they were the last of their kind.

He held the tarpaulin on one side and the girl held the other, the rain beating down upon the two of them and the world alike. At the onset of the storm the raindrops made circles in the tea-colored water, but when the winds rose and the sheets of rain fell in earnest there was created just above the surface a fine mist, and the river itself appeared dark and dimpled before them.

The next morning they sat in some unlearned silence, and the sun missing from above, lost to the cover of clouds and the gathering storm. The wild rye and bluestem bowed to one another with each breath of wind, the blackgum and live oak leaves whispering across the bottomlands of things past and things still to come.

"I'm gonna go see if I can find any wood that's not completely drowned."

The girl nodded.

The girl rose and walked to the water and sat as she had before with her feet half-submerged. She looked out at the river as the first of the rain began to fall, creating scattered ringlets across the surface. Each ripple representing a single drop, growing and spreading until it lost itself in the great body, coalescing with fate and circumstance to become something else altogether.

The girl closed her eyes and smelled the rain and when she opened them again the skies opened as well and the rain fell in earnest and the only sound was static, a hushed accommodation between the storm and the trees. Then lightning from the west, a fracturing of the coruscated sky, and the girl gazed upward and caught the last gasp of purple and pink glow behind the clouds. The following thunder echoed through her, tensing her shoulders. She steadied herself. The rain soaked her face and hair, and she felt it and felt the strength therein. She stood and took first one step into the river and then another. The water reached her waist and she stopped and again closed her eyes. She rested both hands overtop her stomach, fingers interlocked in a powerful symmetry.

The world around her flashed and rumbled, the life of the river swelling, the life within her coalescing with her own soul and in an instant she recognized the wealth of danger long-harbored by the miracle of existence. The river ran faster. It pulled at her. She opened her eyes and saw the world anew and fled for the bank.

Somewhere in the distance a single shot sounded and the girl froze and called for the boy. She heard the crashing of underbrush and the sound of the storm and she readied herself for the threat she knew was coming.

The boy burst from the thicket dragging two large branches. The girl rushed to him and hugged him and kissed his face and the boy dropped the wood and embraced her tight.

"You heard it?" he asked.

"I thought you'd been shot."

"I thought the same about you. Probably just somebody using the storm as cover to kill a deer out of season. Doubt there's many game wardens running around in this weather."

"I'm okay," the girl said. She pulled away, as if she were embarrassed of something.

"You're soaking wet."

"Went for a dip."

"Well, if I'd known you were that crazy, I would've brung more wood."

"Always taking care of me," the girl said, and there was a sad realization in her voice.

"You don't make it easy."

"I know," she said, soft.

They sat with their backs against a red oak and the girl made a small fire and the boy held the skillet overtop it and shook cornmeal from the bag and mixed it with water until it was a warm mush.

The boy pinched a dollop between his fingers and blew on it and popped it into his mouth and chewed.

"Could use some salt," he said, "or syrup, one."

"At least it's not eggs," the girl said and stuck her hand into the pan.

"You're getting better at this whole roughin' it thing," he told her.

"You're a good teacher."

The boy blushed.

"Why do you like me so much?" the girl asked him.

"What?"

"Is it just cause you're a thirteen-year-old boy and I'm an older girl with tits?"

"No. I mean, there's more."

"What then?"

The boy stopped eating and leaned back against the tree.

"You see things how they are, I think. Like when you said god shouldn't forgive people. Or when you were little and thought sending money made more sense than just praying. Everybody talks about forgiveness, you know. But it seems to me that's just the best way for them to go on making the same mistakes. My daddy, he'd say sorry all the time. And I'd believe him. Believe that he was. And I think that made it worse. If I could have seen him for what he was, I think it would of eased things somehow. Not the beatings, maybe, but how I looked at it all."

"You're a smart kid, you know that?"

"I don't think so. Other people think I'm weird."

"Yeah, well, other people are morons. And if the morons think you're weird, that means you're doing something right."

"Maybe."

"Trust me."

"I do."

"Come here."

The boy moved closer and the girl put her arms around him and there they slept in one another's embrace.

39

The office was on the top floor of the only four-story building in Neches County. The receptionist did not make eye contact with John Curtis but turned to watch him walk through the dark mahogany doors.

Inside were hung the busts of wild game, antelope, moose, and bear, and shaggy-haired sheep with great curved horns. Each of them positioned by the taxidermist to look as if they were by some troubling feat of necromancy half alive, immobile but aware. There were tall green plants of all species in the corners of the room and along the back wall of glass, and the floor was a dark tile made to look wood.

Behind the desk at the far side of the room a man in his late fifties with slicked gray hair poured two glasses of scotch and his eyes nearly closed completely when he smiled.

"Mr. Curtis. Come have a seat."

John Curtis stood in front of the bear and looked up at it.

"You like that? Big fucker. Took him from two hundred yards. Up in Canada, somewhere along the Yukon River."

"These bears used to be right here in Neches," John Curtis said. "Gone, like so many other things."

"Well, you know what hasn't ever been here? Elephants. Headed to Botswana next month to bag one of those bastards. Biggest game you can take in the entire world." The lawyer then frowned, as if he'd just thought of something disheartening. "I don't know where I'm gonna put the fucking thing. Anyway, what brings you in?"

John Curtis turned to the man.

"I'd like to turn myself in."

The man waited for more.

"Talk to the feds. Tell them I'll give them everything they could ever want."

"On the cartels?"

"On the cartels, the local law enforcement, the corrupt officials, the DA. All of it."

"Well. Am I out of my mind here to ask why?"

"I want protection."

"From what?"

"Anything."

"What, like witness protection?"

"Exactly like that."

"What the hell is going on?"

"I'm sure it distresses you, but you'll have to find another special client to fund all"—John Curtis looked around the room and the covenant of stuffed corpses—"this."

The lawyer nodded.

"I'll do all I can for you. You know that. But if I'm in some kind of jackpot here, I need to know about it."

"We'll give the feds their trophies, then you can go kill your elephants and never hear from me again."

"I don't understand what's happening. Is somebody threatening you? Does this have to do with that local boy who got knifed at the ballgame?"

"You've always been a good lawyer. One who knows when to ask questions and when to stay quiet. Talk to the feds. I'll get my affairs in order."

"Well. Alright then, if you say so."

"I do."

John Curtis knocked back the scotch and set the glass carefully back onto the table.

"Whatever arrangements are made," he said, "make sure they're for two people."

40

The boy woke and watched the fire, the wind harassing it, the flames twisting and drawing down, diminished with each gust and then rising back in full and stronger than they were before. The breeze would give out, then collect itself and be back nipping at the fire, two elements at play in some game never won.

After the rain, there seemed that night more stars than any one sky could properly accommodate, and the moon thinned itself in the presence of such celestial arrangements, and the boy stared up at the heavens and wondered about them, and wondered about other things, and in such ruminations he found himself, as he often did, thinking of his mother. Of all mothers.

"You think there's aliens up there somewhere?" the girl asked, stirring from her sleep. Her voice was soft and warm and so close by. For a time the boy sat in silence in the question's wake and was happy to feel the girl beside him.

"Maybe," he said at last. "Do you?"

"Shit. Who knows."

"If there are, I hope we don't ever find them."

"Me too. Poor fuckers."

The fire faded. The powerful flames giving birth to a short-lived empire, enveloping all they touched, eating themselves from the inside out until there was nothing left to consume. Until the once bright promise of progress collapsed into ash and ember, and there burned out like the billions of stars watching over it.

When the boy's eyes finally rested, there came a haunting sleep wherein he was carried by giant hawks into the night sky. The great birds of prey flew beyond the known galaxy, navigating between the light of the furthest stars. The boy's arms outstretched toward the glow of such ethereal orbs, but each time he came close to touching their truth, the light before him would flicker and die, and soon the universe held within it an infinite darkness. He felt the hawks release their grip and the boy was falling through an eternal emptiness, and it was from this terror he did awake to the sound of distant thunder.

The thunder came before the rain, rumbling above the earth like a loaded cart passing along an uneven road, jostling the ground and those things set upon it as if the whole world was not but a china cabinet made to rattle.

They paddled through the rain and the boy's arms were tired and so too the girl's and neither complained. At the spillway the two portaged the canoe and the boy took from his backpack the bag of jerky and they squatted on the high bank and ate and watched the water as it fell and crashed from the upper level to the lower.

"Sure is something," the girl said.

"It used to scare me, when I was little."

"It don't no more?"

"No."

"How come? It still looks scary to me."

"Too many worse things, I guess."

They drug the canoe through the mud and mosquito ferns, through pale stands of river birch what grew above the gamma grass, water clovers, and big-footed burheads with their heavy, nodding leaves.

The rain fell heavy and knocked balls of moss and sweet gums from the trees. The boy hacked at a dwarf palmetto and pulled it from the ground and held it over her head as the water poured off its sides.

She laughed.

"What are you doing?"

"Nature's umbrella."

"Uh-huh." She rolled her eyes.

They strung up the tarp between two short laurel trees and slept beneath it to keep off the rain while they slept.

In his dream, the boy followed the panther down a trail covered with leaves and the leaves were dead and turned to ash beneath his feet. For most of the dream they walked, the panther stopping at times to look behind him, ensuring the boy was still there. He was. They followed the path until it reached the river and there they turned along the bank and followed the water's flowing. Night fell in the dream, and the boy lay down to sleep, and he saw himself sleeping in the dream, and with such came a panicked confusion, and for a moment he thought he might wake— either in the dream or from it, and who could tell which. But the panther lowered his head and nudged the boy and the boy felt the wet of its nose, its short fur, the warmth of its breath. The boy rose in the dream and followed on in the twilight. The dream stars were in all ways magnified. They were legion across the sky and burning with an intensity found only in the unreality of the world.

They came at last to the head of a great waterfall and the mist of the pounding water rising like smoke, like the remnants of some steaming geyser wherein lay the path to the hollow earth beneath our own—a hell-like landscape of molten renderings and crouched, half-human creatures, blind in the darkness with elongated limbs and clicking tongues. The dreaming boy could see them, but the boy in the dream did not. Instead, he followed the panther to the water's edge and looked down into the mist and quickly wiped at his own eyes.

At the bottom of the falls where should have been some tranquil pool, the boy saw the entire world inverted. The water fell straight down until it reached the mirror image of itself, a stream falling upward from a ledge even further below. Another bank and shore and starlit sky. And another boy, the same boy, staring up.

In the dream the boy held up his hand and the boy from below likewise in a perfect synchronizing. They remained there, upon their mirrored ledges, staring at one another, at themselves. The overbright stars falling from each sky in tandem. The boy below abruptly jerked his head away from the upturned waterfall and looked behind him. The dreaming boy could feel his fear.

He awoke sweating in the darkness. He shook the girl awake.

"What is it?" she asked.

"Something's coming."

It moved through the underbrush with loud announcement and the boy put himself between the girl and the coming danger and they were still and quiet in their watching. There were five of them that emerged, snorting and grunting, with black matted hair and great humped backs. They each tore at the ground, rooting for food, two with curved tusks, yellow bone caught in the low light of the moon beams.

"Hogs," the boy whispered.

The smallest among them caught scent of the backpack and trotted toward it, squealing.

"Hey," the girl shouted and stepped from behind the cover of the oak. The boy tried to pull her back but she wrenched free.

"Shoo," she said, and the young pig squealed again, and the rest of the passel raised their heads and commenced to growling.

"Get. Go on," the girl continued.

The largest boar lumbered forward and stamped at the mud. The girl was broadside, worrying at the smaller hog. The big beast made his charge and the girl didn't see until it was too late and her eyes doubled in size at the sight of his approach. She raised her arms and turned away from the attack, but it never came. Instead, two gunshots and the dead boar skidded the last few yards and lay at her feet.

The boy held the pistol with both hands, the barrel smoking. His chest rose and fell in rapid succession. The other hogs went crashing through the woods from whence they'd come, the small one squealing after them.

The boy looked at the gun in his hands as if it had acted of its own agency, as if he were merely the instrument.

"Holy shit," the girl said, then she began laughing until she was breathless. "You just saved my life. Again."

"Is it dead?" the boy asked, still unmoved from his firing stance.

"He's dead, alright. Good shooting."

The boy nodded.

"You want to cut off a tusk or anything?" the girl asked.

"Why?"

"I don't know. For, like, a trophy or something."

"No. Let's just get out of here. The sun will be up soon."

"Hey, you don't feel bad about this do you? That thing would've killed me."

The boy nodded.

"I know," he said. "But he was trying to protect the little one. He was being a good dad."

"Jonah. You didn't have a choice. You did a good thing. You saved me."

The boy was tearing up. The girl came to him.

"Hey," she said, taking his face in her hands, "look at me. You saved me. You saved me."

She kissed him on either cheek.

"Thank you," she said.

The boy nodded and took a deep breath and tucked the gun back into his pants.

The hog lay lifeless, tongue lolling, soaking in the mud and the blood and the coming dawn. Buzzards began to circle.

They continued up the river and were all day paddling and into the dusk. The rain was on and off and on again, and at night the North Star was the only thing in the sky save thin gray clouds. The boy watched it and each time he stared at it straight on, the star seemed to dim, as if it were shy or scared or had some other notion that kept it from wanting to be seen true.

They drug the canoe onto the bank and owls called a warning to them or other living things and the frog song came up heavy from the river in trilling tones. The night was alive and the boy knew such nights and was not afraid. The girl startled at each new sound, and the boy would name the sound to her and tell her it was alright, and soon she had taken his hand and huddled close to him. He held thorn branches back for her to pass and told her to watch her head when limbs hung low in their path. From time to time the boy would pause and look toward the river and look toward the night sky and then continue on and the girl never questioning.

The ground before them began to slope into an oft-flooded creek bed, and the boy stopped near the top of the ridge and walked in a short circle and said they'd make camp here. He laid a blanket and told the girl to wait while he gathered wood for a fire.

She had to cut him loose, but she couldn't. He was her lifeline in so many ways. And he was kind to her. More kind than any human had ever been. How could she send him away? How could she say goodbye to something she'd always wanted?

The spotlight from the johnboat came forward to cut the dark and the eyes of frogs shining back at it like spectators to their own executioning. The trolling motor cut and hummed to a stop and the boat veered toward the bank and a shadowed figure crouched over the bow as if adorning one of the great warships of old.

"What are they doing?" River asked.

"Frog giggin'," the boy said.

The boat glided to the bank and the front of the vessel ran ashore and in the light they saw the long pole with three prongs affixed to the end and on the prongs a bleeding bullfrog. The man with the pole swung it around and extended it toward the boat's driver who grabbed the frog and pulled it free then proceeded to twice smash the creature against the side of the boat before tossing its body in a blood-stained bucket.

"That's sad."

"Shit. They're getting out."

The two men climbed from the boat and pulled it half ashore and tied it to a thick cypress root.

"I'll get us a fire going," one said to the other. "You start working on skinning them legs."

"How come it is I'm always the one getting my hands covered in blood and frog shit?"

"Well, there's probably a lifetime of answers to that question, Bud, but the short of it is that we're in my boat."

"Meaning?"

"Meaning I'm the captain and you're the first mate. You do what I say, and I say get to work on them legs."

"Fine."

"How about an 'Aye aye, Captain'?"

"How about go fuck yourself."

The man laughed at his companion and turned on a flashlight and began walking toward where the boy and girl knelt hiding.

"Shit," the girl whispered. "He's gonna see us."

She turned to the boy but he was already rising and walking into the man's light.

"Y'all out giggin' frogs?" the boy asked and the man shouted something indiscernible and clutched at his own chest.

"Who the hell's out there?"

"Two of us," the boy said. "Me and my friend. She's a girl."

The man turned and looked into the darkness as if it might offer him some further explanation. When it did not, he turned back to the boy.

"Well, what in the hell are you doing?"

"Camping."

"Camping?"

"Yessir."

"You're a lying little shit. You ain't camping."

"How come?"

"How come you're lying?"

"How come you to say we ain't camping?"

"Son, I been running this river for going on fifty years. There's camp-grounds aplenty, but not anywhere close to here." The man shone his light at the girl who held her arm up over her eyes. "Plus, you got one backpack and a gunny sack between the two of you; no tent, no bedrolls, and you look like you ain't had a proper meal in your whole life. That, and your friend there is hiding in the goddamn bushes."

"Well."

"I don't need to know. Just c'mon and help me build a fire and y'all can at least eat a bite with me and Bud."

"You sure that's alright?"

"I said it was, didn't I?"

"Yessir."

"I'm Waylon," the man said, sticking his hand out.

"Jonah."

"Alright, Jonah, let's get us a cookfire going."

The girl watched with morbid curiosity as the man called Bud knelt to dress the bullfrogs. He took a paring knife and cut off the feet, then sliced around the belly. He wiped the blade on his pants leg and set it aside. He picked up a pair of pliers and grabbed hold of the cut skin with the nose of the tool, then he set about ripping the skin from the tissue, steadying the carcass with his free hand.

He noticed the girl watching. He smiled.

"Like taking his little ole pants off, ain't it?"

River frowned.

"I'm Bud," he said, dropping the frog and reaching out his hand.

The girl looked at the hand, covered in guts and blood.

"Oh, got some toad juice left over," Bud said, grinning.

She swallowed and walked toward Jonah and the other man.

The four of them sat the fire and the men were both large-nosed and large-bellied and they drank heavily from a bottle with no label.

"Where you kids from?" Waylon asked, turning the frog legs in the pan.

"I'm from down the river," the boy said. "She's from Louisiana."

"Whereabouts downriver?"

"Just near Hog Creek." The boy hesitated. "My daddy's Dwayne Hargrove."

"Christ Almighty."

"You know him?"

"Yeah, I know that no-good rascal. Used to try and get me to loan him money at the Indian casino."

"Yeah, that's him."

"So, what then? You run off?"

"Something like that."

"Well, hell, I don't blame you. I reckon running off and living like outlaws is just about a rite of passage around here."

"You know," Bud said, "I'm part Injun."

"Shut up, Bud."

"You don't believe me?"

"Hell, everybody says that. We can't all be part Indian."

"Why not? They was here before everybody else."

"I don't know. I just mean, you always hear how so-and-so's aunt done tracked the family back to George Washington or Pocahontas or the *Mayflower* or something."

"Naw, it ain't like that. My great-great-granddaddy was a Caddo Chief."

"My ass."

"I swear to god."

"Y'all don't listen to him. He lies like a cheap watch."

"Fine. Y'all don't want to hear the damn story, that's just fine."

"Naw, go on tell it, Chief Bud."

"Keep laughing."

"Hell, I'm sorry, son, I'm just messin' with you."

"Keep on."

"Alright, alright, I'm done. Go on and tell your story."

"It's done ruined."

"Aw, now, don't sull up. Tell it."

"Fine. But not a word from you."

"Scout's honor."

"Alright. Well. All this land here used to be part of the Caddo Nation. They weren't like the warring tribes you hear about from out on the plains or nothing like that. Sure, they got in a scrape or two, but for the most part, they were a peaceful bunch. Well, one day, back before there was ever such a thing as a white man, the chief's wife gave birth to four boys; only, they weren't like normal babies. They had four arms and four legs each, and they grew double their own size every night. The rest of the people begged the chief and his wife to kill the creatures, but they wouldn't do it. So everyone watched as these things got bigger and bigger and started terrorizing the village. One night, the four brothers stood with their backs all to one another and by morning they'd grown together into one four-headed monster. Their arms reached out for miles and they would scoop people up and eat them, bones and all.

"Finally, a powerful medicine man snuck deep into the woods and had a secret meeting with the Great Turtle. The Great Turtle told the man in order to kill this monster, the whole world must be sacrificed. But the Turtle also said for the medicine man not to worry, because in time it would be reborn. The man thought about this and he agreed it must be done. So Turtle told him, when you see the giant reed begin to grow, take your wife and climb inside.

"Some days later, with all the earth being tortured by the four brothers who became one, the medicine man saw a reed growing larger than all the others. He took his wife and they hid inside of it as it grew. And as soon as they were inside the skies darkened and began to rain and the rain lasted until all of the world was covered in water. The monster drowned and when it did the rain stopped and water receded and the man and his wife came out from the reed. But the earth was barren and dead and the wife asked her husband, What will we do? The husband told her of Great Turtle's promise and so they went to sleep in the mud and when they awoke there were green plants all around them. They slept a second time and when they opened their eyes there were animals eating the plants. And so the earth returned to them, but with one big difference. The monster had been washed away out to sea somewhere, but when it first sunk, all them arms and legs and everything had made a bunch of ruts in the ground. The water filled 'em all up, and—"

"And that became the very river we're on this evening."

"Goddamnit, Waylon."

"What? Hell, it's all horseshit. Why didn't they just shoot about a thousand arrows into the big sumbitch? It don't make no sense."

"It's a story, it ain't got to make sense."

"The Shawnee got a different story. I like theirs better. Something about a water panther."

"You don't even know the story."

"I know it's better'n yours."

"I liked the story," the boy said.

"See there, a man who knows a good tale when he hears it. You young'uns want some frog legs?"

They looked at one another, the boy and girl, and both declined.

"Kids these days. They don't know fine cuisine when it's right under their nose."

"I gotta pee," the girl whispered and rose from the fire and walked into the woods.

Bud stood and walked the opposite direction and began to rap the pan against a tree.

"What'll you take for the girl?" Waylon asked the boy, leaning forward toward the fire.

"Take for her?"

"You know, for me and my partner yonder to give her a spin."

"I wouldn't take nothing. She's not like that."

"Well, see, I happen to know that she is. Whether you know it to be true or not, doesn't make much count to me."

"You stay good and far away from her," the boy said. "And I won't kill you."

"Kill me?"

"I believe you heard me."

"You little shit. I was trying to make a fair offer. And here we done offered you food and a fire. We could just gut your skinny ass and throw you in the river. Take her off with us when we leave."

"You try something like that, you'll find your life's worth of blood on the ground, and a hole in your chest where it come out of."

The boy raised the pistol.

If the man was worried, he didn't show it. But he stayed crouched by the fire as the boy backed away into the woods.

"Let's go," he said to the girl. She'd just locked in the button on the jean shorts.

"What?"

"We're getting back on the river."

"Right now? What happened?"

"Just get in," he said, already shoving the canoe into the water. "And tell me if anybody follows us."

They navigated the unnatural inlet through mud and floating wood until the river opened up.

"Tell me what the hell is going on," the girl said, once they'd made the middle.

"Those men were thinking they might do something bad to us."

"What does that mean?"

"It means we had to go. They would've stolen the backpack."

"They didn't even know what was in it."

"They would've figured it out."

The girl stared at him.

"Fine, don't tell me. But I'm going to sleep, so don't flip us over."

The boy watched as the girl laid her blanket in the bottom of the canoe. She took off her shirt and balled it up and put it under her head where she lay curled in the fetal position. The boy paddled slow for a long while and kept watch for movement or lights along the bank. They passed the occasional cabin with a night lamp strung up, but mostly the night was black and the world shapeless, as if they were adrift on the edge of a lost planet where light could never reach, where the shadows of other worlds had gathered and faded into one another, obscuring even themselves.

41

The morning was wet and cool for the season. Still, the old man was sweating by the time he'd pulled on his chest waders, fastening the straps over his shoulders. He backed the trailer end just past the lip of the water and loosed the johnboat from the trailer and dallied a rope over the dock post and pulled the truck forward until the trailer had risen from the river. He put on the parking brake, killed the engine, and climbed out. He walked a little ways into the water and steadied himself against the dock and swung one leg into the boat, caught his balance, and then swung the other. He untied the rope from the bow and left it to hang down from the dock post, then pushed off from the dock and started the trolling motor.

He was out of breath and cursing his knees, but he needed the fish.

He'd always loved the river best in the mornings. It was softer somehow, and that softness seeped out and touched those near to it. He remembered his father talking of the mornings in France, how sometimes, if the light caught a green field just right, or when a songbird mustered the strength of a serenade, a man could forget he was at war. Forget a great many things.

He always liked that. He'd never known such reprieves in Korea. Still, he liked the thought of his father, unafraid in the face of such horror, finding joy in the mornings.

He liked all his father's stories. A great man. A hard time. Would that the world was as simple now, he thought. He'd sat at his father's knee and listened to every word, soaking up the tales of hunting, fishing, war, and comradery. When his own son was born, he'd reveled in the thought of sharing with him all he'd learned, a passing down of wisdom and wont. But such times never came, his boy disinterested in the river and the way of life alongside it. Turned, perhaps, by his mother. Or perhaps not. Nevertheless, they'd gone. And not just his own family, but countless others. Generations of homesteads on the banks of the Neches were abandoned in mere hours. Those who remained were, like him, too old for the notion of a new beginning.

When the economy went dry, despots and criminals slinked into the bottoms, taking hold of the empty cabins and trailers. There was a time, the man recalled, when every boat that passed along the river offered a wave and even words of friendship or good fortune. Now the vessels crawled by with no acknowledgment, only the skulking stares of hard-faced men, more consumed with the worry of a witness than a commitment to community.

He guided the johnboat from the bow. The water was higher than he'd guessed, higher than he would have liked, but the empty bleach jugs marking his lines were still visible and bobbing.

The old man cut the trolling motor. He labored forward onto his knees and reached into the water and got hold of the nylon rope and pulled up. He worked his hands down the rope and the boat followed the path of the staging line and the old man ran each trot at the half drift and found the chunks of carp he'd baited with had been eaten away, yet no fish were on the line.

"Goddamn thieves," he hollered out to the river, or to god, or to no one at all. Then he sunk backward in the boat and sat there, drifting.

For the old man, it was another sign of the times. A trotline was a sacred thing, and yet he'd heard tale of river rats spotting jugs and yanking up the fish for themselves, no matter who the line belonged to.

He considered baiting the line again, but decided against it. Instead, he gathered it up and circled the rope into the bottom of a five-gallon bucket and hung each hook along the bucket's rim. He checked two more juglines, both picked over, likely by the same perpetrator. The thieves had not found his lone limb line and he saw the branch to which the rope was tied, bowed and bent toward the water's surface.

He pulled up the trot and a six-pound channel cat along with. He unhooked the fish and dropped it in the boat's well and collected the rope and turned down river for home. Hours of work had resulted in a single fish. Still, he gave thanks to whatever vestige of god lingered on in his mind.

He took his meager bounty to clean on the stone under the rain barrel and was bent down at his work when John Curtis spoke to him.

"What do you say there, old timer."

Carson turned, then stood. "Do I know ye?"

"Nossir, I don't believe so."

"Well. Thought I heard a truck pull up."

"This ain't Dwayne Hargrove's place is it?"

The old man shook his head.

"It's not. He lives yonder through the woods a piece."

"With his boy?"

"What's that?"

"He has a boy, don't he? Does the boy live there with him?"

"There's a boy, yeah."

"You seen him around?" John Curtis asked.

"Who?"

"The boy."

"Around here?"

"Around anywhere."

"I seen him from time to time," Carson said.

"You see the girl he's with?"

The old man took a long breath.

"What's all this about?"

"That girl stole from me. Run off with things that don't belong to her. The boy's been helping her. Some folks say you and him is like buddies. Figured you might know something about all that."

"I don't know nothing."

"Don't know where they're headed?"

"Naw. Couldn't say."

"Well, that doesn't much matter. I already know where they're going.

I guess what I really wanted to find out was if I was gonna have any trouble from you."

"What trouble?"

"Folks say you was a war hero. I'm a military man myself."

"You want a pat on the back? Thank you for your service," Carson said.

"Yeah. You're a tough old nut. I might should kill you right here."

"I'd rather you didn't."

"You know what's gonna happen to that boy, don't you?"

The old man spit and wiped the fish guts on his overalls.

"Same thing that happened to your son," John Curtis said.

Carson nodded.

"My family was killed in an automobile crash."

"Yeah, but they're still dead, ain't they?"

The old man turned the spigot on the barrel and rinsed his hands.

"If you aim to provoke me into fighting you right here, I won't do it. But you hurt that boy, I'll come for you."

"That's what I figured."

"I'll chase you through hell and back out the other side."

"We'll see."

42

I knew about Splithorn Hill. About the man who lived there. About the types of people went up to that cabin, and what they were looking for when they got there. I knew Mac Stafford. Knew of him anyway. Enough to stay away. His old man, Herman, and me went to school together. There was something not altogether right about Herman, and I mostly heard the same about Mac. Then his body was found floating scalped in the river, and I didn't hear any more about him after that.

I met John Curtis once, before he come out to my cabin. I don't believe I ever told the boy. Seen him at the gas station up by the highway switch. He was coming out, I was headed in. He held the door open for me, called me "sir." I don't quite know what to make about that. About his purpose, about my own.

I spent too long in this world trying to puzzle out such a thing. There were times I thought maybe I'd come close to something that might pass for an answer, but I never really had.

That's the hubris of man. Our endless quest for understanding. The sun and moon and the miracle of mountains, and man needing to know the full regard of each, as if the grasping of some other existence might lead us closer to the discernment of our own. And all the while clinging to the fanciful hope that we might be the first—the first in all the rotations of the earth—to solve the mystery of life's impetus.

I think a wiser soul than mine might come early to the notion that the "why" doesn't matter. Why we choose to act is not relevant to the action itself. The nail doesn't care why we swing the hammer, it cares only about the impact of the blow.

I read about where this scientist got asked about does he believe in the afterlife, and he said we're all energy, and we'll always be energy, whether we're living or not.

Sometimes that sounds quite nice to an old man. Other times, it terrifies me. No sense in lying or being brave. There are moments, days, months even, where I can't fathom the possibility of not existing.

It happens all the time, of course. People stop being, but everything else keeps on.

It takes a mightier mind than my own to accept something like that without fighting back. Especially when there's so many of us preaching the good book and telling you not to be afraid. How lovely does it sound to walk upon streets of gold in a heaven where lions lie down with lambs, to feel the love of an almighty creator wash over you as angels sing and all those folks you've been missing come out to surround you.

To see Daddy again? Just lovely.

He was a long time dying. Thomas Carson. He lingered, in and out of dreams, there but not. It was painful to witness. If that's what was coming, I wanted no part of it. Rather a gun cleaning accident, if my meaning is understood.

I sat with him most evenings. I was at the paper mill in those days, working graveyard. I'd get to the hospital right as the sun was setting, stay until a quarter 'til midnight, then go on to work. I remember how cold it was that winter. I would near freeze every night, walking from the glass doors at St. Juniper's out through the parking lot to my old truck. The heater wouldn't get the cab warm until right as I pulled up to the gravel lot at the mill, and by then I'd have to go on and get back out in the cold. Seems like things just turn out that way.

One night the old man was sleeping, and I was sitting in them chairs like they have for family and loved ones. They didn't have no television set in the room, at least not in his room, and I was sitting there thinking about Delores when in she walked. She'd brought Tommy with her. Daddy was out of it, couldn't barely lift his head up, much less talk, so the three of us just stood there. I couldn't find the right words, assuming there was such.

I asked Tommy about school. He didn't answer until Delores told him to. She was always good to me in that way, even though I didn't deserve it.

"Fine," the boy said. "Is Pa gonna die?"

"I think so," I told him.

"I wish it was you, instead," he said, and then he walked out of the room. Delores stayed.

She asked if I was still sober. I said that I was, and she knew I was lying.

"What can I do," I asked, "for y'all to come back?"

"You know what," she told me, and she wasn't even mean about it.

I hung my head.

"I'm so sorry, Eddie," she said, and she put her hand on my arm, just for a second, maybe not even that. Then she was gone, too. They were dead within the half hour.

The officer said they couldn't quite tell what happened. Maybe Delores had swerved, maybe it was the other driver. Might have been something in the road. A deer, maybe. They met head-on near the center stripe and nobody survived. The officer said it was a tragedy, and that it was nobody's fault. But I knew better. It was my fault, and had been for some time.

We all come to appreciate those things lost to us. The sweetest breath of the day not realized until the night. Such is our reckoning as men. And how do you keep going, when something so meaningful is taken from you? How do you move forward? How do you move at all?

43

They awoke from an uneasy sleep to the trembling of the earth beneath them. In the too-dark of dawn the girl thought herself still dreaming some dream wherein the world was at war again, always, and now her faceless assailants had surely called forth some unholy beast of the Armageddon. She shrieked, and the boy scrambled to his feet and looked wide-eyed toward the black forest.

The air itself seemed to groan and the crashing of limb and trunk surrounded them.

"It's the trees," the boy said. "They're falling."

"The wind's barely blowing."

"The ground's too soft. They're coming up from the roots."

"Is that even possible?"

"We need to get back on the water."

The girl rolled their bags and the boy drug the canoe through the flooded swamp until the bottom was clear of the mud. He went back to the camp and took their gear and packed it to the canoe and the girl sloshed behind him. They climbed in and set out at the first light of the day. In that copper glow they saw the fallen trees. Some flat across the ground, half buried in the mud. Others had knocked into stronger trees and were left leaning against their comrades like wounded soldiers.

The sunlight was short-lived. The sky darkened an hour into the day.

The storms were coming earlier. Once they were on the river, the boy paddled and the girl held the tarp over their heads. The canoe cut against the current in angled encounter, bisecting the water at its bow as if it were fast at work on some great unzipping of the river.

He brought the canoe to the bank that afternoon; the rain had let up but the sky was still gray.

"There's a gully, maybe a mile upriver, and it smacks into what looks like just another little draw, but it's not. The draw turns into the creek running down from the highway. Runs right through Redtown."

The girl nodded.

"I'm gonna tell you something, Jonah. I'm gonna tell you, and you can't ever forget it. Do you understand?"

"Yes."

The boy looked concerned.

"Promise me."

"I promise."

"You," the girl put her hands on his face, "you are a beautiful person. You are the smartest fucking kid I've ever met. The kindest. Do not let your daddy take that away from you. Don't let anybody take it away. You hear me?"

The boy nodded, his cheeks trapped between her hands. She stroked his face, then hugged him.

"I do believe in god," she said.

"What about all that stuff you said? About the ten dollars?"

"I believe that too."

"I don't get it."

"Me neither. But it's the truth. It's something in me that I can't shut off. Maybe I'm brainwashed. Maybe I'm just scared."

"Scared of what?"

"I don't know."

"Dying?"

"Maybe. Or living. Living in a such a shit world and knowing none of it has any purpose. Like, maybe the reason so many folks can accept their lot in life, miserable as it may be, is because they got the promise of heaven waiting on them."

"Maybe."

"I don't know. I just know everybody needs to cling to something. To have some fucking hope. And I guess, despite the shit I see right in front of me, my hope is that god is real, and he does give a shit, and maybe things will be better. In this life or the next. I just . . . I need to believe that."

"You're gonna have a baby."

"Who told you that?" the girl asked, stepping back.

"Nobody. But you are."

"Yeah, I am."

"That's why you need to believe."

"That's why."

"Is he the father? The big man, I mean."

The girl turned her head away.

"Sorry," he said.

"No, it's okay," the girl ran her hands through her hair, holding it back from her face. "I was gonna get an abortion, you know. That's what I told myself. I know they closed all the clinics, but I was gonna figure out a way to get a bus ticket or something, get enough money to have it all go away. Act like it never happened."

"But not anymore."

"No. Not anymore. I saw that bag sitting there, and I thought, there it is. There's the money I could use to get out of here and get everything taken care of. But what then? Even if I got away clean, how long before I make the same mistakes? Like I said, people don't change. I'm no different."

"But you did change."

"No. I use people, because I'm scared to be alone. I'm using this baby to try and be a better person. That's me being selfish, just like I've always been."

"You aren't selfish."

"Yes, Jonah, I am. Don't you see? I used you too. And I'm so *so* sorry. Coming off the drugs like that had me pretty messed up. But I get it now."

"What are you saying?"

"These people who are looking for me, they're bad. Real bad. I don't know for a fact they'd hurt a kid, but I don't know they wouldn't. You understand?"

"I don't care. I'm not afraid of them."

"But I am. And I'm afraid for you. So you gotta go home."

"I'm not gonna leave you."

"You have to. I'm not asking. Don't make me be an asshole about it. You could've died, twice, and I just didn't have the guts to let you go. I couldn't save my sister, but I can save you. Just please, go home."

"But you need me."

"I don't," she said, and the boy looked at her and it broke her heart to have to break his. "I don't need some kid following me around, making me worry about him, too."

"But, I . . . I love you."

"You don't even know what that means."

"I do."

"Jonah, please. I don't want you here. You're a good kid, but it's not like we're gonna get married or something. You're thirteen. You gotta grow up."

It was a familiar pain, a roaring pain, an invitation of sorrow into the boy's stomach. He felt it there, and other places. It caught in his throat and pressed under his chin, his forearms flexed, and his knees weakened and tensed, and all of it a torrent of suffering. The measure of which could only be felt by those with the misfortune of the knowledge, those afflicted beings who in the face of ignorance were unable to accept the bliss brought forth as a companion, but rather sought the desolated state what comes with truth.

"Don't you see?" the boy cried. "Don't you see any of it?"

The words choked him and his breathing was fast. He screamed, primal and desperate and broken, the result of some long line of advancing nature now finally advanced too far.

"I'm sorry, Jonah," the girl said, and she turned to leave him.

"River, wait."

"Jonah—"

"Here," the boy said, and he pressed the arrowhead into her palm. He'd tied the black cord around the carved divots and it hung like a necklace charm.

"Mr. Carson says it's good protection."

"From what?"

"I don't know. He didn't say."

The girl laughed and wiped her tears.

"Thank you, Jonah. For everything."

The boy nodded.

"My name's Samantha," she told him, shrugging. "Just so you know."

Jonah shook his head.

"Be careful, River."

44

The girl wiped tears from her dirt-stained face. She was spackled with mud, her feet blistered and aching. She thought any passerby would surely fear her, some golem come from beneath the ground to wander the bottoms in search of blood.

The trail was washed out with every dip of the earth, and she waded through the sludge until the land pitched upward and she found herself back on broken white rock. She clutched the backpack tight. She was so close to the freedom she desired, and the thought of such a thing was terrifying. She looked at the path behind her no less than a dozen times, checking to make sure the boy wasn't following. A great part of her wished he was.

The trail gave out and there was a once-white paper plate tacked to a pine tree, and from beside it she could see another twenty yards away. She followed the markers to the edge of a tree line and saw there the backside of the Redtown trailer park. She spotted the powder-blue double-wide and followed the chain-link fence to the gate, but no one was there. She fished the cell phone from the backpack and called the last number. No one answered. She called again, and listened. She could hear the phone ringing somewhere inside the trailer. Then someone answered.

"Been waiting for you," he said, and she dropped the phone and turned to run.

Scooter and Ryan were behind her and they laughed as she screamed and tried to fight them off.

They drug her through the gate and the backyard and into the trailer, and there she saw all that had played out, all that had been set in motion since the beginning of the world.

Inside the trailer it was an ancient carnage, a ritualistic bloodletting wherein all manner of demons are called forth unto the same purpose and such purpose can only be a great slaughtering, a war won without variance, a cleansing of some long languishing foe. Through the histories of men, always the world written into existence by battlefield butchers, the blood still wet upon their blades.

In the kitchen, a man with a shaved head was slumped down in the corner near the fridge, his throat more than slit, almost sawed, his head teetering to the side as if it might come off. There was red blood on the white handle of the fridge where he had reached for something, anything. Black blood pooled beneath him.

The men ushered her through and into the living room where another skinhead lay sprawled in a recliner. He was naked save his white boxers and a knife was shoved into his forehead all the way up to the hilt. His mouth gaped, his eyes stared blankly forward.

The girl was pushed down the hallway and into the back bedroom. She screamed and gagged and covered her mouth. A woman, dead on the floor, stabbed through with what appeared to be a dozen wounds, and next to her a child, a girl no older than five, still and forever unmoving, the fire of her life snuffed out, stolen.

The big man sat on the bed. He slid his knife back and again on the block, passing the blade just above his knee, the rhythm of the practice as pure as the bells on Sunday, a measure of time and trade and a marking of the space between realization and action; an accommodation of sorts, for the girl to take in the scene, to understand what had happened, to weigh the choices left to her.

He quit the motion, lifted his head. Her time was up.

He stared at her. His eyes a black, raging death.

"Been looking for you," his voice hard scattered gravel. "Finally poked your head up."

"Stay away from me, Cade," the girl warned.

He grabbed her by the throat.

"You steal from me. Run out on me," he said, squeezing. "Humiliate me."

"You're a goddamn murderer," she said, choking.

The big man let her go. He shook his head.

"Naw. This here blood's on your hands."

"Fuck you."

"Didn't have to be like this. But you done what you done," he said. "I might can be persuaded to forgive you though. If you say sorry real nice like."

The girl spit at him.

"I hate you."

"Yeah, I figured as much."

He motioned and the two men pushed her forward and he grabbed her beneath his giant arm and put his face just in front of her own. She winced and closed her eyes.

"You embarrassed me, girl. Made me look weak. Now you'll get a lesson."

He raised the knife up to the side of her face and dug into her skin with the tip of the blade. She cried and screamed as he slowly brought it scraping down across her cheek."

"Enough," John Curtis said, stepping into the room.

The scene stilled.

Scooter and Ryan looked confused.

The big man frowned.

"I didn't think you were coming," Cade said.

"I wanted to ensure everything that was mine was returned to me."

"Crystal's in the backpack," one of the men said, tossing it to him.

John Curtis caught the bag and set it aside without opening it.

"That's good to hear. But there's something else here that belongs to me. I need to guarantee its safety. So, gentlemen, for that I do apologize."

John Curtis leveled his pistol and fired two shots and the two men crumpled to the floor with the woman and her daughter.

Cade shoved the girl away from him and stood staring at John Curtis who was pointing the gun directly at his heart.

"You better kill me with the first shot," Cade told him.

John Curtis smiled, then lowered the pistol. He grabbed the girl around the waist and pulled her to him.

"In here, boys," he called over his shoulders and four deputies pushed past him and into the room.

"Come on," he told her, and they walked back down the hallway and past the lifeless bodies and they heard the struggle in the bedroom and heard the gunshots. Outside, the red and blue lights washed over the girl's face and she heard the static of radios and a voice confirmed "suspect down."

John Curtis held her gently and they moved past law enforcement of all kinds and no one stopped him or even looked their way. He put her into his truck. She was slack-jawed and shaking. They drove away from the scene and pulled onto the highway headed south, and out of the passenger window she could see the sun sinking behind the trees, and she believed in her heart it would be the last sunset she would ever see, and she wished the boy were with her. She put her hands over her stomach and wept.

45

The boy launched the canoe and climbed in and lay crying in its bottom. It drifted south and from the banks it appeared as some unmanned ghost craft, floating through a dimension not its own.

At midday the boy raised up and found the river was still, as if it were saving its strength for some provocation yet to be determined. As if some great dispute was forthcoming, and with it all the troubles of the world, and all the difference between good and evil, and such difference that might be made by the river's choosing. The sun overhead was white hot, its bright light overpowering the brown and blue hues of the water and turning all the surface into a blinding reflection where sat a glistering blanket of diamond.

The boy watched as the sun was passed over by a cloud and its crawling shadow laid waste to the shimmering river and revealed once more its murky constitution. The boy liked it better this way. The mud-brown channels like a truth uncloaked. Too much of the world was adorned in a saintly sheen and the boy knew enough of life to know this was not the way of things.

"It's just mud," he said to no one.

The rain came again, and the boy had lost count of the days and none of it mattered anyway. He could feel the drag of the spillway nearly one hundred yards before he reached it. He veered toward the shore and pulled the canoe from the water and drug it down the embankment west of the spillway and drug it another fifty yards or so before putting it back in the river and setting the course for Old Man Carson's keep.

The return journey was much quicker and the boy only spent one night on the river, pulling the canoe ashore near Mr. Carson's dock just after noon the next day. It had rained all night and all morning and the top of the dock was barely visible as the high water had swallowed it almost entirely.

The current lapped over the highest boards, as the boy drug the canoe further up the bank. The old man wasn't on the porch and the boy thought he might be napping after lunch. He considered knocking, but decided against it. Instead he trudged through the woods until he hit the river road and followed it to his own driveway and walked through the high side of the yard to avoid the rising water.

The trailer was locked and the boy's father was gone. He sat down at the picnic table and rested his head in his arms. He fell into an exhausted sleep.

He woke to the sound of a pattering rain. He closed his eyes and slept again. The sleep was so deep, so total, and he dreamed of the girl and of his mother. But the boy remembered none of it, and when he awoke even the feeling of dream had not lingered, and it was as if nothing had happened at all.

The sun set below the tree line, being called home to some other world, as if the light given to the earth was contracted to expire and the country would soon go about its existing under the cover of a deep and permanent darkness. The boy wondered about those first men, whether or not they figured out the sun—at least to some degree, at least to the point they quit the fear of it leaving and never coming back. And yet it had left, blocked by ash, the world frozen over. What did men, if there were any, think then?

He watched the sky through the trees as it was set afire with an orange-and-purple glow, the trees themselves as black against the horizon as the coming night. The flood waters had almost reached the picnic table. It was like the world was drowning, and the boy along with it. He imagined, not for the first time, some apocalyptic happening.

A pied-billed grebe swooped down, materializing somehow from the sky, and landed in the standing water near the edge of the sunken yard.

"You'd be a king," the boy told it.

He watched the duck for a while as it splashed in the muddy pools. It grew too dark to see much of anything, but still the boy sat. He thought of the girl and the things she'd said to him. He didn't believe her, but he understood why she needed to say them. She was not the same as everyone else, he told himself. She didn't mean those things.

He remembered her laughing at him, not unkind, and the feel of her arms around him and the way she'd kissed him. He could see the small of her back and the indentation of her skin near her ribs. He tried to remember her smell but he couldn't and it left him momentarily panicked and he felt the tears welling again. He crossed his arms atop the table and buried his face in them and soon he was asleep again and dreaming of rising waters and people with gills and a floating graveyard wherein pieces of driftwood served as headstones, and each one was tethered to a lifeless body floating six feet below the surface.

46

The truck lurched onto the highway and headed south. John Curtis drove with one hand on the wheel and one hand in his pocket. He mumbled to himself in different voices, grinning and laughing, and the girl thought him mad.

She tried to keep quiet, as if he might forget she were there. She looked out the window at the rain. The water was standing for miles along the highway's edge. Soggy fields stretched out on either side of the pavement, crops flooded under. Rain barrels were full, gutters weighted down and threatening to come loose, and the sound of dripping water belonged to every acre of forest as if it had always been there, some forever leaking network of moisture releasing from the trees. Yet the sun still appeared each morning and the people of this world seemed not to notice.

The boy had noticed, she thought, and the thought of him sent her weeping, and John Curtis spoke to her at last.

"You're not crying for Cade are you?"

She shook her head.

"You have the meth," she said. "Please let me go."

He looked at her, and she thought he looked hurt.

"Let you go? What is it you think is happening here?"

"I don't know," she said, sniffling. "Just let me go."

"You've got something that belongs to me."

"What?"

He reached over and grabbed her by the hair, yanking her down into the middle seat.

"Now is not the time to play dumb, darling. You think anything happens on this river that I don't know about?"

"It's not yours," she said, but her voice betrayed the lie and John Curtis laughed.

"I know the big man wasn't much of a talker, so maybe he never told you how it happened. But I was there that day. I drug him out of that pile of shit and loaded him onto the evac. I know what it cost him. And I know for a fact that his line ended that day in the desert."

"That don't mean it's yours."

He shook his head.

"That's my baby inside of you, and you're going to stay right here with me until it's out."

"Then what?" she whispered.

John Curtis again seemed hurt by the question.

"Then I'm going to raise my child. See that they never want for anything. Give them the love and protection I never had."

"I won't let you near my baby."

"Ask yourself: If you leave here, where will you go? What will you do? How will you afford to have a child, much less provide for it once it's born? You know how hard it is to grow up with nothing. So do I. But with me, none of that will be a problem."

"Because of your drug money."

"Wake up, girl. Look at what just happened. I made a deal. I'm done with all that. I gave the law a trailer full of dead pushers. I cut ties with the Mexicans. I'm retired."

He looked over at her.

"So, now me and you are going home to the Hill to take care of a few things. In a day or two, we'll head up to Montana or wherever and find us a little ranch to raise our family."

"I don't love you."

He laughed.

"I don't care. Not one goddamn bit. I don't need your love, just your obedience."

"And if I say no?"

John Curtis shrugged.

"I'll wait until the baby is born, then I'll rip it right out of your arms and slit your throat."

The girl began to cry again.

"Seems like an easy choice to me," John Curtis told her.

John Curtis walked the tree line at Splithorn Hill and gathered fallen branches from the day's storm. The girl had fallen into an exhausted sleep, but he'd locked her in the bedroom just in case. He looked down the hill and thought the river might have been as high as he'd ever seen it. He stood there, his arms full up with wood, then he turned and went inside the cabin.

He crouched down and opened the side hatch on the iron stove and it groaned up at him. He hadn't had a fire in near three months. He stuffed the wood in piece by piece, then threaded the gaps with strips of an old newspaper, and he lit the paper and watched it burn and blew on the flames until the wet branches finally took. He closed the door and stood up and stepped back and stood with his arms folded while the room grew hot around him.

He unstrung the leather pouch from his belt and set it on the table and turned a chair around and sat in it backward with his arms crossed over the back of it.

"I want to tell you something, Mac. Something that's been weighing me down as of late. Back when I was a kid—somewhere between Mr. Quarles forcing me to fondle his balls and Ms. Cook putting cigarettes out on me in the name of Jesus—they herded us into an after-school program at the public library. I read every book I could get my hands on. And when I was finished, I started back at the beginning and read them all again. I liked the stories, true and fiction, about people who were bigger than their circumstances. Because that was going to be me, you understand? I was going to rise above, to overcome."

John Curtis laughed.

"As I got a little older, I started reading more about philosophy, chemistry, psychology, and the like. I wanted to know what makes people tick, find their weakness and exploit it. I wasn't gonna let the world shit on me one second longer than I had to. But that ain't what I wanted to talk to you about. See, it was in one of them books, and I can't rightly recall which, I read a line from some old shrink who said a man is, in one way or the other, solely a product of his father.

"Solely. A product of his father. I don't how I felt about it back then. Probably not too good. But for whatever reason it's come back to me all these years later. I couldn't tell you why. Not to a certainty. But I'll tell you what I think. I think maybe I've finally become the man I was meant to be. The man you never could be. And I don't want you to think you had a goddamn thing to do with it.

"Whatever claim you may have to my success, or even my failure, I'm cutting you loose from it. I thought I'd ended things with this same blade once before. I've been carrying you around like a goddamn trophy and the whole time it weren't but a last thread holding us together. No more. No fucking more."

John Curtis untied the strings around the leather pouch and opened it. He pulled from it a tuft of thin black hair clinging to what remained of a gnarled, calloused scalp. He took it to the stove and with his empty hand he picked up a rag and opened the hatch. The heat rushed out and the flames used the new air to climb higher. John Curtis looked at the shriveled scalp.

"Just know, that if there is a hell, and you're down there right now, I'll be coming for you again. I'll be coming for you until the end of time."

He flung the last of his father into the fire.

47

The thin man drank his coffee. He held the Styrofoam cup under his nose before bringing it to his lips. He closed his eyes and sniffed at the contents like a man tasked with identifying some rare aroma from his own childhood. A mystery only he could unlock.

He sat the cup on the small table and crossed one leg over the other and used two fingers to pull back the window curtain. The trees stood in shadowed dissent to the growing light. The thin man could see the headlights passing on the highway in each direction like warring orbs in the early morning. He let the curtain fall back into place. He drained the rest of his coffee and stood and walked to the dispenser and refilled his cup and returned to the table and sat it on the edge nearest the window, the steam rising to fog the glass.

He opened his sketchbook and took the pencil from behind his ear and began to draw.

The heavyset man behind the desk was looking at him. The thin man raised his head and smiled and nodded, and the man spoke as if this was a permission given to do so.

"You after the worm, friend?" the man asked.

"Pardon?"

"Early bird gets the worm. Figured you might be after it this morning."

The thin man smiled again.

"I see."

"You here on business?"

"Indeed."

"If I'm bothering you, feel free to just tell me to 'shut up, Wes.'"

The thin man nodded and returned to his sketchbook.

"'Cause some folks say I'm a little too friendly," the man continued. "But I don't think there's such a thing. I just really enjoy visiting with folks. How come me to open this little ole place."

The man came from around the desk and stood leaning back against it.

"My grandma died and left me some money. Everybody said I should put it into the stock market. You know, invest it and whatnot. But I just told them, 'Nope, I'm gonna buy the old motel out near the county bridge.' And then of course they said, 'Wes, you are one crazy SOB.' And I said, 'Nope, just friendly.' I mean, why not make it my job to meet new people?"

"Can you help me?" the thin man asked, at last looking up from his book.

"Well, I'll sure try to, friend."

"Do you know this place?"

The thin man pointed to the map.

"Sure, that's Splithorn Hill."

"Can you take me there?"

"Take you there?"

"Yes."

"Raining like it has been. You'll likely need a boat to get anywhere near there."

"Do you have one?"

"A boat?"

"Yes."

"Well, yeah, I gotta boat, but it ain't for guest use. What do you need to get up there for?"

"Where is it?" the thin man asked.

"Where's what?"

"The boat. Where do you keep it? Where do you keep the keys?"

"It's out back by the dock, but like I said, it's not for—"

"The keys? Where are the keys?"

The heavyset man looked toward the desk, then back at his customer. "Listen, friend, I don't think you're understanding."

There was more to say. More words he had planned. Like so many plans, they fell away into darkness.

The thin man found the keys on a ring behind the desk. He stepped over the body and went out through the back door.

He guided the boat upriver, passing through an unfamiliar world of swamp and mud.

He passed under the highways, their bridges crossing over the water like some strange river all their own. Each one another pathway, held up and balanced by the pairs of *T*-topped pillars—set in a row and fastened to the bridge's underbelly—the bottom of which disappeared somewhere below the water's surface, as if they might go on forever, extending deeper than the river and deeper still through the earth's crust and come to some speculated counterworld where they were at last attached to the reflection of the same bridge they'd descended from.

48

The boy woke with headlights on him. He shielded his eyes until the engine stopped and the lights disappeared, then he stood.

His father walked toward him, then stopped. He looked at the gun.

"The hell are you doing, boy?"

"You know her."

"What? Know who?"

"You met her before, at the casino. That's how come you to say those things about her."

His father put his hands on his hips and looked away.

"I ain't said the first thing that wasn't true."

"Did you pay for her?"

The man didn't answer.

"Did you?"

"What do you want me to say? I was trying to protect you, son. I love you."

"And the beatings? The name calling? You trying to protect me then?"

"I'm trying," the man said, in a rare moment of vulnerability. "I don't know no better."

The boy lowered the gun.

"You really believe that don't you?"

"What?"

"I thought for the longest time that you were just a liar. That you hated me. But I see now. And it's worse this way. You've convinced yourself it's not your fault, that you're doing the best you can, even though you're a complete failure."

"You better watch what you say, boy."

The boy laughed. His laugh echoed across the clearing and into the woods.

"No. I don't think I will. What are you gonna do? I've took your beatings my whole life. I'm not afraid of you anymore. Maybe you really do love me, and if you do, that's the saddest part. Because I'm gonna leave, and I'm never coming back. And if you love me, it might actually hurt you. But you'll blame me in time. Or blame someone else. You've made yourself the world's victim and you'll do the same with this. It's your only nature. I'm glad I won't be here to see it. Because it's pathetic. You're pathetic."

The man's face was flush.

"I've had about enough of this. You ain't gonna disrespect me and think I'll just stand here and take it."

The man moved toward him, the way he had so many times before. The same look and posture and unmistakable intent.

The boy raised the gun again.

The man froze.

"You wouldn't fu—"

The boy fired.

His father collapsed sideways, as if someone had pulled a chair out from under him.

The old man was standing on the porch with a shotgun when the boy emerged from the trail.

"That shot come from your place?"

"Yessir."

"They following you?" the old man asked, pumping the shotgun.

"Who?" the boy looked behind him.

Carson lowered the gun.

"Whoever was doing the shooting."

"It was me," the boy told him. "I shot my daddy."

The old man took the news as if it were nothing.

"Kill him?"

The boy shook his head.

"Just a kneecap."

Carson nodded.

"Well. Alright. I thought maybe you was mixed up with all that what happened up in Redtown."

The boy's eyes widened.

"What happened in Redtown?"

He'd read the newspaper report and listened to Carson tell some of the details he'd heard at the feed store. Now the old man was hustling after him, calling for him to stop.

"She's in trouble," Jonah said. "I've got to help her."

"We don't know what she's in, but whatever it is, she put herself there."

"I'm not just gonna sit here and do nothing."

"You don't even know that she's up there."

The boy splashed across the flooded dock and untied the boat. The old man was trying to get down the slope.

"I'm sorry, Mr. Carson," the boy called, and as he did the old man slipped and fell and rolled onto his stomach.

The boy started to turn back but didn't, instead pointing the boat upriver and taking off, leaving the old man lying on the bank behind him.

49

John Curtis was in the porch chair. His back was straight and his hands were placed one atop the other, as if he were attending a service for which he had the utmost reverence. Were it not for his eyes, the boy might have called out to him. Instead, he walked up the porch steps and crossed the wooden floor boards to where the body sat.

Blood covered most of the face, and the eyes themselves had been removed entirely. Great gaping holes of black and blood and loose, hanging tissue. His head was cocked to the side, staring up, blind, toward the corner of the porch roof, as if all the answers of men were writ there and he could never again look away.

The boy swallowed down the sickness in his stomach. He looked closer. Amid the blood-matted hair across John Curtis's forehead, the boy saw a single bullet wound. He moved around behind the body and saw where the bullet had exited the back of the head, leaving another dark cavern and bits of brain matter which stuck to the back of the neck.

The boy braced himself on the chair and as he did so the body slid to the side and took the chair toppling over with it. The boy jumped backward.

"River," he called. "Where are you?"

He peered through the window but the lights were off and he could discern nothing of the inside. He moved to the door, took a breath, then swung it open. The heat from the stove swept forward and past him and into the night. The boy squinted into the darkness. The burning end of a cigarette danced toward the center of the cabin.

"River," the boy said, and felt along the wall for the lights.

When he threw the switch the girl was not there. Instead, a thin man sat smoking on the couch. He wore black jeans and a gray silk shirt. His legs were crossed and there was terry cloth wrapped around each boot. His hands were gloved and he was, the boy saw, at work on the disassembly of a handgun and its adjoining silencer.

"Come in," the man mumbled without looking up or removing the cigarette from between his lips. "Shut the door. Fucking mosquitos."

The boy did as he was told.

"You killed him," he said.

The man stopped his work. He placed the parts on the glass table in front of him and ashed the cigarette in a deer antler tray. He looked up at the boy.

"I did."

"And River?"

"Who is this?"

"The girl. There was a girl."

The man nodded.

"I see," he said.

"What do you see?"

"The same thing as you."

The boy's words caught in his throat. He felt weak. He staggered back against the door.

"No," he managed. "I don't believe you."

The man went back to work on his weapon.

"Yes, you do," he said.

"No," the boy repeated, louder this time. "I want to see her."

"What difference would it make?"

The boy slumped down to the floor and wept.

"I loved her. I want to see her, goddamnit."

The man paused, then nodded his head and continued.

"I will show you. But it will not help. You will never unsee. It is better to know her as she is now, in your memory."

The bedroom door had been kicked in. She sat upright in the bed, as if she was expecting someone, as if it was the natural thing to do. And yet there was nothing natural about it. Her eyes were open but unseeing, and if she did see it was on some plain yet to be discovered. The dried blood pooled on the sheets beneath her.

The boy traced the blood's path in reverse and saw there a deep-red stain just above her left breast, and the white of her gown turned dark. Her hair hung in purple and blond streaks and when the boy reached out to touch it the girl's head lolled forward. He recoiled and cursed and cried, and then he turned about the room as if there were someone else to whom he could appeal his case.

He bit his lip and tasted the salt of his tears and looked back at the bed and the blood and the truth of things. The girl's head was bowed and tilted to the side as if she were in the throes of some solemn thought, a problem to which there was no solution. The boy collected himself and approached her again and used his hand to close her eyes, and then he embraced her, sobbing.

"It's okay," he said. "It's alright. We can still go to the ocean. We'll still go. We can just—we gotta figure out a better way. We'll go though, I promise. We'll go."

The boy drew in a choked breath and shook his head and held the girl close.

"Goddamn," he cried. "Goddamn everything. I told you, didn't I? Goddamnit, didn't I tell you. Why didn't you listen? I told you and you should of goddamn listened."

He rocked back and forth with the girl still in his arms and her weight fell against him, lifeless and awkward, as if she were a child playing at some game meant to frustrate her companion. He tumbled over with the girl's body and there he lay, rocking and crying, until the thin man's shadow fell over them.

The boy sat up.

"You're a goddamned murderer."

"Your time is up. I must be going. You would do well to also leave. This scene would not look so good for you."

"I'll kill you," the boy said and pulled the gun.

"And I will be dead. And my story finished." The man sighed. "The greatest stories are stories of death, are they not? It is the one true commonality of all men. The story of Christ would mean nothing without his death. And in this, are we not like Christ? Like god?"

"You don't know anything about god."

"God." The thin man smiled. "This is a world built and held delicate upon those most fragile of pillars. There will always be some disaster on its way. Every step we take is overtop a grave atop a grave and so on to the center of the earth wherein our reckoning lies hidden and built over. If there was a god in this world we buried her under our own ambitions long ago—sacrificed her upon some limestone altar turned black with blood, then used the selfsame blade of her demise to war with one another, each dying man passing on this tool of death like an ill-starred inheritance and each progeny accepting of their charge through generations untold; and why not, when meaning is so handed to us and otherwise such terror to find on our own. When our existence is defined for us, there can be no true choosing. We may choose god, but this is a false choice. There is no god."

The boy was crying and shaking his head. He let the gun rest by his side.

"You're him, aren't you," he said. "You're death."

The thin man smiled again.

"But let us say there is a god," he said, ignoring the boy's question. "As so many believe there to be. Well. Here were all the worlds to choose from, and god laid this one at our feet, created the day and the night and gave to us bounties and love and gave to us his wrath and gave to us free will to choose between them. A choice we've long since made. A choice made for us by ancestors we'll never know save in spirit. They started us in a direction, some thousands of years ago, and that direction was built upon and hastened by each new generation until the direction was itself our only destiny, all the while pulling us further away from god. So tell me: If there is a god, and if we are to be judged by him in the end, do you believe it will be love or wrath with which we are met?"

"You didn't have to kill her," the boy said, his voice weak. "She didn't deserve to die."

"Deserve. Ameritar. No. No one is deserving to die. No one is deserving to live. Each is an accident. Each is an inevitability. Do you know why it is I come here to your mud river and kill your mud people?"

The boy shook his head. He ground his teeth as the tears fell silent.

"I think you know."

"I don't, goddamnit."

"Some might say it is the drogas. This would not be wrong. But drugs existed before me. Before these people. They will stay after we are gone. So why then am I here? Choices, and each one leading to the next. This man has made many choices, each one leading to me. At any point he could choose differently. Choose to turn some other way. And then, I am not here. He is not there."

"But she never did anything to you."

"To me? No. But still, she made her choices. As we all do. You came here to kill this man, did you not?"

The boy wiped his eyes with the back of his arm and nodded.

"Yes. I have seen this," the thin man said. "You have visited me, I believe, in my dreams."

"I hadn't visited nobody."

"Then how is it I have seen you in them?"

"We can't account for what all we see in our dreams."

The man clicked his tongue.

"Do dreams not belong to the dreamer? What is a dream, if not a story you tell yourself?"

"You don't have no control over it, though, your dream."

"Why must there be control for it to be yours? When the doctor takes up his instrument and taps at your knee, are you in control of your leg as it kicks outward?"

"No."

"No. But it is still your leg, is it not? Yes. And so it is with a dream. A story your subconscious tells you. A story inside of you that you have not yet heard."

"If it's inside me, how could I have not already heard it?"

"Something causes the leg to kick. Something else causes the story to be told. But both reactions are already there, waiting."

"I dreamed the world was flooding, that don't mean it's true."

The man shrugged.

"Perhaps you are seeing something yet to come, or perhaps you are seeing what has already been."

The boy looked away.

"Do you aim to kill me?" he asked, wiping his nose.

"Do you want to be killed?"

The boy was silent.

"I am thinking the answer is no. And this is good. I do not want to kill a child."

"But you would."

"I have."

"So why not me?"

"You are not a supplier, not a dealer, not a pusher. You don't use the drug. You cared only for the girl. You are a poor boy. You have no means. You do not know me. You will never see me again. What threat then are you to me? Unless . . ."

"Unless I shoot you in the back as you're walking off."

"Si. Unless this."

"I ain't going to."

"And so now, the choice is mine. Believe you, or no."

"I guess so."

"Ah, yes. Each choice is a guess. A guess at good or bad. Right or wrong. So I must guess if you are lying."

"I'm not lying."

"Is this not what a liar would say?" The thin man raised a brow.

"Why not just kill me, then you won't have to worry about it?"

"If I kill you, I will never know if I made the right choice. So, I will turn now to leave. You will have perhaps two dozen steps until I am gone forever. I have made my choice. Now you must make yours."

"I already said I ain't gonna shoot you. Just get out of here and leave me with her."

"Very well."

The thin man turned and left the room and the boy heard the cabin door open and shut and he heard the man's footsteps on the porch and they stopped short of the stairs.

"Very well," he heard the thin man say again, then the shotgun fired, and the boy could hear Mr. Carson calling for him.

50

One night, with Daddy in the hospice, before Delores and Thomas had come to visit, the old man gets to moaning in his bed. Of course I shot up and went over to him, as if there was something I'd know to do other than call a nurse.

"Daddy, you hurting?" I asked him.

Then he quit. Just like that. He opened his eyes and there was a light there, like a spark of life, that I hadn't seen since they first put him in that bed.

"Daddy?" I said again.

"Ed," he said. "Ed, you've got to hold on for a minute."

Well. I knew he weren't talking to me. I'm Eddie, and he never called me anything different. His brother was called Ed. Uncle Ed had passed nearly twenty years before from throat cancer.

"Your brother's dead, Daddy," I told him. I don't know why I said it. I felt bad as soon as the words came out. But Daddy didn't pay me any mind. He looked straight past me, like there was something in the corner of the room he was trying to see.

"I can't, Ed. Please. Just for a minute, now," he said.

The hair raised up on my skin. I took a step back.

"I think them shells are in your coveralls," he said, and then he closed his eyes. Went back to sleep.

He didn't die. Not that night, or the next. It was another month or so *before he went on. But that night has stuck with me for a good long while, and I don't know what to make of it. I know what the preacher would say, and I know what the scientists would say back. I just wish I could ask Daddy what it was that happened in that room. Fact is, I wish I could ask him a great many things.*

51

The air was cool and wet with the front end of a false fall and the boy's bare arms were prickled goose flesh. The porch light was still on despite the morning and the boy heard nothing from within and when he reached up and tried the door it opened without fuss and he lifted himself inside.

There sat his father. On the floor, slumped, his back against the couch and his arms resting on his knees brought up toward his chest. He smoked. The lights off and the shades drawn, his father was but a shadow of a man and neither the boy nor the shadow spoke. The boy stood in the doorway, silhouetted by the outside light he kept from coming in. His father raised his arm and drew from the cigarette and the burning cherry cast a soft glow upon his mouth and chin and the sidestream smoke rose and swirled and then stopped, hanging in the dark room as if it were air made visible.

"I'm back," the boy said at last, holding the gun at his side.

His father coughed.

"Yeah," he said, sour. "Yeah, I can see that. I thought you said you were gone for good. What happened? You come to finish me off?"

"No."

"What about your little whore?"

The boy tensed and swallowed and said nothing.

"Well, I hope you at least got some pussy out of it."

The boy closed the door and walked past his father and into the kitchen and turned the faucet and nothing came out.

"Jug in the icebox," his father said.

The boy opened the fridge and no light came on and the air was stale and warm. He took the water jug and drank from it and put it back and closed the door.

"I thought about killing you," he told his father.

"Yeah. I thought about killing you back."

The man drew at the cigarette and coughed and laughed and winced in pain all together.

"You remind me of her, you know," his father said. "Your big fucking eyes."

"You miss her?" the boy asked.

"Your grandfather told me there was only three things I should never do. Join the military, get a tattoo, get married. I figured two out of three wasn't so bad. Meatloaf wrote a fucking song about it. Anyway. We bought this trailer, moved out here to live free from the rest of the world."

"Did she like it here?"

The man's words caught, eyes watering. He nodded.

"She loved the river. Loved the animals and the forest. Like a goddamn woods witch, the way she walked barefoot through the trees."

"Why'd she leave?"

"I done told you why."

"I don't believe you."

The boy's father readied a harsh word but stopped. He looked tired.

"Believe what you want."

"She wouldn't just leave me."

"But she did."

"Tell me why."

"Would that all fathers and mothers loved their children, but they don't. What do they call it? The circle of life. That's all it is. A way to keep the circle tracing over itself again and again, until one day the pen pokes through the paper."

The man shook his head.

"So you tell me," he asked the boy. "How was I supposed to look at you after that?"

"I don't know why I came back."

"I don't neither."

"All I wanted was for you to . . ." the boy let his words trail. "I guess it doesn't matter what I wanted."

"Never does. Now go on. Get out from here. I ever see you again, I will kill you."

52

The truck sped north through the night—the driver's eyes wide, hands tight on the wheel. The passenger cracked his window and discarded a used needle. He slumped down in his seat.

"I don't even know nobody in Canada," Lonnie moaned, then giggled, writhing against the back of his seat as the meth and his body began to pulse together. "Shit, I don't even speak Canadian."

Frank shook his head.

"If I never thought in my whole life that Momma was right about things, I do right now," he said. "Right here in this moment."

"How come, Frank?" Lonnie asked, his head tilted up, mouth hanging open.

"Because here I am running from the cartel, and who am I stuck with but the dumbest sumbitch that ever drew breath—a feat, by the way, that I still ain't sure how you continue to pull off."

Lonnie looked hurt, then he giggled again.

"I don't know about going to no socialist country," Lonnie said. "Why can't we stay in America?"

"We're gonna drive this truck until the last road in all the world gives out. And when it does, we're gonna hope the Mexicans have forgot all about us. We'll wait until things cool off. Then, maybe, we can come home someday," Frank told him. "And Canada ain't socialist. They just have some socialist-adjacent policies. Like we do."

"Who's we?"

"America."

"Bullshit. We're a goddamn democracy."

"You really don't know anything about anything, do you?"

Lonnie sat up in the seat.

"You keep on being mean to me," he said, "and I'm liable to come across this console and whip your ass."

Frank slammed on the breaks and Lonnie flew forward into the dashboard, then crumpled down, ass-first, in the passenger-side floorboard.

Frank laughed. The first time he'd done so since he heard about what went down in Redtown and up at the Hill.

"Pull over," Lonnie cried, his body folded up on itself. "I think I broke my goddamn nose."

"Hang in there, bud," Frank said, smiling. "Canada has a great health-care system."

53

The boy took the canoe and left the old man a note and headed south. He worked the canoe down river and found the terrain familiar, though the pace of the flowing water quickened every half-dozen miles. When the darkness and the river's fast flow made navigation near impossible, the boy made for the flooded coves and there tied his vessel to cypress trunks along the shadowed shore.

On the third morning the river opened into a great lake and the lake into the gulf, and the sun rose gray behind clouds of smoke from the towering steel cylinders of the refineries. The rain had stopped. Everything stops, eventually, he thought.

The boy drifted near the shoreline and passed small fishing vessels and shrimp boats and crabbing nets and all of them dwarfed by the industry built up around them.

A man in a stained white tank top sat smoking on a short dock and the boy nodded to him and the man touched his cap and it was as if they knew, the both of them, what others were too afraid to understand.

The boy passed below the back of a ramshackled seafood diner with a wooden patio extending over the bay. The umbrellas shading the picnic tables began to bend and stretch as the winds commenced, and the boy continued on.

He passed through a shipping channel and under the last roadway and the river was long behind him and the ocean ahead, the enormity of which caught in the boy's throat. The tears came, and the boy closed his eyes and listened to the sound of the waves surrounding him.

EPILOGUE

We broke about every rainfall record there was that summer. A bunch of flood damage, a bunch of money to clean everything up after it was all said and done. At the same time we were fighting the water, they had the worst ever heat wave on the other side of the world. Something like a million people died in India alone.

It was years later when the boy come back. He wasn't a boy no more. Still skinny, but a man in full. He told me he caught on with a tugboat captain out of South Carolina. Some old man who didn't mind that he wasn't but thirteen. The boy followed him back to the East Coast and worked for him until the man died, then he worked the harbors for a bit, fishing boats, loading docks, you name it. Said he wanted to do everything he could to stay on the ocean. Said that's where they had been gonna go, him and that girl.

He'd sent me a postcard from Gloucester. I still had it on my icebox. I showed it to him. I asked if he'd got my return letter telling him about his daddy. He said he hadn't, but that he'd got word anyway. That's why he was back, he told me, to see if there was anything worth saving from the trailer.

We sat the porch after dark and listened to the night bugs and I asked if he could tell me what all happened back then, but he said he couldn't. Said sometimes he didn't know if anything had happened at all. Or if it had, maybe it happened to somebody else. I told him I understood. And I did. I look at old pictures of myself and wonder what I must have been like when I was whoever I was back then. A hundred years was not something I expected to see.

I don't know what all the boy had seen, but the way he sat there, staring, it occurred to me that he could have seen everything. Everything there was to see. He could have been born and reborn a thousand times over, his soul and the memory of his soul soaking up all the world's struggles and delectations alike, then spiriting from one life to the next like some ethereal marauder.

You think they're in hell? he asked me.

Who? I said.

Anybody.

I wish I could have told him one way or the other. I wish I could have given him just a small piece of certainty in such an uncertain existence. Instead, I said that if he wanted someone to be in hell, that's where they'd be. And if he wanted them in heaven, they'd be there too. I said that the best I could figure, after all these years, is that we make of god what we want. We make him exist or not exist, make him good or evil or apathetic. It all comes down to us.

Well, he said. I'm not sure we're right for the job. He told me that, the boy, and I nodded. I stayed up with him as long as I could, then I took his hand and patted it and went on to bed.

The boy sat the porch for a long while yet. The eastern stars began to dim. Soon the horizon would trace itself in shadow against the soft gray light of the coming dawn; the dayspring chorus from the pine warblers and brown thrashers giving proof of the night's retreating. The boy would witness it all: the forest come alive, the river singing out, and the sun rising overtop an unchanged world. And there the story begins and ends and begins again, as each rhythm of the earth's turning draws the water darker still. As each rhythm of the earth's turning draws the water darker.

ACKNOWLEDGMENTS

Thanks to Josh Stanton, Rick Bleiweiss, and the Blackstone Publishing family. Thanks to Josie Woodbridge, Lauren Maturo, Megan Wahrenbrock, Jeffrey Yamaguchi, Greg Boguslawski, Mandy Earles, Anne Fonteneau, Bryan Green, Brad Simpson, Brandon Bobkowski, Chloe Cotter, Isabella Bedoya, Ananda Finwall, Kathryn English, Lysa Williams, and Hannah Ohlmann, for all of your tremendous efforts with this book.

Special thanks to Mark Gottlieb, my agent and earliest champion. I couldn't do any of this without you.

Thank you to Clint Stone, who taught me everything I know about running the river.

Thank you to Natalie McBrayer, my dear friend and meditation coach.

Thank you, Albi Sabani, for your friendship and for reminding me to always look within.

To my friends and family, I love each of you far more than my actions might suggest.

To Jordan—my greatest love, my best friend, my always partner—I love you more than mountains. And Juniper, my tiny adventurer, Daddy loves you so much.

And, finally, to East Texas, and the pine trees that helped raise me.